MW00657281

# God's Love Most Faithful

God's Love Most Faithful

Copyright 2018 by Mary Marie Allen

Farrand Avenue Faith Publishing

When her husband deserts her after his gambling has lost them their jobs and home, a woman starts a new life.

ISBN: 978-0-988-784-4-7

Catalog: 1. Christian Fiction, 2. Spouses of gamblers—fiction, 3. Rebuilding a life—fiction, 4. Strong women protagonists—fiction, 5. Friendship – fiction

*God's Love Most Faithful* is entirely a work of fiction. The names, characters, and incidents portrayed in it are the work of the author's imagination. Any resemblance to actual persons, living or dead, events, or localities is entirely coincidental. Al-Anon is a real world-wide organization.

All rights reserved. No part of this publication may be reproduced, stored in a retrieval system, or transmitted, in any form or by any means, electronic, mechanical, photocopying, scanning, recording, or otherwise, without the prior permission of the author, except for the brief quotations in a review. This book is sold subject to the condition that it shall not, by way of trade or otherwise, be lent, re-sold, hired out or otherwise circulated without the author's prior consent in any form of binding other than that in which it is published and without a similar condition.

Scriptures, unless marked otherwise, are taken from the King James Version (KJV): King James Version, public domain.

Cover photo by Tina Pappas Lee.
Back cover photo Sharon-Mccutcheon-576867-unsplash.

# Acknowledgements

Thank you to Meri Mehaffie, Danielle Thorp, Barb Freese, Janene Grace and Nancy Carlson for editing and story line review.

A special thanks to attorney Gary Schoof for answering all my questions on how the legal system in Indiana works. Also, thank you to Julie Gerick, M.D. for your trauma and emergency care advice. Your friendship through the years has meant a lot to me.

## Other books by Mary Marie Allen

Fiction
God's Love Most Gentle

Non-fiction & Poetry (writing as Mary Allen)
Journey to Christmas (Devotional)
Ten Days to an Empty Tomb (Devotional)
Full Spectrum Living
The Invitation

Dear Reader,

This book came about because many after reading Kim's story in *God's Love Most Gentle* wanted to know how Carol and Trudy had become friends.

While the circumstances represented could happen, the characters in *God's Love Most Faithful* are fictional. Any resemblance to an actual person is coincidental.

Indianapolis and Las Vegas are, of course, real places, but the names of stores and restaurants are fictional. As far as I know, (thank you, Google) there is no place in Iowa called Amesville. That's just my imagination being playful for the intent of making a play on words.

The scripture for this book is I Corinthians 10:13 KJV. "There is no temptation that has taken you but such as is common to man: but God is faithful, who will not suffer you to be tempted above that ye are able; but will with the temptation also make a way to escape, that ye may be able to bear it."

Or, stated in my own words, what I call Mary's Amplified, Paraphrased Scriptures: There's nothing unique about the temptations you face; people have always faced these same temptations: but God is faithful. He will not allow you to be tempted past the limit of your ability to say no. He always gives you a way out. (So, if you refuse the escape He offers, and choose to get chummy with sin, don't blame God when you fall.)

I hope you love these characters. I hope you identify with their courage and determination. I hope they inspire you to trust God a little more and discover that you can more fully experience God's most faithful love, too. He redeems us because we do fail.

I invite you to like and follow my Face Book page https://www.facebook.com/PoetAndWriterMaryAllen/ and to post any comments about the book that you might have there or on my website marymarieallen.com where you'll also see more about me and my books. I'd love to dialogue with you there.

Happy reading!

*Mary Marie Allen*

For the women I know who have fought so hard to overcome codependence to loved ones who are addicted whether to gambling or substances. Your stories have inspired me and reveal that in Christ there is life and love after loss.

# God's Love Most Faithful

Mary Marie Allen

# Chapter One

Trudy Bellafonte exited Manicure Mania in high spirits because dark red nails with pearl insets always brightened her mood. She turned toward the parking lot. In front of the window signs advertising the newest beauty products for 1990 stood a young girl barely in her teens. She held out nail-bitten hand. "Hey, lady, can you spare a five?"

Trudy took in the bony figure, stringy hair, dirty fingernails, and slovenly appearance. Underneath that, the girl's eyes were intelligent and bright. This could be her if situations were different. "Sure." She opened her purse and pulled out a ten.

The door to Manicure Mania popped open. One of the nail technicians rushed onto the sidewalk shouting, "You get out of here. I'm calling the cops. How many times do I have to tell you?"

The girl snatched the ten from Trudy's hand and sprinted down the block.

The nail technician put her hands on her hips. "You shouldn't encourage beggars, Mrs. Bellafonte."

"She looked hungry."

"Then let her get a job like the rest of us."

"I don't think she was old enough."

"Please, Mrs. Bellafonte. If you want to give, there are places you can donate for the homeless."

The owner of Manicure Mania joined them on the street. She held the door open. "Fiona, your customer is waiting."

With an exasperated sigh, the nail technician pulled her gaze away from Trudy and went through the open door into the shop. The owner said, "Trudy, I know you mean well, but she's right. If you want to give them something, please, do it elsewhere. I don't want them begging around here, bothering my customers. It's bad for business."

"Okay. Point taken. It's only that I have so much and they have so little."

The owner shook her head. "It's hard, but that's the way it is. You can't help everyone. I suppose you'd give everything away, if you had a chance. Take my advice. Enjoy your success. We'll see you next week. Have a good day."

At her black Lincoln Town Car, Trudy placed one hand on its shiny, dark top and the other against her white cashmere dress. She stroked the fabric with her finger tips. This was what success looked like. She enjoyed the expensive car and sleek clothes, but that didn't mean she had to be callous. She enjoyed the prestige and the special treatment people gave those with money, but that didn't mean she didn't remember how she and Phillip got where they were or why she never wanted to repeat the experience.

With one last glance down the street, Trudy slipped into the car. The engine purred into action, she drove the short distance to their Las Vegas subdivision with fine homes that would look like castles if they were plunked down in the small town where she had been raised. One more reason to keep moving on and not look back, although, how could one ever really forget?

Her beautiful two-story white stucco with the bump bay windows came into view. She pulled into the drive and parked behind a huge van blocking access to her two car garage. She giggled. What had Phillip bought her now? Couldn't be those ruby earrings she'd been admiring. It wouldn't take a van to deliver those.

She couldn't quite make out the black logo on the back of the uniforms, but something wasn't right. Trudy looked closer. Men in jumpsuits, like ants, carried furniture from her house up the ramp and into the van, then returned for more booty.

Her heart beat against her chest like a caged bird. No one was going to steal her beautiful things. Trudy grabbed the mobile phone from the passenger seat and punched 9-1-1. When she put it to her ear there was no dial tone. How could the battery be out? It had a full charge before she went into the nail salon. She threw the phone on the seat and climbed from the car.

The pencil dress prevented large steps, but her stiletto heels clicked an emphatic drumroll as she charged up the driveway to where the men in jumpsuits hoisted her ebony coffee table into the truck. "Hey! What are you doing? Stop it right now. Get out of my house. I've called the cops."

A man whipped around to face her. His scraggly black beard and hair lent him an unsavory appearance. As she neared, the black logo on his shirt pocket matched the one on the side of the truck that read Reynolds Reclamation Service. He waved a clipboard. "We have an order to reclaim this furniture."

"No. That's not right. This is absurd."

Two bulky men bore her lovely white couch down the sidewalk. Trudy blocked their path. "Put it back. Put it all back. You have the wrong house."

The men with the couch glanced at the bearded man. He jerked his head. Obediently, they detoured around her. He glanced at the paperwork on his clipboard. "Phillip and Trudy Bellafonte. Are you Trudy Bellafonte?"

"Yes. I'm Trudy Bellafonte. I don't understand. This is my furniture."

"Not any more, Ma'am. It's being returned to the store. They issued the order this morning."

She glanced at the order and recognized the name of the furniture store. "There must be a mistake. Why are you taking it?"

"Non-payment."

"No. That's not possible. My husband paid for this in full." She yanked the clipboard away from him and checked his paperwork for any detail that proved an error. Everything seemed in order. Trudy shook her head. "I'm telling you there is some mistake. I do not give you permission to enter my house."

"We don't need your permission. Your husband gave us permission." The man held up the keys.

Fear punched her gut. Was it possible Phillip had known? Why didn't he tell her? Where was he? After a moment to collect herself, Trudy stepped through the front door. The foyer with its white marble floor was bare. The lovely ebony dining room table and its white velvet chairs were gone. Even the custom-made Jacquard curtains had been stripped from the windows.

She clung to the door frame a moment, then climbed the stairs to the master suite. More men pulled covers and sheets from the king-size bed and tossed them into the corner. Her high-heels sank soundlessly into the plush carpeting as she made her way to the walk-in closet.

None of her expensive clothing had been touched, but the contents of the missing vanity lay in a jumbled pile on the carpet. A gruff voice said, "Excuse me, lady."

Trudy moved aside so another workman could carry the vanity chair out of the spacious walk-in closet. She clasped her hands and pressed them to her lips. The movement drew her eye to the round vanity mirror leaning against the wall. Beneath her ginger hair, her face was nearly as white as the form-fitting dress with the wide boat neck.

The image disappeared when a white cloth, like a funeral shroud, was tossed over the mirror. The worker taped it, hefted it, and mumbled, "Sorry, lady." as he passed her.

The whine of a drill came from the bedroom. She felt as if the drill was hollowing out her insides, but in reality the men were unscrewing the bolts on the bed frame.

In Phillip's walk-in closet, the empty built-in drawers hung open. Bare hangers lay scattered across the floor. She wheeled around and marched over to the men working on the bed. "You took his clothes? How could you? That's not furniture."

One on them glanced up. "Not us, lady. We didn't touch a thing, except the furniture. That room was empty when we got here."

The bedroom darkened for a moment. The man sprang upright and grabbed her arm. "You don't look so good. Why don't you sit down?" He guided her to one of the window seats which had already been stripped of the softening influence of cushions and pillows. The wood beneath her was as hard as truth. Phillip and his one-stop-shop plan had stripped them bare. No, his failure to pay the store had.

The man's anxious, stubbly face was close to hers. "You okay?"

Trudy looked straight back at him. "How could he do this to me?"

At the pathetic quiver in her voice, the man shrugged and seemed to find the movements of his co-workers engrossing. After a moment, he evidently decided she wasn't going to faint because he returned to the task of dismantling her life.

Trudy noticed the bedside phone sitting on the floor. With shaking hands, she dialed her husband's number and put the phone to her ear. No dial tone. In a flash, she realized the cell phone wasn't out of battery either. Both phones were disconnected. The orders for the repossession and the disconnected phones hadn't taken place in one day. Maybe he'd even shut the phones off himself to get the deposit money.

The men carried the pieces of her bed frame out of the room. Trudy swallowed bile. She thought they were doing well. Phillip had told her they were doing well. She was so sick of their up and down life. She had thought they were done with sneaking out to avoid paying rent or moving to a new city to avoid debt collectors. Repossession was a new and particularly personal violation. How bad was the debt this time? Why hadn't he warned her? More importantly, where was Phillip?

In a slow, dreamlike state Trudy followed the men down the stairs, out the door. She stood on the front lawn looking at the house she and Phillip had bought and furnished together. They'd promised each other it'd always be their home.

The late afternoon air cooled as it did in Las Vegas in the winter. She claimed a Christian Dior coat from the hall closet and pulled it in place, buttoned it, and wrapped her arms around herself against the chill. She felt no warmer so the chill probably had more to do with the shock of it all than with the weather.

Mutely, she watched the last of the furniture disappear into the van. The men secured the back. Three climbed into the van's cab and three crawled into a second smaller truck.

The man with the clipboard approached and handed her the house keys. She gripped them hard and felt them dig into her skin. He didn't move. She looked at him. He glanced away. "I'm sorry, but, um, Mrs. Bellafonte, could you please move your car?"

The men waiting in the truck kept their heads turned away from her. There was no one to ask for help. It was pointless to resist. They could drive through the yard and mess it up. She nodded.

This time the slow *Tick, Tick, Tick* of her heels was like a clock marking the time that had run out on her fantasy life. She reversed the Town Car into the street and waited as the smaller truck backed down the drive and drove away. The van loaded with her hopes and dreams rumbled down the street after it.

# Chapter Two

This was the end. She couldn't go any further with Phillip. She twisted off the wedding band and engagement ring and dropped them in the unused ash tray. Trudy drove the Town Car into the garage. She swung the car doors open wide and popped the trunk. Phillip had wanted the bigger car for its status. It was ironic that all the room it had would come in handy to load up what was left of her life.

Her feet were heavy, clumsy blocks of wood as she reentered the house. She used the banister to pull herself up to the second floor. Switching to sneakers, jeans and T-shirt seemed symbolic of the change from high class homeowner to vagabond. She grimaced.

Trudy opened the largest Louis Vuitton suitcase and threw in the high-heeled shoes she'd worn that day. She pulled expensive dresses, high fashion coats, and lovely lingerie from hangers. She packed more suitcases with clothes from the piles on the floor, stuffing name brand shoes around the edges. Her mind went blank, but her body remained on auto-pilot for the methodical repetition of smoothing, folding, rolling, and packing.

On her third trip in loading the car, she brought plastic garbage bags from the kitchen and filled them one after the other until her closet and bedroom were emptied. Trudy made the rounds of the house stuffing small home decorator items, towels, toiletries, and cleaning supplies in the bags.

She jammed what she could into the trunk of the Town Car and smoothed the bedspread flat over the bags. She applied weight on the lid to close the trunk. Next, she used a little hip action to force the side doors shut. Surely, the car couldn't hold even a sheet of paper more.

A few black bags remained on the garage floor burdened with the shower curtain, extra sheets, and kitchen towels. Beside them were stacks of china, the tableware, and some kitchen gadgets. Trudy shook her hair and lifted it away from her hot, sweaty neck. She'd rent a room, unload some things, pick up empty boxes, and come back.

Trudy backed the Town Car out of the garage and pressed the remote. She drummed the steering wheel. The fresh, red nails gleamed while the garage door lowered like the final curtain on the play of her life.

Was this it? Would there be no encore? Her left hand looked like it should belong to someone else without the usual flash of the diamond ring.

Perhaps she'd been too hasty in packing to leave. Maybe it wasn't too late. Phillip had slipped. He'd be sorry about it. She'd forgive him. It'd take time, but they'd get everything back.

That period of working together to rebuild was always the best part. They'd bounce back. They always did. She wasn't going to leave Phillip. She loved him even if he always left the hard stuff for her to handle. When he got back from his business trip, they'd have a heart-to-heart.

Trudy retrieved the rings from the cup holder and drew them onto her finger. Much better.

She considered driving back into the garage and emptying the car, but exhaustion carried the nay vote. Anyway, camping on the floor held no allure. She backed into the street and shifted into drive. The sun hanging low in the sky blinded her. She braked and rummaged in her purse for sunglasses.

Three vehicles came up the street and pulled into her driveway, one behind the other. Men spilled from the cars and headed toward the front door. Trudy left the engine running and the door hanging open. She sprinted up the driveway. "Who are you? What are you doing?"

One of two men who looked like weight-lifters faced her. "What business is it of yours?"

"I'm the owner."

Another man in a business suit waved to the men to go about their jobs, and they moved toward the house. He pulled a wad of legal papers from a valise on the front seat of the lead car, and leafed through the pages before saying, "I'm looking for Phillip Bellafonte."

"I'm his wife, Trudy Bellafonte. Who are you?"

"I'm Everett Black, attorney for Mr. Avery."

"Our boss?" Trudy shook her head. "That doesn't make sense. My husband is out of town on business, on Mr. Avery's business. Mr. Avery knows that."

"You appear to be uninformed. Phillip Bellafonte no longer works for Mr. Avery."

"What?" A knife of ice seemed to pierce Trudy's brain. She pressed her hands to her temples to still the pain and felt her pulse thumping wildly. What was going on? As calmly as she could, she spoke and heard the quaver in her voice. "What is this about? You can speak to me about what's going on here."

Mr. Black scanned the paperwork again. "I don't see your name on this mortgage."

"That's because my husband moved here ahead of me and bought the house for us."

The man shoved horn-rimmed glasses closer to his eyes and riffled through more papers. "You're not on the deed, either. I can't discuss anything with you."

"This is sheer madness."

Mr. Black eyed her. "I will tell you that in order to clear up his gambling debts, Mr. Bellafonte signed the deed to this house and everything in it over to Mr. Avery. I'm here to take possession."

"You can't do that. Some of those things are my personal items, not Phillip's."

He waved a thick wad of legal papers. "According to what your husband signed, everything on this property belongs to Mr. Avery. In toto. If you have items owned separately, you can contest it in court."

Trudy let out a garbled yelp. She spun around and sprinted to the Town Car. She stomped on the gas pedal. The tires squealed as the car skidded leaving, she hoped, a black mark on the street like an obscene gesture. She pounded the wheel. This was bad. Really bad. A growing dread clenched her gut. Where was Phillip?

Trudy maneuvered the Town Car through the dust and noise of road workers and turned into the nearest branch of their bank. She tried to draw an advance from the ATM, but it wouldn't work. She parked beside the bank and headed for the lobby. A chill wind whipped hair across her eyes. Trudy pushed it behind her ears.

Inside, a pert young teller informed her that the joint checking and savings accounts were empty. As if she were expecting it, the news failed to shock. She thanked the girl and left with a numbing emptiness in the pit of her stomach.

Back in the Town Car, Trudy's heart pounded in time to the jackhammer down the street. She fought panic for several minutes before willing herself to think and plan. Forty-nine dollars. That's all she had to her name. She couldn't afford legal advice. She couldn't even buy a hotel room.

In the eight months they'd lived here, she'd spent all her time working as a hostess in one of Mr. Avery's casino restaurants and never made any friends. Phillip always liked it that way. Just them. Two against the world.

How romantic it had seemed in the beginning for Phillip to claim they were enough for each other. Later he made her feel silly for trying to form friendships when they traveled so much. He said it wouldn't be fair to the friends.

Trudy wondered if he believed this himself, or if it was a purposeful strategy meant to keep her dependent on him alone and more easily controlled. Eventually, it had become a matter of survival. Whenever they had to disappear, no one was left behind to give clues where they might be.

Las Vegas was meant to be different, but there hadn't been any time to form friendships, not even with the people she worked alongside. She could rely on no one. She had nowhere to go. Phillip was gone. She was alone. Tears of frustration, fear, and anger flowed fast and furious.

Once the flow stemmed, she wiped her eyes. Sometimes the paychecks came to the restaurant the night before they were passed out. If ever she needed an early delivery, this was the night. Trudy reentered the bank and spoke to the blonde at the information desk. "Please, may I use the phone? Mine isn't working. I need to call my work."

The blonde hesitated.

"Look, it's a local call. You can punch in the number yourself. I'll make it as quick as I can. I wouldn't ask if it wasn't urgent."

The blonde looked to the right at a man behind a desk talking with a client and glanced to the left at the next teller. "Okay, but be quick." She handed Trudy the phone, her finger poised over the number pad. Trudy rattled off the number for the reservation desk of the restaurant.

Kelly, a girl she worked with frequently, answered on the second ring. Trudy identified herself. "Are the paychecks there yet? If they are, I'll swing by and pick mine up."

Kelly's voice took on an affected tone. "Let me see if we have any bookings for that day."

"What? Kelly, it's Trudy. I need to know if the checks are ready."

The background sound of the call changed. Kelly had moved away from the foot traffic in the main part of the restaurant into the private office where the big parties were booked. Trudy heaved an exasperated sigh and tapped her foot impatiently.

Kelly's voice was terse and low, almost a whisper. "Don't come in. Mr. Avery is angry. He's looking for you."

"Why would he be angry with me?"

"I'm not sure, but he was asking about your husband. Listen to me. The last time he looked like this, a girl ended up in the hospital for two weeks. I'm serious. Don't come back here."

The line went dead. Trudy handed the phone to the receptionist as if it were glass. Her knees were jelly. Even breathing seemed like a big risk. "Thank you," she whispered and stumbled out to the car.

One choice remained: groveling. She'd have to go back to her parents. She'd have to admit she shouldn't have eloped and that the past five years were all a mistake. She'd tell them they'd been right about the exciting young man who'd captured her heart and freed her from that restrictive, mundane life.

She couldn't say that last part, of course. They didn't understand that was what life was like for her living under their strict rules and constant disapproval. She would kowtow to them if they'd take her in for a few months to help her get back on her feet. Even if they hadn't talked in a long time, she was still their daughter. Surely, they'd respond to a desperate cry for help. The setting sun became a blaze of fire on the horizon, burning bridges behind her as Trudy headed for Amesville, Iowa.

Late that night, the white center lines on the road blurred. Trudy rubbed her eyes and turned up the radio until it blared. That helped her stay awake for quite a few miles before the Town Car weaved across the lines. Trudy shook her head and kept going.

Several miles later, the tires bumped onto the berm. She jerked the car onto the blacktop and rolled down all the windows to let the cold fresh air blow on her face. Even so, the emotional roller coaster of the day had taken its toll. When she began to dream with her eyes open, Trudy knew it was foolish to fight sleep any longer.

She pulled into a filling station and parked along the edge of the concrete. The back seat was packed too full for the driver's seat to recline so she leaned against the window. Too hard. Too cold. She covered herself with her coat and pulled a small decorative pillow from the back seat to soften where she rested her head.

She next opened her eyes to the brilliance of a sunny day. A dusting of snow had fallen during the night, but was already melting in the mid-morning sun.

She rubbed the stiffness from her neck and wondered if the aspirin was buried in the back seat or the trunk or perhaps was still in one of the bags she'd left on the garage floor in Las Vegas. Trudy massaged tight neck muscles and tried to rub away her headache. She was unwilling to spend any of her limited resources on something she had, even if she didn't know where it was. She got out and stomped her feet to ward off the chill that gripped her.

The filling station looked old and unkempt. Trudy steeled herself and pushed through the dirty plate glass door. She used the facilities, then braced with a hot cup of coffee, pressed on toward home.

Home. She hadn't called it that in years. Home meant the farm and Skipper. She hadn't minded farm living with its constant, hard work, but the sameness of the everyday routine coupled with her father's increasing restrictions had left her longing for adventure. She liked challenge and Phillip had given her that in spades. His idea of routine had been change.

Excitement at seeing her parents alternated with fear and agitation every time she remembered her sin. For sin is what they had called her elopement. But, you can't pick whom you love, can you? She had fallen hard.

Phillip was a sophisticated city man, three years older than she. His lust for derring-do had enticed her. That and the fact that he was wildly handsome with black wavy hair that would go to curls at the nape of his neck whenever he let it grow. His blue eyes always seemed to be laughing at some hidden joke. He was fun. When he chose, he could speak with an Irish brogue that'd made her heart melt. He claimed he'd gotten that from his Grampa, though she'd never met any of his family.

Phillip had intimated he and his family were well off, but some argument or other had kept them from talking. She'd been appalled at how horribly he'd been treated and had been honored he'd shared such private information with her. Even after they were married, he never did give her more details. Had any of it been true? Still, Phillip was kind and generous and treated her like royalty. How could she not fall for him? Surely that had not been a sin. Hopefully, her parents had softened with the passing years.

## Chapter Three

Trudy surveyed the modest farmhouse from the end of the well-packed gravel drive. The roof had been recently shingled, but all in all, it looked unchanged. Nostalgia mixed with relief washed over her.

Growing up here hadn't been so bad. It was good in fact until she had turned twelve. As she exerted more independence her father had "laid down the law" more and more. She'd chafed under his increasingly tight rein. They were often at odds, except when she competed in the horse barrel races.

Together she and Skipper had taken many blue ribbons. That horse had been her best friend through her teen years and her father had wholeheartedly approved of that activity. He hadn't missed a meet and always cheered her on.

The memory warmed her. Hopefully, her father had softened toward her with the passing years. Hopefully.

She could use a friend before going in to face her parents. What a pleasure it would be to nuzzle Skipper again. He'd probably missed her and didn't understand why she'd deserted him. How could she explain that she'd believed Phillip when he said they'd come back for him? How could she explain her naiveté that when Phillip said he loved horses what he really meant was he loved to bet on horse races?

Trudy parked alongside the corral. She got out and leaned on the fence. Skipper wasn't in the corral. The trough only held frozen chunks of ice. She unlatched the door to the barn and felt for the switch. Light revealed an empty barn. The cows weren't there and Skipper's stall looked as if it hadn't been used. Maybe he was in the field since the winter had been a fairly mild one. Disappointment tightened her chest. It was a familiar feeling. Life had not turned out as she'd dreamed.

In the empty, unused barn, Trudy wondered, not for the first time, if Phillip had stolen, lost the family fortune, or had in some other way disgraced his family's good name. Probably. He couldn't seem to help himself. Once he started, he gambled more and more. In spite of frequent arguments, he seemed driven to it, even when he'd had to sell his motorcycle, his fancy car, and his boat. Gambler's Anonymous had helped. For a while. Yet, here she was back where she'd started.

Trudy closed the barn door and faced the house. Even approaching it was a hurdle. Should she use the front door as a visitor or the back door as a welcomed family member? Choosing the more formal approach in order to test her parents' reception, Trudy stepped up onto the front porch and faced another hurdle. Should she knock or enter? She decided to do both. She knocked and timidly stepped over the threshold.

The lingering scent of morning pancakes and bacon reminded her she'd only had coffee for breakfast while the aroma of bubbling bean soup promised a hot meal of cornbread and butter with her mother's homemade pickled beets on the side.

From the kitchen, the radio burbled. The words were indistinct, but the cadence of the announcer told her that her parents' favorite long-time broadcaster, Paul Harvey, was on the air.

In the dimly-lit hall, the same tired, pressed cardboard photo of a vase with white lilies hung on a narrow entry wall. The same old-fashioned black, corded, dial telephone still sat on a tiny table by the stairs. In the adjacent living room, the same sofa with the gold and green crocheted throw crouched along one wall. The familiar worn and lumpy autumn-gold recliner with crocheted doilies covering the frayed arms sat against a wall opposite the TV.

Trudy shook her head, but really hadn't expected anything else. It wasn't as if her parents couldn't afford nicer things. They simply liked the old better. They felt safer with a fat savings account than with more comfortable or better looking furniture. Now that Phillip had disappeared, she wouldn't have to worry about him wrangling their fat savings out of them in their retirement nor from her, when their time came. She immediately cheered and the well-used furniture assumed an aura of homey-ness.

Above the recliner, a grouping of ceramic cherubs with gold-gilt wings looked heavenward. As a girl she thought they were rolling their eyes at some of the odd things her parents said or did. Other times, they seemed to be thinking of mischief, but perhaps that was a personification of her own leanings. On that day, Trudy thought the cherubs appeared to be mocking her with some secret joke. Her cheerfulness evaporated.

She plucked at the jeans she'd worn since yesterday. She should've changed into a dress, so that her parents would approve. Dad never allowed pants except when riding Skipper.

She closed the outer door and walked through the short hallway. One hand drifted over the framed embroidery on the wall that listed their wedding date and the names Howard and Emma. This tiny proof of their solidarity and constancy fortified her. She smiled to herself and called, "Mom. Dad. I'm home." She stepped into the brightness of the kitchen.

Emma turned from the sink and murmured, "Trudy." Her eyes widened in surprise, but the initial spark of joy fought with some other unidentified emotion. It was probably uncertainty, as she'd be waiting to see how her husband would react before committing herself. Even that hadn't changed. Nor had the dress and the tight poodle perm. However, in five years Emma's hair had greyed, her face had aged a lot, and her blue eyes had lost their color, like water turning white when frozen. She dried her hands on her apron and kept wiping them.

Howard half-turned from the newspaper spread across the laminate kitchen table. His brown-and-black checked flannel shirt had faded from multiple washings throughout the years, but was crisply pressed. His face was sallow and wrinkled, his hair white and sparse. He didn't bother to rise. With shaking hands, he removed wire-framed glasses from his aquiline nose and looked her up and down, noting the jeans. His stare held judgment.

A third person stood at the stove stirring the bean pot. His back looked familiar, but Trudy couldn't place which of her parents' friends it could be. He pivoted. Her universe tilted.

"Phillip."

How did the man her parents despised come to be making bean soup in their cozy kitchen? She blinked and shook her head to clear the mirage. He shot her a saucy smile and, as always, his blue eyes pierced her heart with their intensity. "Hi, Tru."

"What're you doing here?" Trudy stepped toward her mother. "What's he doing here?"

Emma said, "Phillip's been a great help since your father's heart attack."

"Heart attack? Oh, my. When?" Trudy dropped to her knees at Howard's side. "Dad, are you all right? Shouldn't you be in the hospital?"

A cold stare met her. "A little late to be asking now." He turned from her and placed both hands on the table.

"What do you mean?"

"We wrote you two months ago with the news. We were really disappointed that you never came or wrote or called," Emma said.

"I didn't get the message. I never knew."

Emma made a little twist of her head. A sign that she didn't believe what she was hearing, but wasn't prepared to challenge it. She said, "Oh, well. Phillip said you were busy with the new house. It sounds very grand. He's been great. He's visited often. He even finished re-shingling the roof for us."

"He did what?" Trudy stood and gripped the back of her father's chair to steady herself. She may as well have been standing on her head. Life was upside down. Maybe she was still in the car, asleep.

Emma sent a warm smile toward Phillip. "He also replaced the furnace when it went out."

Trudy regarded her husband who never did a favor without figuring the angles. He returned her stare with calm calculation. "He did? How much did he charge you?"

"Phillip didn't charge us anything," Howard said, testily. He placed the eyeglasses back on his nose and somehow still managed to look over them at her. "He got us a good deal, too."

In the face of their solidarity, Trudy struggled to couch her reply in an acceptable manner. "Well. Well. Phillip, thank you for helping my parents. I'm angry you didn't tell me about Dad's heart attack, but grateful for what you have done."

"Yes, you should thank him." Howard continued in an unrelenting tone of judgment. "He's been a godsend. Can't say the same for you. You should be ashamed of yourself, running up debt, spending all the money he made. I understand you're in a real pickle now that he lost his job when the company downsized."

"Phillip, you told me you were out of town on business." Trudy pressed fingers to her temples. The rest of her father's words hit her. "Wait a minute, Dad. I'm not the big spender. It was Phillip who bought the big house and helped me to decorate."

Trudy pointed at Phillip. "Last night I came home to find men repossessing the furniture. Then Mr. Avery's lawyer sealed the house and changed the locks because you lost everything we had on a horse named Blessed Event."

Phillip shook his head. His face filled with sorrow. He covered his eyes with his hand. His voice quavered. "I told you she'd blame me for our situation. I don't know how much more I can take."

Emma stepped forward to touch his sleeve in a comforting manner.

Howard said, "It's not your fault. Nothing was ever good enough for her. Always reaching for the stars. I'm so sorry, son."

Trudy pulled out a kitchen chair and sank heavily onto it. "I didn't do this. They locked me out of our house, Phillip. They wouldn't even let me get my stuff. You said it'd be our forever home."

For a few moments, the soup bubbling in the pot was the only sound.

Trudy straightened in her chair. "Phillip, I'm sick of your sickness. You're a liar and a thief. I've had it. I want a divorce."

"No," her mother said, aghast.

Phillip raised his head to assess her words. Once more he covered his eyes as if he were aggrieved.

Howard removed his glasses again and pinched his nose. An old, familiar sign that he thought her words were the last straw. "If you break your sacred bonds of marriage, little lady, we're through with you."

Trudy leaned across the table. "Dad, you were right about Phillip. This has happened before. I forgave him, but his gambling is way out of control. He was going to Gamblers Anonymous. I thought he was recovering, but I guess even that was a lie. Dad, I came to ask forgiveness."

Howard kept shaking his head. This lips formed an upside down U. "You came because you have no place else to go."

Trudy nodded. "That's also true, because he's gambled away everything. Dad, could I please stay with you for a couple of months?"

"We can't harbor a divorcée."

"Please Dad. Show a little mercy and grace. Jesus did."

"Yes. But he said to go and sin no more. You have every intention of divorcing your husband to continue your highfalutin lifestyle with carryings-on and wild parties."

Trudy pulled back. "What? No. What has he told you? I've never ever been unfaithful and I quit partying three years ago. He's the one who still drinks."

"Pretty hard to believe when that's what you were doing here. Sneaking out. Taking off."

"I never did anything immoral."

"You ran off. We can only imagine why."

"I was an adult. I left to marry Phillip because I loved him, not because I had to get married. Please Dad, I'll get a job. I'll get back on my feet without Phillip's help. Please let me stay."

Emma's voice held a note of apology. She'd twisted her apron until it looked like a rope. "Given your intentions, Trudy that would be difficult. Phillip is already staying in your old bedroom."

Trudy couldn't get enough air. Her lungs didn't seem to work properly.

Phillip kept a solemn face, but his eyes twinkled. Her parents probably thought it was tears, but she thought he enjoyed her shock. Life was a giant chess game to him. Checkmate, Trudy. He said, "I love your daughter. Maybe if she stays, she'd change her mind about the divorce."

"You're a good man, Phillip," Emma said.

Howard glanced from his wife to Phillip to Trudy. His eyes were moist, but resolute, behind his glasses. "You see, we know all about what you've been doing, missy. The kind of trouble you got yourself in. Trudy, we love you enough to let you get yourself out of it. We'll be praying for you. If you want to truly repent and change your ways and make up with your husband, we'll welcome you back."

His words trickled into her understanding like water through a filter. The moment stretched into eternity. "Until then, I think it is best you be on your way."

Emma gasped. In a familiar ultimate signal of distress she held her wadded apron to her mouth. Phillip kept one hand over his eyes and making a fist pressed the other to his face, covering his reaction. He turned back toward the stove. His shoulders heaved in slight rhythm. Her parents may think this was grief, but Trudy suspected he was laughing at her.

She was reduced to that silly, unsophisticated girl she'd been when he'd first flirted with her. Once their love had seemed extraordinary and immortal. Along the way, she'd been demoted from soulmate to that dependable someone who supported him while he played the ponies and went to the casinos. She'd become the person who always stuck around to pay his debts and clean up his messes. Somehow, he'd guessed she was at her limit even before she knew she was. He was intuitive like that.

Now that she'd drawn the line, she was of little use to him, except as an in-road to her parents' money. This was her fault for letting it slip how much they had socked away. Trudy reached across the table to her father. Howard pulled his hand back. Palms down, she spread her fingers on the table. "Phillip lied. I'm your daughter. Please believe me."

"Phillip has proved himself over the last few months. We wouldn't have made it without him. No thanks to you."

Trudy rose slowly. "Okay, Dad. I know once you make up your mind there's no changing it. I'll go, but please, please listen to me. Do not let Phillip touch your savings. Don't lend it. Deal with retailers and suppliers directly. And don't let him talk you into investing in any of his schemes."

Howard and Emma exchanged a glance, but said nothing. Trudy hoped her warning had come in time. "Remember that and remember this. I love you both." Trudy's voice broke. She swallowed and tried again. "Even when I eloped with Phillip, I loved you. I'll always love you."

Emma sobbed into her apron. Howard stared at something out the window. Phillip with a face arranged in a show of sadness reached a hand toward her. Trudy spun on her heel, went through the dark hallway, and out the front door as Paul Harvey wrapped up his radio program with "and that's the rest of the story."

Trudy drove down the dirt road, through the town of Amesville, onto the paved county road. Lovely brown horses were grazing in a field by a farmhouse. The sight of them reminded her of Skipper. She hadn't had a chance to see him. Thoughts of him tied in with a multitude of good memories with her parents. The tears came so hard she couldn't see. She pulled the car over and gave herself up to them. She sopped them with the last of the tissues in the glove box. She hated crying and here she'd broken down twice in as many days.

She pounded the steering wheel. She hated that despicable rat, Phillip. She was done with him. The electric window opener gave an almost inaudible *whir* as the glass descended and cold air rushed in. She pulled the big diamond ring and the wedding band off her finger.

# Chapter Four

The diamond glinted in the winter light and Trudy thought better of tossing away such precious stone and metal. She zipped them into a tiny pocket in her purse.

For the hundredth time she wished she'd never let slip that her parents had money. She knew she had to pay for her youthful folly, but it was worse that it continued to hurt her parents and had left them exposed to a master manipulator.

Like Eve with the apple, Trudy's eyes were opened, but her warnings were not enough to stop the events that were in play around her parents. They bought the good son-in-law act, the same way she had been mesmerized five years before. They saw only the part he wanted them to see, and there was nothing she could do about it.

Her own situation commanded attention. As scary as it was, at least the frequent moves since her marriage had taught her how to survive. She'd make it on her own. She could. She would. With a voice dripping with sarcasm, she said aloud, "Thank you, Phillip."

When Trudy reached the highway, she drove east because going west reminded her of the bitter fruits of Las Vegas.

As she reached Indianapolis, Indiana, the gauge indicated she had a quarter tank of fuel remaining. City in the Land of Indians. She remembered this from a report she'd made in sixth grade geography. Except it wasn't the land of Indians, anymore. There were few Indians left in Indianapolis, or even in Indiana and those who remained didn't live off the land as they had before the settlers drove them out.

Trudy empathized. Her name remained, but her marriage didn't, her lifestyle didn't. Now, she too had been driven from her childhood home and her secure identity. The thought somehow bonded her to Indianapolis. She turned off the highway and wound through the downtown area looking at the capitol building and the Market Square Arena sports stadium and other tall buildings.

She passed a huge sculpture that said LOVE. She could use love. A lot of it. Vast amounts of it to make up for the love she'd lost when Phillip pulled the trust rug out from under her, and for the love she'd lost from her parents by her choices and naïveté.

The fuel needle hovered over E. She flicked the plastic covering the gauge a few times and the needle dropped below the red line. The engine coughed and shuddered. Trudy turned sharply into a fuel station as the Town Car sputtered to a stop and died. She rested her forehead on the wheel and said, "That's it."

She got out of the car and kicked the front wheel. The damp, March air seemed colder here. Trudy reached into the front seat and pulled on her jean jacket. A couple of bikers in black leather left the pumps and headed her way. She glanced about searching for an escape.

The first man had a red bandana over his head, an earring, and a spider tattoo on his neck. He said, "Hi. Car trouble or out of gas?"

Trudy waved her hand toward the car. "It's empty."

"We'll push it to the pumps. Put it in neutral and steer." Trudy sat in the driver's seat as they moved behind her car. When it was pushed into place, the second man flipped the gas tank lid open and stuck the nozzle in. He was more broadly built than the man with the tattoo. His long brownish-blond hair was tied back at the nape of his neck.

Trudy climbed out of the car. "Thanks guys. You don't have to do that."

The one filling the tank said, "No problem."

"$5.00 only please." She shuffled her feet. A brisk wind made it seem colder than it was.

The man with the spider tattoo pointed to the car full of her belongings. "Moving here or passing through?"

"Moving here. How's the job market?"

"The best thing to do is go to a temp agency. They'll find you something, especially if you're drug free."

Trudy nodded. "That's good to know. That's enough gas. Thank you."

The spider tattoo on the first man's neck quivered as he continued. "If you show up and don't mind working, you can stay employed practically full time, even if it is at different places. If you go to All-Star Temp Agency, ask for Kathy. She tests all the new temps."

"No benefits. No insurance." The guy pumping gas at the back of the Town Car said.

Trudy shrugged. "Right now a job is more important than benefits or insurance. That's enough gas. Thanks."

He grinned in a friendly way. She noticed a scar at the corner of his mouth made the smile lopsided. "Naw. We'll fill it for you. Don't worry about it."

"No. Really."

The man with the spider tattoo broke into a smile. One gold tooth glistened. "Mike likes to do this. He pays for your gas and asks that you pay it forward sometime to someone else."

Trudy sighed with relief. "Pay it forward. Thanks. I'll do that."

Mike placed the hose back in the pump, screwed the cap on the tank and paid the attendant in the glass booth, gesturing to the bikes and the car.

The man with the tattoo shook her hand. "I'm Spider. Welcome to Indianapolis. Remember, any place is as good as you make it. You just have to have a little faith." As he walked away she noticed the Christian Motorcycle Association logo on the back of his leather jacket. Mike and Spider strapped on helmets and mounted their bikes. With a wave, they roared out of the gas station into traffic.

The whole exchange was rather baffling. She could expect this kindness to strangers in Amesville, but it hadn't been her experience that it happened in a big city. After using the restroom, she checked the phone booth for a directory. Finding none, she asked the attendant for one.

The girl behind the counter flipped long blonde hair over her shoulder. She bent down and pulled out a thick phone book. "You have to look at it right here."

"Okay."

"It can't leave the store. And don't tear out any of the pages. And return it immediately."

"I promise on the life of my first born," Trudy said, making the Girl Scout pledge sign.

The girl fluttered half-closed eye lids and gave a soft grunt of disgust, but she hefted the directory over the counter into Trudy's hands.

Trudy copied the addresses and phone numbers of temporary employment agencies, including All-Star Temp onto the back of her useless bank checks. She handed the directory to the attendant. "Do I owe anything for the gas?"

The girl looked at her like she was stupid. "No. The guy who filled the tank paid."

Trudy nodded, too relieved to give a snarky response. At least this time, someone did what he said he'd do. It meant she still had money for food.

In the service station bathroom, Trudy cleaned up and exchanged the clothes she'd traveled in for an old off-the-rack blue skirt and blouse and blazer she had in her suitcase. Not long afterwards, she presented herself to the receptionist at All Star Temp Agency. "Is Kathy here?"

A broad-shouldered woman in a long sleeve black sweater decorated with white geometric designs stood. Her blonde hair was pulled back in a ponytail at the base of her neck. "I'm Kathy."

"I'm new in town and looking for work. A couple of guys helped me out this morning and suggested I talk with you about a job."

"Spider and Mike?"

Trudy blinked.

"Don't look so shocked. They've done this before. If they see someone they think might be a good candidate, they refer them. Of course, from here on you have to prove yourself."

"Of course."

Kathy tested Trudy on typing, numbers, and problem solving. When all the forms were done Kathy said, "You've neglected to fill in contact information."

"I'm in the process of moving here. I don't yet have a place to stay. I don't even have a phone, but I'll check in with you every morning when you open to see if there's work."

Kathy's grey eyes softened with understanding. "Okay. That'll do, but only for a week or two."

"Also, I'd appreciate it if you didn't contact my last employer. I wasn't fired, I left, but we didn't part on good terms. I don't want him to know where I am."

Trudy left All Star Temp with a bounce in her step. To keep the positive glow, she drove around until she found a pawn shop. There she pawned some of the belongings she considered expendable. She breathed a little easier holding the cash in her hands. The added benefit was after rearranging the bags, she had enough space to recline the seat when she wanted to sleep.

Trudy left the pawnshop with directions to the nearest laundromat. From there she checked out some of the coffee shops around the university and colleges. In each place she perused the bulletin boards for leads on a cheap room to rent. Everything she found was more than she could afford for the next few months.

It was a reminder of how far she'd slid down the ladder of success. In fact, her ladder didn't even have rungs to climb anymore. Her face grew hot at the thought of how prideful she'd been of her and Phillip's success. All pretense. All smoke and mirrors. Her father would quote the Bible, "Pride goeth before the fall." She sure couldn't argue that point.

The next morning, Trudy waited for Kathy to unlock the door, anxious to see if a job had materialized. By the weekend she hired on at a grocery store to smile at the public and hand out samples she cooked in a toaster oven while encouraging them to try Breck's Best Sausage.

Bright and early one Monday morning Kathy sent her to an office job at a factory that needed a temporary secretary for a week. Trudy continued to sleep in the Town Car, but the factory parking lot had a gate and a security guard, so it wasn't as terrifying as being on the street. Every evening she spent in coffee shops, laundromats, or diners searching the bulletin boards for leads on room rentals.

Trudy moved a copy of 'The Indianapolis Star' someone had left on the coffee shop's chair and laid it on the table next to her cup of coffee. The rentals section offered no better leads. Turning the page, a color photo of two familiar faces caught her eye. Posing with other men and women in leather jackets, Spider and Mike smiled broadly enough that Spider's gold tooth was obvious. The header read "Christian Motorcycle Association Raises Funds for Children with Cancer." Someday she'd thank those men for helping her get a job.

A couple of slim co-eds stepped up to the nearby bulletin board. The board bulged with ads for cars, motorcycles and bikes, musical instruments and text books, beds and home supplies, as well as advertisements for upcoming events. Starting at opposite ends, they worked their way through the postings skipping over the apartments and rooms listing. Trudy followed them with interest wondering what they were searching for.

"Here," said one girl with dangly earrings and hair cut so short, Trudy considered it a boy's crew cut, except it was dyed red at the tips. "Size 9/10 satin prom dress. Green. Full length. Worn once."

The other girl with a short layered bob stuck her hands in her jacket pockets and swung them out away from her body a couple of times. "Nah, green's not my favorite."

Trudy said, "If you're looking for fancy dresses, I have a few. I'm new to the area and doubt if my new lifestyle will require formals."

The girls turned and looked Trudy up and down. She was wearing the same conservative, but high-end skirt and jacket she'd interviewed in and had worked in that day. She stood so the girls could see she was their size. She shook her head to set her full length of ginger hair a-swirl. It was a youthful gesture she hoped would give the girls an impression that their ages weren't that different.

"What color?" Said Miss Layered Bob.

"I have several. They're outside in my car." Miss Layered Bob exchanged looks with Miss Crew Cut, who nodded. Together they walked out to the Town Car. Trudy pulled out a couple of suitcases, shut the trunk and laid them on top. She unzipped the first one and lifted out a blue dress.

"Oh," Miss Layered Bob cooed as she stroked the material. They pored over the choices and tried on their selections in the coffee shop's restroom. Miss Layered Bob bought the blue dress and a low backed red dress. Miss Crew Cut settled for a sleek style with white sequins and a low cut bodice trimmed in ostrich-feathers. Trudy packed up as they counted out the agreed on price. "I've got a couple of friends. What's your number?"

"No phone yet, but I expect to be here tomorrow night at the same time. I have shoes and accessories that I can show you then."

Miss Crew Cut's attitude had warmed up considerably during the exchange. "Say, if you're looking for an apartment, I know a place."

Apartment was a strong word for the place. It was a single pale green room a little larger than Trudy's walk-in closet in Las Vegas.

Trudy was certain it had been a closet even though it held no rods. Shelves for storage were built in between the unfinished studs on one wall.

Furnished was a strong word, too. It was comprised of a long couch with a deep seat that she would have to use as a bed and a large, bulky beat-up coffee table. The one window was painted over and the green color pooled at the bottom to keep it permanently shut. Trudy thought in this neighborhood that was a plus. There was no kitchenette.

Oddly, the bathroom was larger than the main room. An iron claw-foot tub sprawled in the center of black and white tiles. Wherever the wall paper wasn't torn, pink flamingos tip-toed among lily-pads. Misshapen black spots where the enamel was chipped dotted the enormous white sink. An ancient toilet with a tank mounted high on the wall still gave a mighty flush.

The price was outrageous for the size, but cheap compared to what else was available.

"I'll take it," Trudy told the old woman who showed her the apartment.

The woman sighed. She said, "Great." She tugged her pink sweatshirt over the too-tight matching sweatpants. "My son will be so pleased. I own the building, but he manages it. He's gone for a couple of weeks. His name is Brett. He's a real nice boy. He never gets into any trouble. He's available, you know."

"I'm not looking for a boyfriend, just an apartment."

The woman sighed. "Too bad. I'm not getting any younger, you know. I'd really like grandchildren."

Trudy smiled tightly. "Is there a lease I can sign?"

The woman sighed and tugged at her shirt again. "Follow me down to the office."

Trudy signed the lease and paid. "May I have the key to the apartment?"

The woman sighed again. "You're such a nice girl. Maybe you'll feel differently when you meet my Brett."

"Really, the apartment is all I'm interested in."

The woman sighed twice this time then handed Trudy the keys.

Trudy immediately dubbed her new digs 'The WC.' She was down to a few dollars again, but at least she had an address to give the temp agency.

That night, Trudy spread her quilt over the couch. Ah. What luxury to spread out. She snuggled into the back of the couch as if she were spooning with someone. She closed her eyes. The words to a childhood prayer sprang to mind. "Now I lay me down to sleep. I pray the Lord my soul to keep."

Her next thought was, "What time is it?" The glowing dial of her watch indicated 3:00 a.m. She'd slept hard, feeling safe.

Trudy rose and stumbled into the bathroom. She turned the faucets on full and let the steam fill the room. Lowering into the huge tub reminded Trudy of a night in the fabulous first class suite of the St. Regis Aspen Resort when she and Phillip took a ski trip. They'd had such fun during the days and the nights had been so romantic. His eyes. His nose. His mouth. Why did she miss him so much? It wasn't fair.

Later that morning, Kathy unlocked the temp agency door and Trudy followed her inside holding two cups of coffee. Once the lights and computers were switched on and the answering machine checked, Kathy greedily reached for one of the cups. "God bless you. I overslept and didn't have time to make coffee."

Trudy wasn't sure the gesture merited a blessing. She was purposefully trying to be friendly to keep on Kathy's good side, which was a Phillip ploy – be friendly without being a friend. She didn't want to be like that so she decided she'd welcome the blessing because she intended her new lifeview to be opposite of what Phillip had taught her. She purposed to be friendly to everybody and to develop a few worthwhile friendships as well. Kathy was so nice, her friendship seemed worth cultivating. "I found a place not far from here."

"Wonderful."

"Well, it's not exactly wonderful, but it beats sleeping in the car. Am I still at the factory today?"

"Yes. One more day at this job. I spoke with the supervisor last night. He was pleased with how well you handled that shipping snafu. The regular gal will be back Monday, but they said you were their preferred temp choice from now on."

"That's good," Trudy said.

"Good? That's great. They want you in a different division next week to cover for someone taking vacation. How do you feel about line work? You'll want to wear old clothes and it'd be wise to cut your nails."

Trudy looked at her perfectly manicured hands with the long acrylic nails. Without a regular manicurist and nail artist, they'd be difficult to keep anyway. She paused. "I'll take it. Say Kathy, can I have a few sheets of typing paper and an envelope?"

Kathy nodded and pointed to the paper as she answered the ringing phone. Filled with a warm glow, Trudy grabbed the paper and headed to the factory. She determined to work equally hard at the line job next week as she had at the office job. Unlike Phillip, she'd be friendly with co-workers and those under her, not only those she thought could do something for her. She would make it clear she wasn't after their jobs, didn't mind taking instruction, and would do any job they gave her without complaint.

That night she posted half-sheets on bulletin boards with descriptions of her less expensive gowns. It only made sense because a college kid couldn't afford the name brand ones. She added times she'd be in the coffee shop and decorated the edges to add a little class and to draw attention to them.

After noticing several upcoming gala events announced on their community calendars in the "Indianapolis Star" and the "Southside Times", she advertised the higher priced items there. With each sale the Town Car looked more like a car and less like a storage container.

Despite working most days at the factory, Trudy showed up each morning at the Temp Agency. She and Kathy would visit for a few minutes before the office opened for the day. One Friday morning Kathy handed her an envelope. "Oh, I've got some mail for you. This was delivered for you yesterday."

Trudy recognized the envelope as the same one she'd sent her parents using All Star Temp Agency as the return address. Trudy accepted the envelope. "Return to sender" was written across the front in her father's hand.

# Chapter Five

On the other side of Indianapolis, Carol Streeter unlocked the door to Andy's office and peeked at his desk. It had piles of paperwork stacked on it, evincing the idea that in this busy place, at any moment, Andy would return. Andy would never return. Had it already been a year since his death? How could that be? It seemed like yesterday.

The smell of stale cigarette and cigar smoke hung in the air. Carol coughed. Andy had let the crew smoke and would occasionally light a cigar himself, if they were shooting the breeze after a long day. It smelled as if the crew had continued the practice.

She pushed the door open a little further and tried to step inside. Someone grabbed her jacket to keep her from entering Andy's workspace. She dropped the cardboard box she carried and whirled around. No one else was there. The tugging came as the pocket of her heavy blue winter jacket caught on the door knob. Still, it was almost enough to convince her to leave. She sighed. This was one more distasteful task that must be done and there was no one else to do it. Carol freed the fabric from the door handle and stooped to pick up the sturdy box that had once held bananas.

She coughed again and opened a window. She waved the box over the desk to whisk away some of the smoky smell into the cold March air. The box caught the edge of a picture and sent it clattering to the floor. Carol bent to retrieve it.

The framed photo was of Andy and their daughter Kim when she was little, smiling as they staggered under the shared weight of a watermelon with a big blue ribbon affixed to the top. Good times. Good memories. She placed it in the sturdy banana box and picked up another photo. Her oldest son, Nick, with beaming face sat in a wingback chair with one arm around the shoulders of his smaller brother and the other holding a tiny baby propped against his side.

Carol wiped the dust from the glass. The two younger children were gone and had been for a long time. Sometimes it felt that way about Nick, even though he came home every few years from South America. She couldn't let herself think about how she longed for her children or she'd never finish clearing the office. She carefully placed that picture in the box. She picked up the next photo. Carol caught her breath.

This one showed her and Andy on their twentieth wedding anniversary. He'd surprised her with a cruise to the Bahamas. A photographer caught them on the dance floor. He'd called out to them and they'd turned from gazing into each other's eyes. The look of love was still on their faces, their eyes shining with happiness. Her blonde hair pulled up away from her rosy cheeks and blue eyes. His slightly darker head still bent toward hers. Andy's arms held her, leading her, just as he had through their marriage. They'd been so happy.

A sharp pricking like a runner's stitch caught in the area over her heart. She pressed a hand to it while blinking away tears. Aloud she ordered herself, "This is not the time or place to break down."

Quickly she placed the photo in the box and added other personal items without lingering over them.

When the box was full she carried it to the car and returned with another empty box.

"Good morning Carol." The job foreman preceded her up the steps and held the door open for her. An orange stocking cap covered his curly brown hair and caused his ears to protrude like handles on a sugar bowl. His normally broad smile was subdued, but kind.

That pinching in her heart happened again. She placed her hand on his arm. The material of his duck fabric jacket felt stiff to the touch. "Thank you for all you've done, Martin. You were a good friend to Andy and then to me. You've kept things going here this last year. I couldn't have done it without you. It means a lot."

Martin looked away, up toward an empty corner of the office. "Sure thing. No problem."

Carol said, "I'm sorry it turned out this way."

"Yeah. Me, too." Martin quickly moved away and closed the window.

"Will you be staying on now that the business is sold? Mr. Wolfenbarger said he'd keep all the men that wanted to stay."

Martin nodded. "Probably. Although it won't be the same. Andy—and you—were good people to work for."

Neither mentioned Andy's partner who had left the country after taking out loans against the business and emptying its checkbook. It was something she only became aware of when the checks automatically paid from the business account started bouncing.

Carol surveyed the office. Andy had worked so hard to build the business, now it was gone in a moment with a signature on a piece of paper. She tried to smooth out the catch in her voice. "I don't think there's much left. I should be finished in a few minutes. Don't let me keep you from your work. If you find anything else personal, would you drop it by?"

"Sure thing, Carol." Martin shuffled his feet and looked at the floor. "However, I've been instructed by Mr. Wolfenbarger to stay while you get Andy's things."

"Oh." Carol gazed over the messy office. What did he think she'd take? Current client files? "Not a problem," she rushed to add. "You can check what I took already. Some photographs and personal items."

Two red spots appeared on Martin's cheeks. He shook his head. "No, that's okay."

He busied himself with something on the desk. When she finished, Martin offered to carry the box. Carol declined, hurried to the car and drove away. Tears streamed down her face, whether from relief that the business and its burdens were in new hands or from the fresh sense of her deep loss, she simply wasn't sure.

Either way it wasn't something that a trip to Dairy Queen could solve. On the other hand, it wouldn't hurt. A peanut buster parfait seemed the perfect way to salute Andy's business good-bye in the same manner as they'd celebrated with one when the business opened all those years ago.

She yanked the wheel to turn the car into the DQ drive a moment before she passed it. *Honk. Honk.* The car behind her swerved slightly. "Sorry. Sorry," she muttered.

The cool creaminess of the ice cream, the hot sweetness of the fudgy chocolate, and the crunch of the peanuts were comforting as she sorted through memories.

That first year the business had struggled and they'd made many sacrifices. Then, it grew robust. Andy took on a partner and the business expanded even more over the years. Until, everything reversed.

The fatal heart attack, the partner's betrayal meant a year of scrimping for Carol to make ends meet while trying to keep the business going. All that while dealing with the lonely nights without her husband and comforting Kim over the loss of the father who had doted on her.

Andy's foresight meant that upon his death, the mortgage had been paid on their nice, but modest home, so she and Kim at least had a place to live. Carol toasted her husband with the last spoonful. "Thank you, Andy." She threw the empty container away and pulled out of the parking lot.

Two blocks later she pulled to the side of the road and threw up. It was too much sweetness after all those months of doing without. Or, maybe it was the knot in her stomach about how much debt was still left. She'd been fasting and praying, but a world of uncertainty remained. Kim would graduate a year from June. Would the college plans have to be scrapped?

Carol's heart beat faster as she pulled back into traffic and headed home. If she wasn't careful, she'd have a heart attack, too. She opened the window to the brisk air and chose to be invigorated. She shivered violently and closed the window again.

When Carol pulled into the drive, she saw Kim was waiting for her at the front door. Kim jumped up and down and came running along the brick walkway to the car. She waved a letter in one hand. "Mom. Mom. I got in. I'm going to Boston University this summer for that special two-week program."

Carol pulled herself from the car and accepted Kim's hugs and looked at the letter. "Kim. How exciting. I'm so proud of you."

"We'll have to go shopping. They put us up in dorm rooms, but I'll need to bring all my own linens, and blankets, and stuff. They sent a list. I'll need a new wardrobe. It'll be perfect because I'll be familiar with the area and I'll know everything I'll need for next year when I go to school there."

"Kim, that's a year and a half away."

"Sure, but I still need stuff for this summer. We have to send them a check for $2,000 right away."

"$2,000," Carol yelped.

"Yes, to save my spot in the program."

Carol herded her daughter into the house. She set her purse on the table by the front door. Kim continued to ramble while Carol removed boots and coat and hat and gloves. At last she headed for the kitchen and put on a kettle of water. She pulled hot chocolate packets from the cupboard.

"…it's going to be perfect," Kim enthused and melted into one of the chairs at the table. Her face shone and her gorgeous dark hair floated around her shoulders.

"I'm proud of you, honey. But we don't have that kind of money. I've been meaning to talk with you about this. We can't manage your tuition there next year. It's not a full ride. Even with your scholarships we can't afford that university. If you help, you should be able to go to one of the local universities here in Indianapolis."

"But mom, of course I'm going to go. We've talked about this for years. Dad would want me to. We planned on it."

"Kim, haven't you been paying attention to what's been going on around here this past year? There isn't any money. The bank accounts were wiped out, including your college fund."

"But you've sold the business, now. That had to be a lot of money." Kim reached out and patted her mother's hand. "You're afraid, that's all, because Dad's gone, but it'll be okay."

"Sure, we'll be okay. Yes, I'm afraid. But the money from the sale of the business is spoken for already. It's gone. It went to clear up debt, to pay suppliers. There isn't anything left and there's more debt to pay."

Kim's full lips trembled. Tears welled in her large brown eyes. "But Mom, it's not fair. I thought—"

"What did you think, Kim? Didn't you notice that the cupboards have been practically bare? Didn't you notice that I wasn't eating at supper? Didn't you see the bills stacked up in the mail box? Or that Minnie missed her last vet appointment? Or that you didn't get your dental checkups this year? What about the six weeks we didn't have electricity? What did you think that was about?"

A frown worked over Kim's forehead. Tears came fast and furious. "Don't yell at me. I thought you were missing Daddy and forgot to keep things up. Does Nick know?"

"What would be the point of worrying your brother? He's a continent away and can't do anything to help."

The tea kettle sang. Carol ignored it, slumping into the kitchen chair opposite Kim. She put her head in her hands, too weak to do anything else now that her anger was spent.

"Can't you get more hours at the hospital?"

Carol lifted her head and stared at her daughter's hopeful face. She'd been wrong to continue to pamper Kim the way Andy had. She really was a pouty princess at times. "No. I can't. I've already been working extra-long hours at the hospital typing my fingers raw so your junior and senior years could be fun."

The kettle whistled more insistently. Carol shut the heat off under the water. The whistling subsided to a hiss, then quieted. "What have you done around here? You haven't helped. You wait for me to fix your food. You spend your time with friends. Never once did you ask if you could help by getting a job or fixing supper or cleaning house or doing laundry or, or getting a job."

"But you never wanted me to do those things before. You've always been so particular."

"I was always the homemaker with the time and energy. I wasn't the sole provider in a household that was going under."

Kim's beautiful face screwed into a frown. "I didn't know. Are things really that bad?"

Carol reached for a yellow envelope that had been sitting on the table for a few days. She pulled the notice out, unfolded it, and showed Kim. "Gas and Electric - Final Notice". Carol picked up the stack of mail Kim had dumped on the table. She took a table knife and slit open the top envelope. "Here's one from The Department Store, $68. I thought I told you not to charge anything anymore."

"But the sweaters were half price."

"You'll take them back. Here's the Visa and the high school wants your tuition paid before the end of the year. Grant's wants the balance due from replacing the hot water heater."

"I suppose this means I won't be going to Paris with my friends either this summer." Kim frowned and her lip puckered as she collapsed against the back of her chair.

Carol sighed. "A little bird will sit on that lip one of these days."

Kim scowled harder.

"What's this?" Carol held up a letter.

Kim shook her head and shrugged to indicate it wasn't anything that was her fault. "Not mine. I didn't charge anything except those sweaters."

"Please, God," Carol prayed. She picked up the table knife. It felt cool in her hand. With one slice she opened the envelope. She gasped as a check fluttered to the tile floor. With two fingers she picked it up by the corner and held it within sight.

The publisher had accepted her book manuscript on grief and was paying an advance on it. "Thank you, God. Thank you, God," Carol said. She clasped the check to her chest.

No one else knew how much it meant that the check would come today, the last day to pay the electric bill. Kim picked up the attached letter to read it. She said, "I didn't even know you were writing a book."

"At first it was to get through the nights with your father gone. Then, I thought maybe somebody else would be helped by it. They're going to print it. This is the advance." Carol waved the check in the air.

"That's good, huh? Right, Mom?"

"It's fantastic."

Kim picked up the utility bill. "Come on, Mom. We can still get there before they close." They both giggled as they stuffed their arms into jackets, grabbed purses, and ran out the front door. They nearly knocked over a man who stood on their front porch poised to ring the bell. The man wore a long dark overcoat, which along with protruding eyes, made him appear somber.

"Oh, Hello," Carol said.

"Mrs. Streeter?"

"Yes."

He held a business card toward her. She took it and studied it.

"I'm Everett Digger from the Internal Revenue Service. We need to speak."

# Chapter Six

Carol said, "I'm sorry, but we have to be somewhere important. Can I set up an appointment?"

"I'd prefer to do this now. You haven't replied to any of the letters we've sent."

Carol frowned. "What letters? I didn't get any letters."

"They were sent to the Abbers Road address."

Carol sighed. She handed the keys to Kim. "Honey, go start the car. I'll be there in a moment."

Kim walked down the sidewalk, glancing backward a couple of times.

"That address is, was, my husband's business partner's address. He's disappeared. I didn't know about any correspondence," Carol said.

"This regards unpaid business and employment taxes."

Carol gasped as if someone had dumped a bucket of ice water on her. She studied his bulging eyes and the round fur cap on his head. She waved the business card. "I really don't have time now to talk. I've got to be somewhere before they close. I'll call tomorrow for an appointment later this week."

"But, Mrs. Streeter."

Carol hurried to the car and didn't wave as she drove away. Dread, like a lead weight, pressed the pleasure out of being able to pay the electric bill. Still, she did her best to keep in high spirits for Kim's sake.

The heaviness of learning about more debt dogged her. On her first day off work, she entered the IRS office. The open office with grey cubicles and orange plastic chairs was spare, utilitarian, and ugly. The one redeeming feature was that it was located in an old store front property with glass windows that looked out over the busy street. She thought, "Out there life goes on, while in here..."

Carol licked her lips. She took the plastic chair the man with bulging eyes offered her. Revenue Officer Everett Digger, without his black coat to bulk up his frame, looked less imposing. His manner was polite and straightforward as he laid out the extent of the business indebtedness for years of non-payment along with the resultant late fees and interest.

His lips kept moving, but Carol stopped hearing what he said. She simply couldn't take in any more. The amount was staggering. How could Andy not know his partner was embezzling? How could he not see the tax notices? Would she lose her home?

Everett Digger handed her a form detailing the full amounts owed and pages and pages of forms to fill out for a payment agreement. Stunned, she wordlessly took the paperwork, and drove home.

Once there, Carol climbed the stairs to her bedroom, fell on her knees at the side of the bed. "God, please help us. You know we did not try to defraud anyone. Please show me what to do."

After a while her knees grew stiff, and she felt chilled, but calmer. She kept thinking about the box of stuff she'd removed from

Andy's desk. She rose with the conviction she'd prove Andy had not done anything wrong.

She hauled the box up from the basement and carried it to the dining room table so she could paw through the paperwork and the files that the new owner hadn't felt pertained to his carrying on of the business. In the bottom of the box, inside one of the files was a red bound journal with several pieces of paper sticking out of it.

The journal was heavily used, the binding weak and almost ready to tear. The first entry was the year Andy had dedicated his business to the Lord. Carol remembered well the night five years before in church when Andy had gone to the altar and said he was giving his business to God. The first entry read: "'Whatsoever ye do, do it heartily, as unto the Lord, and not unto men.' Colossians 3:23."

After that, each day had been recorded, its ups and downs listed, usually with a sentence, occasionally with a paragraph. He noted when he'd paid the bills and if something couldn't be paid immediately. Carol found references to donations that she never knew he'd made, including research for Sudden Infant Death Syndrome and a survivors of drowning victims group. These reminders of their losses as a couple brought tears to her eyes. Andy also noted when he'd paid the taxes and how much.

A later entry revealed his suspicions that something wasn't right with the taxes. His partner claimed an error and corrected the accounts. Andy even wrote that when he'd checked up on his partner the next time everything was fine.

Reassured by this proof, Carol called the accountant. He advised her to bring proof and speak with the IRS to see if they would reduce the amount or even allow an Offer in Compromise. Hope burned within her as she set about finding evidence to clear Andy.

First, Carol explained her dilemma to Mr. Wolfenbarger. He allowed her to search Andy's old business records in the basement and make copies of anything she needed, as long as Martin was there to oversee what she did. Carol felt better about being in the creepy, dimly lit basement with Martin present.

She learned that after Andy had checked on the partner, everything was normal for several months. Then, comparing the paperwork from the IRS with Andy's records, found that the partner changed the billing address filed with the IRS. "Thank you, God. Thank you, God," she exclaimed.

Carol came out of the basement feeling filthy physically, but mentally clean of any thought that Andy had known about the embezzlement. She didn't bother to go home, but took her evidence straight to Mr. Digger at the IRS office.

After laying out all the evidence, he agreed with her. The heavy fines and late fees that had been levied were removed from the account. She was liable for only the tax itself.

"Yes." Carol jumped up. She felt like giving Mr. Digger a hug. She came around the desk. His bugged-out eyes widened. She took mercy on him and shook his hand vigorously. He relaxed, again. She dusted her grimy hands against her jeans. "I would like an Offer in Compromise."

Mr. Digger shook his head. "You're not eligible for an OIC. The taxes were employee trust taxes. They can't be waived."

Elation waned. The amount remaining was still enormous. Carol ran a hand through her hair and felt a cobweb cling to her fingers. "Ew." She brushed it out and dropped it in his wastebasket.

He eyed the basket, as if he might empty it as soon as she left. "Do you still have the paperwork for a payment agreement?"

"Yes."

"Fill it out and get it back to me as quickly as possible. That's the best we can do."

She thanked him, and hurried home to shower off the dirt of Andy's, no not Andy's any longer, but Wolfenbarger's basement.

The soap bubbles gathered at the drain and disappeared. If only the heaviness of the remaining taxes could be drained away as well.

"Lord, you led me to the information to clear Andy of illegal activity. You dissolved the extra fees. I know I owe this money and you said pay to Caesar what is Caesar's. Even though Andy already paid it once, they didn't get it. It was stolen. It's not fair, Lord. I don't know why I have to go through this, but I am. I can trust you to bring the embezzler to justice. You know where he is. Please help me be gracious under this load, even as you've helped me with every other heavy load in life. I know you'll bring me through this one as well."

The verse "Bear ye one another's burdens and so fulfil the law of Christ" came to mind. It stayed with her the rest of the day. This Ephesians scripture didn't make sense until she was sitting at supper with her daughter. "Kim, do you remember that man that came to our door the day we were rushing off to pay the electric bill? The day I got my advance?"

"Kind of. He had big eyes and a fur hat."

"He was from the IRS. It turns out that not only did the partner steal our money, he also embezzled money that your dad owed to the IRS."

Kim's dark brown eyes fastened on her mom. "That's bad."

"Really bad. I'm telling you this because you're grown now, and I think you should know what we're up against. I'm not going to keep you in the dark, anymore. We'll share the burden." Carol named the amount due.

"That's a fortune. I guess this means I can't go to college." Kim's dark brown eyes filled with tears.

"Hold on, until I've told you everything. I've been working all week to find the paper trail. I can prove where he showed falsified records to Dad. Dad knew nothing about it. I met with the IRS today. The good news is they reduced it."

Kim considered the new amount. "That's a lot better, but it still seems impossible."

"It'll be difficult, but not impossible."

"Well, I have some good news, too. I got a job as receptionist in a talent agency downtown."

"A talent agency? What do you have to do? Do they want you to model?"

"I know what you're thinking. It's not that kind of agency. No porno. This is legit. I got the job through the school. I'll be answering phones, making appointments, taking the people back for interviews and auditions."

"Well, if the school helped you find it, it must be okay."

"I'll give you all my wages. That'll help." Kim brushed at a tear.

Carol hugged her daughter. "That's so sweet. You're generous, but I'm not asking you to pay the taxes. That's on me. I think I can work something out, a payment plan that's not too horrible. However, I will need you to save for college and to help with gas money plus car insurance. It means you can't do any special program in Boston."

Kim pulled a long face. "Aw, Mom. Don't you have any savings?"

Carol willed herself to not waver. Firmly she stated, "I have a couple of bonds, but with everything else gone, we'll have to save that for a dire emergency. Summer programs in Boston are discretionary."

Kim slouched with her arms folded for a few moments. Her face cleared and she straightened. "I know. I'll take a job dog-walking and dog-sitting, if you'll help let the dogs out while I'm working at the Agency."

"Sure," Carol said, caught up in Kim's enthusiasm. Then, she re-thought her reply. "No. I will if I'm here, but don't count on me. You'll have to solve that problem yourself. Kim, even with two jobs, Boston is out of the question, but there'll still be prom and parties and lots of things you can do. As long as you understand the bills have to be paid and college is your primary goal. We'll sit down and set up a budget."

Kim hugged Carol. "I'm sorry all this is on you, Mom. I know it stresses you out."

"Yes, but it was a lot worse when I wondered if your dad knew about it. It's a relief that he didn't. In fact, it was his dedication to God that brought the proof." Carol told Kim about the journal which led her to the other records.

"I always liked Dad's partner. I can't believe he'd do that to us. He was our friend."

"Yes, betrayal always hurts more because it is someone you've trusted."

# Chapter Seven

Trudy held the envelope Kathy had given her and felt the heat of embarrassment rise in her cheeks. Being rejected was something she never wanted anyone to witness, particularly Kathy. With a sense of loneliness, she tucked it into her purse without saying anything about what it meant.

Kathy smiled encouragingly. "Boy, you look tense. Sit down."

"Why?"

"Come on. Sit down. I'm going to give you a neck massage. Come on." She patted her black swivel chair. "Sit."

Trudy complied. Kathy moved around behind her. "Wow. You're muscles feel like iron bars. Relax."

Kathy's fingers expertly worked a few of the knots out. Trudy felt the tension fade. "If I'd known you were this good at massage, I've have looked pathetic earlier."

"I'm being especially nice to you because I have a favor to ask."

Trudy stiffened.

Kathy hurried to say, "I got a couple of tickets for my birthday to see that Elvis impersonator next Saturday night. Would you go with me?"

Trudy swiveled around to face Kathy. "Yeah. Of course. I love Elvis. How is that a favor to you?"

"My boyfriend doesn't want to go and I don't want to go alone."

"Done." Trudy swiveled again. Kathy resumed kneading her neck. "You're still massaging. Uh-oh. What else do you need?"

"Monday, I'd like to send you to Peter Faulkinroy. He's the owner of Faulkinroy Publicists. The man is kind of a pretentious jerk. I've sent him four secretaries in six weeks."

"What's his problem?"

"He's a perfectionist, which is good for his business, but hard on secretaries who aren't familiar with the office. He's impatient and expects them to know what he needs before he needs it. You've already proven you can handle pressure and can see what needs to be done next. Plus you're good at managing people. I think you can manage Mr. Faulkinroy."

"What happened to his regular secretary?"

"Nothing. He's starting up his business so he's looking to hire full time. He expects a lot, but he's driven. I have a feeling he's going to be a huge success. He can be very personable and persuasive with his clients. They love him. If this business goes where I think it will, you could hire on permanently and grow with the company."

"What's he paying?"

"The regular fee for temps, but if he wants to hire you, you can buy your contract from me and negotiate for your wages. I'll let you pay the contract in installments, but I don't do this ordinarily, so don't tell anyone."

"That's generous. I'll give it a try."

Kathy heaved a sigh. She twirled Trudy around to face her. "Whew. I was worried you'd say no. Hey, don't forget me when you settle in there. We'll still be friends won't we?"

"Of course," Trudy said. "Any friend of Elvis is a friend of mine. Say, you want to come over to the WC tonight for pizza? We could watch old Elvis flicks. I bought a TV from a St. Vincent de Paul's second hand shop."

"The Vay-Tsay? Where's that? It sounds like something from a Vietnamese restaurant."

"No. It's spelled WC for Water Closet, but it's the French pronunciation. That's what the French call their toilets. It's what I've dubbed my apartment because the bathroom is the biggest room."

Kathy laughed. "You're funny. What time?"

"I'll meet you back here at closing. We can pick up a pizza and take it back to the WC."

Kathy laughed again. "Okay. The 'Vay-Tsay' it is. I'll slip out at lunch and rent a couple of movies."

That night Kathy brought the VHS tapes while Trudy carried the pizza. Its smell tantalized them every step down the dark hall. Trudy groaned. "Oh, great. The light's out. I'll have to call the apartment manager to replace it."

"How many years will that take?"

"The landlord is an old lady. She likes me. So does her manager son. Hopefully they'll be pretty good about that kind of maintenance stuff." Balancing the pizza box with one hand, Trudy bent to insert the key in the keyhole. She never got a chance to turn it. At the slight pressure, the door swung open.

A man with long, greasy, brown hair stood near her couch. Her TV was in his hands. His face registered surprise. At his feet the

VCR sat askew in a box with a set of sheets. The corner of her jewelry box, still filled with her favorite pieces, poked out the other corner.

A surge of rage flashed within her. Shrieking like the proverbial banshee, Trudy dropped the pizza and grabbed a floor lamp. Swinging it like a bat, she charged the man. The thief dropped the TV and ducked. The TV crunched as it hit the floor. The sound infuriated her. Trudy roared, swinging again. Missed.

He bolted for the door. Kathy did some quick poke-jab moves with her hands. The intruder doubled over. She bent to the side lashing out with her foot. "Oof," he grunted as he landed flat on his back, both arms flung out.

A second figure, heavier, older, and greasier than his accomplice, appeared at the door, a gun in his hand.

Kathy straightened and stepped backward. Trudy halted in mid-swing with the floor lamp suspended in a tight grip over her head.

The man on the floor scrabbled to his feet and stumbled out the door. His partner waited a moment and followed.

The room filled with loud panting. Trudy realized it was herself. She set the lamp on the floor and bent over with her hands on her thighs, trying to catch her breath.

Kathy stepped to the door and peered down the hall. "They're gone." She closed and latched the door. "Did they take anything?"

Trudy did a quick inventory by sight and determined they'd left empty-handed. She shook her head, and crouched to pick up the television. The screen was cracked all the way across and a big chip was missing from one corner. She groaned. "My TV."

As if there had been no intruder and they'd accidentally knocked the TV off the beaten-up TV tray, Kathy calmly said, "Plug it in. See if it still works."

Trudy set it up and plugged it in. A picture came up, even though the crack interrupted a seamless view. "It's okay."

"In better shape than this pizza," Kathy said. She scraped a piece off of the lid and tasted it. "Still good though. That's what's important. Let's eat. You can hook the VCR up later."

Trudy followed Kathy's lead, but found her hand trembled as she lifted a slice to her mouth. The warm, gooey goodness was soothing. She took a second bite.

Kathy finished her first piece, and used a napkin to wipe grease from her fingers and mouth. She tapped the top on a can of soda and popped it open, quickly sucking off the fizz that rose from the shaking it had taken when it was dropped on the floor. She set it on the bulky coffee table for Trudy, and opened the second can. She giggled. "Boy, Trudy. You were a real wildcat. I thought that guy was going to wet his pants when you charged him with that lamp. What were you thinking?"

Trudy sipped her pop. "I was thinking, 'Oh no you don't. That's my new TV.'"

Kathy pulled a wad of stringy cheese off the cardboard box. She gestured to the TV. "You call that new?"

Trudy snorted and sat up quickly. Soda pop bubbled out her nose. They laughed and laughed, grasping each other's arms, trying to speak, before going into a paroxysm of laughter, again. Tears ran down their eyes. Finally, they wiped the tears, still chuckling. Trudy's nerves quieted. She let out a big breath, and sank back into the couch. "I've been ripped off too often. I wasn't going to let it happen again."

Kathy said, "I guess not. I pity anyone who tries such a thing. At least now you won't have to file an insurance claim."

That absurdity set Trudy to laughing again. They finished the pizza and settled in to watch the movie. During the middle of "King Creole" Trudy paused the tape. She studied Kathy and said, "Where did you learn to kick like that?"

"I take karate classes. I like the discipline it takes. You really should, too. This isn't the safest area of the city. Even when you move from here, it's better to be prepared."

Trudy nodded. "Yeah, but what does that cost?"

Kathy looked around at the little room. "How strapped are you?"

"Very. I'm trying to clear up debt."

"That's commendable."

Trudy shook her head. "It's necessary. My husband's gambling destroyed my credit. I'm starting over from scratch."

"Where is he?"

Trudy shook her head. "I don't know. Maybe still with my parents. He told them I was the one causing the financial troubles."

"They believed him?"

"Once I became a teen my dad always found it easier to believe I was out doing wrong. To my dad's way of thinking, when I eloped on a Harley, I proved it."

"Were you?"

"Not really, although some of the kids I ran with were bordering on juvenile delinquency, at least by Amesville standards."

"What was the worst thing you did?"

Trudy leaned back against the couch. "One Halloween, some of the boys had firecrackers. I suggested we take them to a couple of vacant houses and blow up the mailboxes."

Kathy laughed. "You hooligan, you. How old were you when you ran away?"

"I didn't run away. I was eighteen and old enough to leave and get married."

"Ah." Kathy said and drained her can of pop.

Trudy ran her fingers through her long, thick hair and sank back into the good memories. "You know, it was the first time I ever traveled. It was so exciting. I didn't mind living in motel rooms and touring the country. We went from Iowa to Florida to California and everywhere in between. He was a big roller. We lived really well and kept moving around for a couple of years. Then I wanted to settle down."

"How'd that set with your husband?"

"Phillip said he'd do anything for me. We rented a furnished apartment and a car. I got a job as a cashier, and he worked at a casino as a dealer. He came home late one night frantic. In an hour we'd packed up our clothes and left everything else behind.

"It became a pattern. New place. New jobs. We'd dine at fancy restaurants, wear fancy clothes, then he'd lose it all and we'd barely be able to eat. Slipping out of apartments in the middle of the night to avoid the landlord. I was so ashamed. I hated that lifestyle, but like my father used to say, you make your bed and you lie in it."

"Did he actually say that to you?"

"I heard him say it plenty of times about plenty of other people. I knew it applied to me. I felt like a cheat and started paying off the debt. After all, Phillip was my husband and what was his debt was mine. Right?"

Kathy leaned back into the couch and turned her head to face Trudy. "Let me guess. It got worse?"

"Yes. Phillip said he hated it when I paid his debts, but it kept happening. The highs got higher and the lows got lower. I tried separate checking accounts so I could at least keep the household together. It didn't help, so why go to the extra bother? He kept telling me it was my fault we didn't have money, that he'd never had these problems until he married me."

"Did you believe him?"

"Part of me thought that it wasn't accurate. After all, before I got married, I'd always been a big saver. I always lived within my means. I mean, I was still living at home and that's the way we always lived.

"He was so adamant and self-assured that somehow I thought he must be right and I must be wrong. I worked harder to keep us afloat. After another year, the weight of the debt was crushing me. The idea of being untrustworthy and cheating or turning a blind eye to stealing was killing any self-respect I had. I told him he had to get help or I was leaving."

"Is that when you came here?"

Trudy shook her head. "No. He quit gambling. At the time I thought it was because he loved me. Now I wonder if maybe he needed me to keep cleaning up his messes."

"How long did he stay clean?"

"Almost a year. He took a high-paying job in finance in Reno. In a few years we'd have paid off the credit cards and the loans. I was proud of him and of myself. It was going so well. We talked about starting a family. At least I talked about it.

"He transferred to Las Vegas and bought a big house in a fine neighborhood. I gave notice at my job in Reno and moved to Vegas to be with him. It was so much fun picking out furniture, going to fancy fundraisers, getting jewels and dresses as presents, meeting a few celebrities. I thought we were settling in. Living the life we'd always talked about.

"Then his job took him on the road. He'd be gone a week or two at a time, sometimes a month. Maybe that's when it all went south, or maybe it had all soured already and he was preparing to run.

"Either way, I came home one day to find they were repossessing everything including the house. He'd racked up more debt than ever before. He forged my name and cleaned out both our accounts and disappeared."

"So, you don't know where he is?"

Trudy thought about the horror of finding him at her parents. Somehow she couldn't bear to tell Kathy that part. She evaded the question. "That's how I got here."

Kathy touched Trudy's arm. "That's tough. No wonder you're reeling under it. You sound really bitter."

"Well, wouldn't you be? It follows me wherever I go. I can't get away from it. I sometimes feel as if it'll choke me. Like I can't get my breath. I'll be paying for the rest of my life. I never know if someone new will come knocking on my door demanding more money because he's used my name somewhere."

"That'd be awful."

"Worst of all, I think he's scamming my parents." Trudy blurted out the truth of their last meeting and bounced out of her seat. She paced the apartment. "I don't know how I got here. Why didn't I listen to my parents? Why didn't I see him for what he was sooner?"

"It wasn't bad in the beginning. How could you know? Gambling, like every other addiction, is a downward spiral."

Trudy gripped the back of the couch. "I thought he loved me."

Kathy pivoted to face Trudy. "I'm sure he does."

"Then why didn't he stop?"

"Gambling is a sickness. A person can't stop an addiction without help. Even then, it takes a lot of effort. What about you? What are you doing to get well?"

Trudy reared back. Her hand went to her chest. "There's nothing wrong with me, other than a deplorable lack of wisdom when I was much younger."

"Wrong. You have issues that you need to work through, or the bitterness will eat you up and make you unfit for other relationships."

"The thought of a relationship with Phillip, or any other man, makes me want to vomit."

Kathy stood and looked over the back of the sofa at Trudy. "Exactly. His sickness, his addiction, made you sick, too. You stopped participating, but you're still struggling with codependency issues. Fact is, without getting help yourself, when you see Phillip again, the same pattern will surface. And if you ever start another relationship, you'll repeat the same mistakes with whatever problems that person has."

"I don't think so. I won't ever live like that again."

"Trudy, you're still doing it. Because you feel guilty, you're clearing up his mess instead of contesting it. That's not right. You're removing the consequences for his actions. That helps him keep doing what he's doing." Kathy reached across the couch and gently tapped Trudy's forehead. "You know that because you already took some steps to clear your name and separate financially from him."

Trudy was confused. Kathy's words made sense, yet a stronger urge drove her to deny it. "No."

"You're the victim, not the perpetrator. Addicts can be skilled manipulators. He used your love and morality against you. He turned your strengths into weaknesses. He capitalized on your sense of right and responsibility. Meanwhile he went scot free."

"That makes me so angry."

"Take my advice. Get yourself some help. Go to Al-Anon. Break the cycle and get yourself healthy."

Trudy looked at Kathy in a new way. "Have you been through this, too?"

Kathy sank into the couch. "My man drank. He was a great guy when he was sober, but he couldn't stay sober. We lived together for ten years. The more he drank the more out of control he got. I did the whole hide the bottles, and dump the juice thing. On paydays, I searched from bar to bar to find him and drag him home before the paycheck was completely gone. I'd call him in sick when he was hungover."

"I used to do that when Phillip wouldn't come home from the casino." Sensing kinship, Trudy sat beside Kathy.

"We argued. Then, we fought. One day he split my skull open." Kathy leaned forward and parted her hair to show a huge scar at the back of her head. "So, I left him."

Trudy sighed and touched Kathy's arm to offer sympathy. "It's hard, even when you know it's for the best."

"Sure, but he begged for forgiveness and promised to change, and I went back. Six more times. He broke my finger, my ribs, and then my self-confidence. I kept to myself and quit going to family functions. When he broke my nose, a gal at work had this same talk with me. Said I'd changed so much I wasn't like myself anymore. I finally listened. I was scared, but I went with her to Al-Anon. I'm convinced it saved my life."

Trudy felt uncomfortable without knowing why. "I had no idea. You seem fine to me."

"I am better now. That was four years ago. I still go to meetings. When I don't, I notice I start slipping back into the old behaviors when he comes around again. I still love him, you see."

"You do?"

"Emotions are complicated things. You can love and hate at the same time."

"Are you still with him?"

"No. In all that mess of my life, I also found Christ. He helps me stay away from that old life. I'm dating some nice guys now. If I get a feeling of déjà vu, I don't date that guy again."

Trudy thought about the nights she cried for Phillip, missing him, the nights she raged at him, not caring if she ever saw him again, the times she grieved, wishing he'd change so they could be together, and the times she imagined how much life would be easier if he were dead from an accident or heart attack, and she'd finally be free.

"If you don't want to go to meetings alone, you can go with me."

"I don't see how dredging up the past will help."

"Some of that may come up, but basically it's not about him and what he's done. It's about you and how you react. It's about getting you better. You only share what you want, when you're ready."

"I think I'm doing okay, now." Trudy picked up the VCR remote and punched play.

"Okay," Kathy said, not sounding convinced. She settled back on the couch to watch the rest of the movie. "Remember, the offer stands."

"Really. I'm okay now. I've got my life under control."

# Chapter Eight

According to the wall directory in the lobby of the bank, the offices of Faulkinroy Publicists was on the fifth floor. Trudy stepped to the left where a metal gate stood between her and the elevator shaft. She and pushed the embossed metal button. The elevator moved into place without even a creak. The inner solid door opened and then the metal gate. Very retro.

She pressed the button with a gilded 5 and the metal gate shut followed by the solid door. With a tiny jolt the elevator moved smoothly upward.

She removed her coat and draped it over one arm, arranging herself for the best presentation possible. She smoothed her navy blue skirt and checked her silk blouse for smudges. The elevator nudged to a halt on the correct floor.

Trudy pulled back the gate and the solid metal door opened to a green and white marbled floor extending down a wide hallway. She passed two lawyer's offices and a notary public before coming to the frosted glass window at the end of the corridor. Black paint on the glass spelled out her destination.

Inside, a person of medium height stood at the desk talking on the phone. The man was better dressed than a secretary would be. He had an athletic body without being bulky. His hair was dark, well cut, and, yes, he was handsome. His voice was soft, sweet, and persuasive. Mellifluent. Trudy smiled to herself. Where had that word come from? She'd never used that word in her entire life, although she'd once read it in a book. The man oozed the type of aura that made you want to use big words and take your game up a notch.

The desktop was not messy, despite a number of files stacked to the side or standing upright in a black metal rack. Pencils and pens poked from a black metal cup, available to clients, as well as the secretary. Through the open door behind him, a large desk with a shiny clear top dominated the space in front of a ceiling-high window. That room appeared to be unoccupied.

Trudy waited, pretending not to listen as he conducted business and made an appointment. He ended the call and placed the phone on the multi-button base. If all the lines were operational, she could possibly have to field five calls at a time. On the other hand, since Faulkinroy was a start-up company, probably only one or two lines would be used. The man pushed another button and punched in some numbers. He turned his gaze on her. "May I help you?"

"I'm Trudy Bellafonte. I'm here about the temporary secretarial position."

"You're five minutes early."

"I like to be early enough to feel comfortable and unrushed for my appointments."

"Good. I like that," the man said. "I'm Peter Faulkinroy. Come into my office. I've set the phone to voice mail so we'll be undisturbed during the interview."

She followed him into his office. He took up position behind the enormous desk. He waved a hand at one of two visitor chairs of a good quality black Naugahyde. "Sit down, Ms. Bellafonte."

Trudy complied, remembering not to cross her legs and to allow her hands to rest comfortably on the arms of the chairs in a confident, relaxed manner. She judged appearance would be important in this job.

Peter Faulkinroy settled into the leather swivel chair, set his elbows on the arms, and touched his fingers together in a steeple. It was an affected look meant to tell her he was superior and thoughtful and not to be trifled with.

Trudy pressed a finger briefly against her lips to stifle a giggle. She scratched her nose with the knuckle of her right hand and hoped he thought she was nervous, rather than amused. This man would not tolerate someone laughing at him. She raised her eyes to meet his as he scrutinized her.

"You're well dressed. That's important in this business. What experience do you have as a secretary?"

"While I've been working as a temp, I've worked four different businesses, answering phones, filing paperwork, acting as receptionist, doing a bit of bookkeeping. I'm good with numbers. I'm also good with people. I've handled a few problem situations that arose with employees or clients, all to the satisfaction of my employers."

"Are you an experienced typist?"

"I type thirty-seven words a minute."

He frowned.

She added, "I know that is far below standard, but since I graduated high school, I've never had to type. Before I moved here, I was a hostess for a large, upscale restaurant. However, I'm accurate and gaining speed."

"What type of computer experience do you have?"

"I've not been trained on a computer, but I'm not afraid of them. I learn quickly."

He looked unconvinced. Her stomach knotted. She wanted this job very much. "Mr. Faulkinroy, I understand that you are an up and coming business, making your mark in Indianapolis and beyond. I'm on my own and looking for a permanent job. I'd be invested in growing this business, not merely putting in time."

The steeple came down. He reached for a pen in the pen holder on his desk. He took it and twirled it. This, Trudy thought, was a natural gesture for him. She gave him a moment, but when his faced relaxed a fraction, she said, "What type of wages are we talking about?"

He told her. "If I hire you, after a trial period of course, I'll pay off your contract with the temp agency for you."

"Why don't you start me at $2.00 more an hour and I'll pay my own contract?"

Peter Faulkinroy appraised her. He laughed in a mocking way. "That's absurd."

"No. I'm worth more, but I understand I have to prove myself. I'm investing in this company. Your success is my success."

With a hint of respect in his eyes, he considered. "I'll hire you as a temp for a six week trial period. If your work is acceptable and your typing speeds are up, I'll hire you for a dollar more than your temporary contract pays you. After six months you'll get a raise, and another raise at a year."

Trudy studied him. She could feel it. This job would require finesse and negotiating skills. She may be a secretary, but she wasn't going to be inferior, especially to a demanding man who also had an ego that would need to be pampered. "Hm. Yes. That is acceptable. After all, Mr. Faulkinroy, like you, I wouldn't want to commit myself to a job long term if I didn't like working for you."

He frowned again.

Trudy sent him a big smile. "However, I think we'll work very well together. We will renegotiate in a year. When do you want me to start?"

"Now."

"Where should I store my purse?"

"You can put it in the large bottom drawer of the desk up front. It can be locked." He came around his desk to lead her to the front reception area. When his back was turned, Trudy made a little fist and pulled it down in a sign of triumph.

He pointed to her personal drawer and handed her the key. He showed her where to hang her coat. He ran through how he wanted the phone answered, how he preferred messages to be taken, how to prioritize them. He also reviewed how he liked the files kept, where to put the different types of information, and where the supplies were. As he released the answering machine, he said, "Refer to me as Mr. Faulkinroy with first clients and whenever answering the phone. Otherwise, call me Peter and refer to me as such with established clients."

"I understand. It gives them that personal touch."

He appraised her. "Exactly."

As soon as he was done punching in numbers, the phone rang. Trudy answered as if she'd been doing it for years. Life at the Faulkinroy Publicists began.

That Friday when Trudy dropped off her timecard, Kathy asked, "So how was it?"

"I can work with him. He's got oddities, but who doesn't? He doesn't like foolish or lazy people, but I'm neither. I blew a little smoke at his ego, but after two days, I think my words were more prophetic than pampering. This guy is going up the ladder of success. Not fast, but steady. I like that about him. I think we can build a working relationship around mutual respect."

"Wow," Kathy said. "I knew you'd be able to do the job, but you're the first that had anything good to say about him."

Trudy put in the hours and made sure the clients were happy. She had a way with them, and a way of making whatever Peter promised them, however improbable, happen when he said it would happen.

When he asked for the impossible, she told him outright it couldn't be done, then suggested alternatives until they worked out a new plan. Trudy worked as hard as Peter. After a while, it was as if he were an older brother, annoying, but loved. Well, at least well-liked.

One of the tasks Peter assigned her was to read the local newspapers to look for business opportunities. While reading the Indianapolis Star she saw an advertisement for an upcoming church event with the CMA raising money for children with cancer. The accompanying photo pictured the same two motorcyclists who had filled her tank when she first reached the city. The group was going to have a cycling rally following the service. Trudy decided it offered a fine opportunity to thank them.

That Sunday, Trudy walked past about twenty motorcycles on her way into the church. It felt odd, sinful even, entering a church dressed in a black pantsuit and fake snakeskin jacket instead of a dress, but the newspaper indicated casual wear. In fact, she was overdressed. Almost everyone wore jeans.

After worship, the pastor introduced Spider and Mike as speakers. When the service concluded she moved forward. Spider shook her hand. "Say, you look familiar."

"Yeah. I'm the lady with the Town Car and the empty gas tank."

"Oh, yeah. How are you doing?"

"Things are going well. Thank you for that tip. I landed a permanent job through All Star Temp Agency."

"That's good. Hey Mikey! Look who's here. It's—" Spider pointed a finger at her.

"Trudy. I'm Trudy."

Mike excused himself from a conversation and approached. He shook her hand vigorously. "I haven't noticed you here before. Do you attend this church?"

"No, I saw your photo in the newspaper and came to say thanks. I wanted to make a donation for the kids. It's not much, but—" She pulled a pre-filled check from her purse and handed it to him.

"Thanks." Mike accepted the check without looking at it. "This will make a difference."

Trudy sighed with relief. It was a pitifully small donation carved out of her coffee and lunch money. The first paycheck of each month, Trudy hid a portion of her paycheck in the WC, as Phillip had taught her. The second paycheck, she sent an equal amount back home to her parents' pastor with instructions to take care of her parents. She always included a letter to her mother. After sending money to clear up debt and meet living expenses, there was nothing left.

Spider said, "Are you going to ride with our group this afternoon?"

"No, I don't have a motorcycle."

"We've got lots of room. Lots of single riders. I know the perfect person to team you up with. Hey, Hodges, come see who's here."

Trudy glimpsed a pony tail of yellow hair snugged against the back of a head and held in place by a black forehead band. The broad-shouldered woman excused herself from the group. Trudy gawked at the tattoos covering both arms up to her red, short sleeve shirt. She noted a warm smile. Then, Trudy was enfolded in a big hug while a familiar voice spoke welcoming words. Trudy pulled back.

Kathy laughed. "It's me. Didn't recognize me with all my tattoos out in public, did you? They're stunning. Did you catch this cobra?" She pointed to her left elbow so Trudy could admire the green tattoo snake winding up her arm.

"I'm stunned," Trudy stammered.

Spider said, "Kathy, can Trudy ride with you?"

"Sure. I have an extra helmet," Kathy said.

"Oh, I don't know. I didn't plan on—"

"Come on," Kathy said. "It'll be great. We ride around the downtown area and the city parks and go out for a late lunch at Bertolli's. Then, we come back here and drop off any riders."

Trudy tried a few more times to refuse, but the group was so insistent that she got caught up in the excitement of riding a motorcycle on such a lovely spring day.

When Trudy got home to the WC she fell onto the soft couch. She thought about what a good time she'd had. The group loved their bikes. The banter revolved around bragging about new parts and bigger bikes. It was a friendly manner that created a lot of laughter. They shared with her about places they'd ridden and some of the incidents that had happened on other fundraising rides. They also spoke of situations and prejudices they'd encountered simply because they were bikers.

At the end of the day, she'd been invited back to the church for future services and back to the group. Trudy had accepted both invitations. They assured her this church was Bible-based. Trudy determined if she ever once felt that someone was judging her because of something she said or did, she'd be out of there in a flash.

A knock on the door brought Trudy to her feet. No one except Kathy knew where she lived and Kathy was with Mike. Cautiously she opened the door.

# Chapter Nine

Cocky as ever, Phillip leaned on her door post, a leather duffle bag slung over his shoulder. The light in the hallway had been replaced, but even so the lighting was poor. Trudy didn't need light. She remembered every detail about him. He was still as handsome as ever.

"Hi, Tru. How's my wild Irish rose?" He said, using his Irish accent as he proffered a single red rose. He bent to kiss her. She stiffened and turned her face away so that the kiss fell on her cheek. He brushed past her into the room and set the rose on the coffee table. "Whatever made you move to Indiana?"

"I was trying to get away from you."

"That hurts Trudy, me love, but you really didn't go very far and you mailed your parents your address, when you knew I was there, so I know you don't mean it. Besides, I'll always come looking for you. I'm your husband."

"Why is that not a comfort? Have my parents changed their minds about me?"

"Afraid not, sweetheart. Your father said you were walking the road to perdition."

"He would. You lied to them about me."

"No, darling. I stood up for you. I said you were one of the finest people I knew. True and honest and loyal."

"In the kitchen that day you laughed at me."

"No, no, no. I was choked up and too embarrassed to show it. I told them I loved you and wanted to be with you. I ran out after you, but you left so quickly, I didn't have a chance to stop you. I didn't know where you went. When I figured out where you were, I said if they couldn't accept me wife, then I couldn't be a-staying either." The accent grew thicker, the longer he talked, somehow making him sound more sincere.

Trudy snorted. "You're talking as if they're your parents, not mine. They probably threw you out."

"After everything I did for them? I don't think so. They think I'm a saint, darlin'. They didn't want me to go."

"You did do some nice things for them. Thank you." Trudy closed the door.

Phillip flashed her his special smile. Her heart leapt. He walked across the room and touched the painted over window. "Man, Tru, this is practically squalor. What a third rate, shoddy apartment."

The feeling of joy evaporated. "It's all I can afford, and that barely, thanks to you. Why are you really here, Phillip?"

"I told you. I missed you."

"You need money."

"No, although I don't have a lot." He dropped the accent. "I'm making a fresh start, Tru. Like you are. I'm leaving that old life behind. I'll get a job and we'll build us a life, like you want. Slow and steady. We can do it, darling. Let me come home to you."

Trudy stood where she was and shook her head. "We've tried this before. You left us in a real mess in Las Vegas. You didn't even have the guts to tell me. You left me. That really hurt."

He hung his head. "I know. I should've told you, but I felt so badly. I couldn't stand the thought of disappointing you again. You deserve the best. I was sure I could turn it around before it got worse. Then out of the blue, Avery pulled my marker. He was looking for me with intent to harm. I had to get out of there. It was better if you didn't know where I was in case he came asking."

"He did come asking. I had to leave without my paycheck or I'd have wound up in the hospital."

"I'm sorry. I never thought he'd do that." Phillip drew close. He stroked her hair. "Come on, darling. I don't like it when you look at me like I've let you down. I love you so much. Give me another shot."

"Phillip, I—"

"Come on, Tru. It's you and me against the world. You remember that oldie. It's our song." Phillip put his hands on her waist and started to sway as he sang. In a moment, Trudy let herself soften.

As he danced her around the room, his explanations seemed more logical. Her resistance weakened and the confusion that it brought quieted. She believed she could try again. As if on cue, he kissed her. The flame that burned in her belly at his touch roared to life, making her forget all the bad stuff that had happened.

In the morning, Trudy slipped her engagement and wedding rings back on her finger.

Over breakfast at a nearby diner, Phillip opened the newspaper to the employment section.

Trudy said, "If you get tested at All Star Temp Agency, Kathy is sure to place you."

"I'm not settling for some second-hand job. I'm skilled. The places I want to work will advertise directly."

Trudy let that comment pass even though he was talking down the job she held.

As the days passed, Phillip answered job ads in the newspaper. He always seemed to be too late in line or the jobs weren't suitable. Trudy knew the market was tough so she was pleased that he stuck with the job search, even if he chose not to go through Kathy.

When she tried to get him to go to a CMA meeting with her, he said he'd run into an old friend, whom he didn't name, that he would visit instead. Trudy suspected it was someone from his gambling days. She decided it was better to stay home with him, than risk him getting tied up with a gambler.

The following week she dressed for her karate class and kissed him goodbye. The kisses he gave her in return caused her to miss her class. The next time, he picked a fight with her. She again missed her class.

Somehow Phillip took up more and more of her time so that Trudy barely saw Kathy anymore. Often she missed church as well as her karate classes. She told herself that was to be expected. After all, they were trying to rebuild a life together.

Phillip pitched in more than he ever had, not that there was much to do in the tiny apartment. Still, Trudy considered it a sign of his intent to improve. He cleaned the bathroom, swept the room, and even did the laundry. Trudy showed him her gratitude with abundant kissing and, since his funds had run out, offered to take him shopping for necessary items at the mall. Although she had to talk him down from the more expensive brands, she paid for good shirts for the new job he'd landed.

Phillip was ecstatic about his boss and his job for two weeks. When the complaining started, Trudy encouraged him to stick with it until he found a routine, despite the enmity building between him and his boss. "It's not challenging," he said. "I'm bored out of my mind."

"Perhaps for now, but if you show them how well you do this, they may find other, more interesting jobs to assign you."

"You don't get it. You don't understand what it's like."

By the middle of the following month, Phillip's growing restlessness made Trudy increasingly uneasy. A sense of exhaustion gripped her as she tried everything she could think of to keep him from being bored.

They attended a lecture, open to the public, by a man who felt sky-diving had changed his life and was the spiritual answer to everything. They swam at the YMCA on a free-for-a-day pass. They visited the zoo and parks and created stories about the people they saw. Together they walked different parts of Indianapolis admiring the architecture, the old homes, and dreaming of the home they would own together some day. Still, her anxiety bled over to her job.

One day near closing time, Peter asked, "Where's your mind today, Trudy?"

She startled and raised eyes to him. Peter stood at the edge of her desk. She answered, "I'm editing the promotional materials for the client."

"No. You've been staring at that same screen for ten minutes without making any changes at all. I've been standing here, and you didn't even know it. Besides that, I found three errors on the plan you gave me. We're doing the campaign this year, not next. You misspelled my name and left in one of the programs we decided against."

"Sorry. I do have something on my mind. I'll concentrate." Trudy vowed to herself she'd keep her mind off Phillip and on her work and check everything three times to make sure she didn't make any errors.

Peter continued. "I need those changes by 6:00 p.m. I've got a dinner meeting with that man."

"I'll finish them up right now." She glanced at the time and picked up the phone. She left Phillip a message at his office that she was working an hour later than usual and would bring something to eat.

When Trudy finally reached the apartment building, carrying a bag of burgers, she wanted nothing more than to put her feet up and relax. Maybe Phillip would even give her a neck rub.

Phillip was sprawled on the couch. As she closed the door she sensed he'd been waiting for her. Her entrance was his cue to perform. Before she even said hello, he sat up and threw the newspaper down. "There's no decent jobs here. Let's blow this town."

Trudy clutched the bag of burgers more tightly. "What happened?"

"I quit."

"What? Why?"

"My boss treated me like a slave. She was always asking me to do lame things that someone in my position shouldn't be doing. The people were such nerds. I hated that job."

"You were drinking again and lost that job, didn't you? You were fired."

Phillip jumped to his feet. "You always think the worst of me. It's easy for you to go to the same prosaic job, day in and day out."

"My job is interesting and challenging. If you're saying that it's commonplace, then, one, you are ignorant of what I do, and two, you actually mean that I'm commonplace."

"Well, if the shoe fits, darling."

"Why did you ever marry me, Phillip?"

"You were a ball of fire back then. Lately you've grown so," He drew the word 'so' out as if trying to put a name to her malady. "tame."

"Tame? You mean boring. If you think I'm boring, why are you still here?"

"Did I say boring? I didn't say boring. I didn't even mean that. You're putting words in my mouth. It's just that, Trudy, love, I'm itching to travel. You don't seem to care about that anymore. You've lost your sense of adventure. Come with me to Atlantic City. I'll be able to make a killing there. Fresh ground and all that. That spark of adventure you used to have will come back once we're on the road again. I'm sure of it."

Hairs on the back of Trudy's neck rose like hackles on an angry dog. She dropped the bag of burgers on the coffee table which doubled as their dining room outfit, and tugged at the buttons on her coat to get it off. She kicked her shoes off so hard they flew across the room. "You're right about one thing. I don't care to travel. I'm not going anywhere. I like my job. It's challenging and interesting. Besides, it keeps us eating and pays for this apartment."

Phillip walked the short distance to the end of the room. He waved an arm to include the tiny space. "That's too generous of a word for this rat-hole. By the way, those burgers you bought aren't exactly cuisine, dear heart."

"You managed to eat your fill over the last several weeks on my dime."

Stiff-legged he advanced toward her. "It always comes back to that, doesn't it? Stick the shiv in old Phil and twist it. You make the money and I'm nothing but a no-good sponge."

Inside she felt herself backing down, her anger buckling in the face of his quick-tongued aggression. She feared he would leave again. Somewhere from the back of her swirling thoughts, a conversation with Kathy surfaced. Kathy had said that fear he'd leave would remain a threat, even if she left Indianapolis with him.

Trudy widened her stance and straightened her back. "I didn't say that. I only meant that we haven't starved. We don't always have to have fine dining."

"Well, Trudy, maybe I do."

"But you don't, Phillip. You don't. Oh maybe for a little while you eat caviar. Then, the next thing you know, we're not eating at all. Wake up. Something has to change."

"Change? Baby, you don't want change. You want everything to stay the same, down-home-on-the-farm-nothing-ever-happens same. I'm sick of it. I'm sick of this place. I want to live. We wouldn't be in this mess, if you ever supported me in my dreams."

Trudy drew back as if she'd been slapped. "What? That's all I've ever done."

"I don't see it that way."

Her stomach knotted. How could he not see what she'd done, how she'd tried? She was so weary. Trudy covered her mouth to stifle a sniffle. The tears came anyway.

"Oh, good grief. Are you starting that?" Phillip grabbed his coat off the back of the couch.

"Where are you going?"

"Out."

The door slammed. Trudy cried harder. Same old argument. Different town. It was always the same. Phillip never changed. She never changed. Well, that was one thing that was going to change. She could do nothing about him, but she could about herself. Trudy swiped at her tears while she punched in a number on her cell phone.

"Kathy, we had a big argument…"

When the tale was complete, Kathy said, "Sounds like Phillip knew which buttons to push. He's trying to deflect attention from himself. He knew that calling you tame or boring would spark a reaction."

"I think you're right. Kathy? Is there an Al-Anon meeting tonight?"

"I was getting ready to leave when you called."

"I'm coming." Trudy listened for directions as she re-buttoned her coat. She looked back at the bag of burgers and snatched them up. She'd eat them both. And all the fries. He could starve, for all she cared.

Kathy was scuffling her feet against the concrete in the cool night air as she waited on the sidewalk at the side of the old stone building. She waved as Trudy pulled up. "Hi. I'm glad you came."

Trudy held out a visibly shaking hand. "Look. I'm shaking so badly, I could barely open the car door. My dinner is churning in my stomach."

"I was like that at first, too. It gets better. Come on."

Together they entered the old school, and quick-stepped down a walkway into a spacious well-lit room that once was a school cafeteria. A group of fifteen women sat on folding chairs in a circle. They kept their coats on because the room wasn't heated. It looked like a prayer meeting, but none was said. Some faces were friendly, the women chatty. Other women were quiet and reserved. One sat rigid and kept folding and unfolding her arms, as if she were ready to explode. Trudy recognized the look as the way she herself felt.

Someone handed her three books to use during the meeting, explaining they were available for purchase. One lady with short cropped hair and hoop earrings read off a laminated paper. She welcomed newcomers, explained about the group, and laid a few ground rules for the meeting, including anonymity.

First names were said all around. A volunteer read from a blue book, "One Day at a Time", and commented on what it meant to her. Other members spoke up to add their views. When there were no more comments, the next reading was done.

The hour passed quickly. Trudy watched and listened. Some of them had gone through similar events, while others endured far worse. The woman who was about to explode, burst out with her tale of woe.

When the woman's sharing was over, others mentioned what they'd done in similar situations and referred her to a couple of pages in the book. Nobody tried to tell her what to do. Nobody said what she'd done was stupid.

Trudy sighed with relief, both that the emotional discharge had calmed down and that the woman had been heard without being judged. Having a safe place to be heard would be priceless. The burgers in Trudy's stomach decided to stay put.

The Lord's Prayer was said to close the meeting. One of the attendees refused to say it. The others simply went on without her. Trudy repeated the familiar words, glad to seek the help of the Lord. She needed help to know what to do about Phillip. Afterward, everyone in the group hugged each other. It felt uncomfortably odd and, inexplicably, satisfyingly good.

Kathy handed her the blue book. "Here. It's a gift."

Trudy said, "I can't accept this."

"Sure you can. I'm paying forward what someone did for me. You do the same, someday. Read it every day. Right along with your Bible."

Trudy didn't say she wasn't reading the Bible every day. She tucked the book into her purse. "Thanks."

Several in the group headed for coffee afterward, but Trudy resisted Kathy's urging and went to the WC to check on Phillip. He still hadn't returned. He was probably finding some bar or backstreet place to gamble, thinking somehow that a big win would make everything better, although what he had to gamble with, she didn't know.

She tried to go to sleep, but sleep eluded her for a long time. Once she did sleep, it was so deep from exhaustion that she never heard him come home.

In the morning, she first noticed Phillip wasn't squished against her on the couch. She called out to him, but he didn't answer. She sat up and noticed his coat wasn't on the peg. Had he never returned? As she looked about the room it was obvious all his stuff was gone. She found a scrawled note on the dented coffee table with a set of keys. She picked it up and quickly scanned the message.

Tru, I've had a job offer out east. I didn't wake you because you were sleeping so peacefully. I hope you had good dreams when I kissed you good-bye. I'll let you know when I settle in, then you can come to me. Love, Phillip.

P.S. I took the money you hid in the tampon box. I knew you wouldn't mind. Also, I needed the Town Car for the job. I have to make a good impression. Don't worry, I know how you love horses, so I'm leaving you the Ford Pinto (ha ha). Be careful driving it. I think it needs some work done. XXX

# Chapter Ten

Trudy yelled, pounded the table, and kicked the couch. She paced around hardly knowing what to do with herself. She caught sight of the rings and wrested them off her finger. She poked them into the zippered pouch of her purse, muttering to herself. She flung the purse down and paced some more.

Feeling as if she could jump out of her skin, she grabbed her gym bag and headed for the dojo, where she worked on kicking and punching, using Phillip as an imaginary target. It didn't change anything. At night, alone, she wrapped in a blanket and curled against the back of the couch, wishing life wasn't so hard, so painful.

Trudy did her best over the next week to maintain a professional demeanor and to hide the depression that threatened to squash her. She recognized it as the invisible elephant she'd been so familiar with for the last few years. Simply identifying it, didn't make it go away.

The "One Day at a Time in Al-Anon" book said that refusing help was like bumping about a dark room, refusing to turn on the light. Trudy was ready to admit she could do nothing about Phillip, but the hurt and anger that created the elephantine depression still was firmly planted on top of her, making it difficult to draw a deep breath.

To be honest, the Psalms, which Kathy had suggested she read, helped shrink that elephant a bit. She could really get into some of them, calling on God's wrath to vindicate her from her enemy, aka Phillip. She took pleasure in imagining his retribution.

Afterward, these thoughts always led to wishes that he would change so that they'd be together again like it was in the beginning.

As the days passed, Trudy quit wishing for retribution and simply wished he'd come back so that they could start again. She sang Sinead O'Connor's new hit, "Nothing Compares 2 U" over and over. It was as good as a country western song to wring emotion out of her.

Remembering how good it had been at the start of their relationship, Trudy put her rings back on her finger. "God if you'll only bring Phillip back again and stop him from gambling, I'd be willing to try again."

Spring turned to summer and then summer passed without hearing from Philip. Trudy wondered if she ever would hear from him again. Every time her diamond flashed while at work or she put lotion on her hands, she'd touch her rings and think of him.

Eventually, in an effort to clear her mind of distracting thoughts of Phillip, Trudy removed the wedding and engagement rings and once again zipped them into her purse.

A respite from her internal dilemma presented itself in the form of a tricky client negotiation that required her complete concentration. The hours she devoted to it were hours she didn't think about Phillip. Trudy was keenly disappointed when the potential client took his business elsewhere without giving a reason why.

Upon hearing the news, Peter ranted and raved in his office. Finally, he stormed into the outer office and pointed a finger at Trudy. "This is your fault. If you'd only…"

She stopped listening. The breath froze in her lungs. Phillip. It was as if Phillip were standing in front of her. Her brain went into hyper-drive. This wasn't Phillip. It was Peter. His words became crystal clear. What he was saying wasn't true. There wasn't anything more she or he could have done. He was simply upset and bullying her. She might have trouble drawing the line with Phillip, but it wasn't too late to set boundaries with Peter.

Trudy commanded herself to breathe. Air rushed into her lungs filling them with almost dizzying power. She opened her desk drawer, withdrew her purse, and stood so abruptly Peter took a step backward and closed his mouth. She pushed her arms into her raincoat and shrugged it on.

"Where are you going?"

Like listening to a book on tape, Trudy heard herself calmly say, "I'm leaving. I'm not your whipping boy. I'm your secretary. I do a terrific job. I did nothing to lose that account."

"If you leave, you're fired."

"Too bad. I enjoyed working here. You know where to send my check." Head high, Trudy stepped out of the office and closed the door with the rippled glass.

She made it into the elevator. There, her knees wobbled so badly that she leaned against the wall to stay upright. She was scared, but vindicated. She'd go immediately to the temp agency. Kathy would place her again. Why couldn't she have been like this with Phillip before things had gotten out of hand?

The bell announcing the first floor pinged. She forced herself upright and blinked back tears. The elevator's solid door slid open and then the metal gate.

Peter burst from the stairwell. He halted in front of her, slightly out of breath. "I apologize. I was out of line. I was angry after all the work I did."

She set her jaw and stared at him through narrowed eyes.

"I mean, after all the work we did. You did do superb work on that job. We both did. It only stands to reason that through no fault of our own, sometimes a client will choose to go elsewhere. Please come back."

Decision time. Trudy drew another breath. It came a little easier. She liked her job. The line was drawn. "Understand, if it ever happens again, I will not come back."

Peter nodded.

"I'm going for an early lunch. I'll be back in an hour."

He nodded again and stepped aside. Trudy marched past him and out the door onto the sidewalk. She had no idea where she was going. A large drop of rain hit her full in the face. She ducked into the little pastry shop next door and ordered a coffee.

The rain drops became a full-fledged downpour, hitting the shop window and streaking down the sill. She blinked back tears. She would not cry. She'd let the rain do it for her. In an effort to compose herself, she thought about the deliberate moves of karate. Her hands shook as she sipped her coffee, sloshing it a little bit.

The encounter was proof that the Al-Anon ideas were working. With Peter, she knew the client's rejection was not her fault, therefore she wouldn't accept his accusations. If only she could be like that with Phillip. With her parents.

A piece of peach pie appeared in front of her. Trudy looked up at the pudgy shop owner. "I didn't order this."

"Maybe not, sweetie, but you need it. It's on the house."

"Thank you, Francie."

"No problem, Trudy. You're a good customer. I hate to see you so down in the mouth."

Trudy took a bite. "You know, pie doesn't solve everything."

"Of course not, it just makes you care a little less. Like a touch of home."

It sounded much like what her Mom used to say. Trudy thanked her. As soon as Francie walked away, Trudy covered her mouth with her hand to stifle a sob. More and more Trudy missed her Mom and her Dad.

Mom would be canning green beans and tomatoes from the garden. Dad would be harvesting. When the weather changed, he'd bring Skipper up to the corral near the barn. Maybe even ride him, because Skipper needed to be ridden. Would her father think of her? Miss her?

How she missed them. She'd risk being rejected if she could see them and know they were okay. She'd go this very weekend.

Trudy pounded the table with her fist once. She wasn't going anywhere. The Pinto Phillip had left her was a ten year old clunker that took longer and longer to start each morning. She needed the job with Peter to save enough to get a new vehicle and to replace the emergency money Phillip had taken. Why hadn't she deposited that money in a bank where it was safe from him? Why was she still squirreling money away as if she'd have to run at any moment?

Before the showdown with Peter, this same question popped out of her mouth at an Al-Anon meeting, prompting a discussion. She hadn't done anything about it, but she would. When she received her next pay check, Trudy vowed to open a savings account. It would be a small step forward in sorting through what she was responsible for and what she wasn't. It would be a healthy change to make.

Trudy remembered one night after a meeting, Kathy had said, "The reason this program works so well is that it's based on God's Word. That's where you need to be, Trudy, in God's Word. Jesus will show you the way and give you strength."

Trudy hadn't protested, but thought the meetings were doing more to instill her with inner strength and change, the same as her body was changing with the twice weekly karate classes.

As if Kathy could read her mind she said, "You know the Bible says in Isaiah, 'He gives power to the faint and to them that have no might he increases strength.' For me, he did that through this program."

Trudy considered her friend's words again as she drank the last of her coffee. Whichever it was, or maybe both together, it's how she had stood up to Peter. She was improving. If she got better and acted differently, change in her situation with Phillip was sure to follow.

Heartened by this thought, Trudy swallowed the last bite of pie and returned to work.

Peter acted as if nothing had happened. Although he never mentioned the episode again, he continued to treat her with respect.

Trudy shared the exhilaration of her success at the next Al Anon meeting. They warned her not to expect immediate results like that all the time because change usually came slowly and painfully.

They didn't know her, though. Didn't know how strong and determined she could be. Trudy couldn't shake the idea that she could make things better if she kept her cool, with Peter, with Phillip, and maybe with her parents.

# *Chapter Eleven*

Carol folded her legs beneath her and let the glider rock back and forth. The pungent smell of marigolds pervaded the air. She'd planted them because Andy always had edged the walk around the house with them. The gold and yellow certainly brightened the area. Next year maybe she'd plant something different, something new, something that didn't make her think of Andy.

Of course, he seemed to be nearby all the time anyway, as if he hadn't come home from work yet, or was watering plants around the corner of the house, or upstairs when she was downstairs, and downstairs when she was upstairs. Somewhere close, yet out of reach. At times, she even imagined she glimpsed him, but it always turned out to be a curtain ruffled by the wind or their beagle Minnie burrowing under a blanket.

A year and a half ago, they might have been sitting on the glider together, his arm draped over her shoulders, sharing a glass of lemonade and the events of the day. She missed being held, missed sharing the day with a male who's view was always so different from hers, so masculine. She missed his closeness, his strength, even the heat of him. Even so, she certainly wasn't ready to have anybody else step in.

The loneliness weighted her with its intensity, but then, it was their anniversary. They'd long made a tradition of celebrating by going out to eat or getting together with family. No more. No one even said anything. No one sent anniversary cards. Why would they?

She was no longer a couple. They feared mentioning him would make her sad. They all acted as if saying something would make her think of Andy, when in fact, he was never far from her thoughts.

Carol understood this thinking. She'd experienced it after losing her parents and her children. Despite her own losses, she still felt shy when someone else grieved. It seemed as if the corporate loss would bind people together. Instead, each loss was a private loss, an individual loss like none other, so how could she know exactly what to say? She didn't even know what she wanted to hear, for nothing could change her grief. Still, not mentioning him made her sad.

"Rejoice with them that do rejoice and weep with them that weep." The gentle Biblical words from the book of Romans reminded her that it wasn't her responsibility to take the grief away, to make someone laugh because it was uncomfortable to be around their sorrow. No, she merely needed to be open to acknowledging their sorrow, accepting it, and be willing to share in it to the extent the other person was willing.

Carol tilted her head back and peered through the dark trying to find a star that shined through the light-filled sky of the city. The stars were there, even if she couldn't see them. God was near, even if she couldn't see him.

She recalled scripture after scripture. Soon peace and calm wrapped her. God was sufficient. As she'd done many times before, Carol recounted the many mercies God had sent. She thanked him for the time she'd had with Andy, for the comfort that they'd see each other again someday as children of the Lord. She thanked God that Jesus understood and shared her sorrow and loss.

"Great is thy faithfulness," she whispered. "I will choose to enjoy the little things of life that remain. After all, I can see and feel and taste and hear and have people to love. There are so many things to be thankful for. You are with me, God, all the time, forever and ever. I'm never alone."

The heaviness receded to a tolerable level. She stayed on the glider a while longer listening to the cicadas and crickets while a breeze rustled the leaves of the tree. Everything around her was alive. And so was she.

A half hour passed. Carol went inside for the night and added these thoughts to the others she'd written. Maybe somebody else would be comforted and encouraged by these words in her book.

# Chapter Twelve

Whenever Trudy allowed her thoughts to dwell on Phillip, she told herself his prolonged absence made her stronger. In the car on the way to work each morning, she practiced responding to various scenarios until she was certain that when he did come back she'd be able to stand up to him, whatever he said. And he would return. He said so himself. He loved her. He'd always find her. The thought increased her confidence.

A more pressing question was how could she use that new found confidence to gain her father's respect and be treated like an adult? She was a responsible adult. She was cleaning up the mess of her life. It might not be perfect, but it was progress. She was trying. If she didn't argue, make excuses, or beg, maybe her father would finally see her as an adult instead of a child, even if he didn't agree with her decisions.

The thought nagged as the hot, humid summer turned to the rainy chill of fall. She rehearsed aloud, responding in a mature, unemotional way to every accusation her father might level. Trudy decided to use the five day Thanksgiving weekend to go home before she lost her nerve, or before the Pinto, which Spider and Mike had fixed, went defunct in some new way. She didn't call ahead, reasoning rejection would be a bit more difficult in the face of a stalwart and determined daughter.

Wednesday dawned cold and clear. Trudy claimed it as a good sign. She dressed in a T-shirt and blue jean skirt, anklets and tennis shoes. By nine o'clock she headed west. This time, Trudy knocked like any other visitor at the front door of her childhood home. She huddled in her coat while a sharp wind pelted her with crisp, dry leaves.

The curtain moved briefly. Emma swung open the door. The whitish-grey hair was frizzy, needing a perm. She looked frail and worn. The hug was warm and Emma didn't immediately let go. "Trudy."

"Mom, are you okay?"

With a sob, Emma released Trudy. "You better go before your father sees you."

Trudy grasped her mother's arms. "Please. I came home to surprise you for Thanksgiving."

Her Mom bit her lip. "Your father is still upset. Months ago Phillip disappeared with our savings."

"Mom," Trudy whispered. "I told you not to have anything to do with Phillip. He gambles."

"Phillip made it sound as if you wanted us to invest with him to help you. Your father's very angry at Phillip and at you. Phillip was your choice against our wishes. He feels you brought all this on us when you married him."

Trudy grasped her mom's thin arms and tried to look into her eyes. "Do you believe that?"

Emma wiped tears from her eyes. She didn't say anything.

Her mom would side with her dad. She'd never confront or contest anything he said. A chill blew through Trudy's heart that had nothing to do with the gusting wind at her back. "Have you been getting the money I send through Pastor Higgins?"

"Yes, but I haven't told your father. He'd never accept it, and we need it or we'll lose the farm."

"Mom, I thought the farm was paid off."

"It was, but your father mortgaged it again to invest in Phillip's business."

Trudy's stomach clenched and bile rose in her throat. She swallowed it down. "I don't know how, but I'll try to send you more."

"Who's here, Emma?"

Emma pressed a fist to her mouth. She shrank away from Trudy.

Trudy had never heard her father call his wife anything other than "mother", so he truly had disowned her. It was as if her birth had never happened. In her father's eyes, she didn't exist as a daughter anymore. Trudy almost turned and ran.

Using a cane, Howard hobbled from the kitchen into the hall. He stared at Trudy without saying anything. He'd become shrunken and his skin yellowed. The sun glinting through the open door reflected off his glasses, so she couldn't see his eyes. His balding head and gaping mouth made him look like a pale Halloween pumpkin that had endured hard freezes until it turned mushy and fell in on itself.

"Hi, Dad."

"Trudy." His voice was little more than the rasp of a sanding plane on wood.

"I've come home for Thanksgiving. Is that okay with you?"

For a long moment, Howard didn't answer. Furrows creased his forehead and his lips moved to form words that didn't come.

A new look of determination crossed Emma's face. She stepped forward and put an arm around Trudy. Its meaning was not lost on Howard.

"Close the door, girl. You're letting in the cold." He reversed direction, returning to the kitchen. As he did so, she thought he wiped his eyes.

Trudy heaved a sigh of relief. She closed the door. Emma hugged her, and held her close as they followed Howard into the kitchen. Emma fussed about the room, putting on a pot of coffee, and pulling an apple pie from the refrigerator.

Howard remained quiet while Emma chattered to Trudy about all the Amesville news. He ate his pie. He drank his coffee. He stood.

"Howard, don't forget to take your pill," Emma said.

Howard nodded. He went to the sink. From the lower open shelf at the end of the upper cabinets he plucked a bottle. It had been half-hidden between a ceramic bull with a flower tucked behind its chipped ear—thanks to Trudy's clumsy five year old hands—and a little porcelain girl in a red, hooded robe who was kneeling to pray. Wordlessly, he swallowed the pill, drank some water, set the glass back on the counter. He shuffled out of the room.

Trudy heard the *ka-thump* from the living room as the recliner's mechanism dropped into position. The TV came on louder than she remembered. "How bad is his health, Mom?"

"The doctors say his heart is paper thin. They don't know how long he'll last. He seems to have lost all hope. He was bad after you left, but since Phillip disappeared, he does nothing but mope around and watch game shows on TV."

Trudy's stomach knotted. A dull throbbing started at the sides of her head and inched across her forehead. "I've got a secure job in Indianapolis. I've been trying to pay off Phillip's debt or I'd have sent you more. I'm supposed to get a raise soon. I'll send more then. While I'm here I'll look at what you owe and your expenses and see what can be done. Maybe we can let someone use Skipper in return for boarding him. That should help. I've missed him and looked forward to riding him while I'm here, but I'll do it for Dad and you."

Emma frowned. She tilted her head. "We don't have Skipper anymore, Trudy. Phillip said you didn't want the horse. He sold it when he first started living here."

"He sold Skipper?" The throbbing in her head turned to pounding. "My Skipper?"

Emma looked at her strangely. "You know that. You sent him a letter saying to sell it. I saw it."

"No, Mom. He made it up. He's done that before. He forged my name."

Her mom's face puckered and tears glistened in her eyes. "I'm sorry. We thought—" She wadded up the apron she wore and pressed it to her lips. A sob escaped. "It upset your father so much to think you'd sell Skipper. It was the worst cut of all."

The kitchen blurred as Trudy choked back her own tears. Taking her mother's hands, she squeezed them. Her voice squeaked. "Well, it's done. We have to move on. I'll find something else to sell to take care of things. Do you and Dad still want to stay on the farm?"

"This is our home."

"I know Mom, I know. If Dad can't work it anymore and can't pay someone to work it, I hope at least you're leasing it out. It'll bring in some money that way. Surely some neighbor would like to farm it."

Her mom's eyes brightened a little bit. "Do you think so?"

"Sure. It's good land."

"You're right. Evan Biers might be interested. He's hinted in the past about it, but I've been so involved with taking care of your dad, I didn't follow up. Maybe that will help pay off the mortgage and keep the household running."

Her mother considered the plan while Trudy got a drink of water at the sink. She wanted to scream or pitch the drinking glass through the window or something! If Phillip were present, she'd stick the carving knife in his chest. Was there no end to the hurt and deception of that man? She returned to the table and plopped into the seat.

Emma leaned forward and clasped Trudy's hand. "I'm so glad you came home."

"Mom, is that why you haven't gotten a perm lately?"

"Yes," She whispered as she glanced toward the door. "We don't have the money. It doesn't matter. I can't leave your father, anyway. He's dependent on me for everything these days. He's frail, Trudy. And defeated."

"I'll help as much as I can while I'm here. You can go visit your friends or go to the store. Maybe we can try a home perm."

A smile played about her mom's lips. "You always did like to dress up and do your hair."

It was pitiful that such a little thing brightened her mom's day so much. "I've never done it before, but we can at least try."

"That's fine, Trudy. That's fine. Now let's get some supper on the table."

At bedtime, Trudy watched Emma dole out the medicines because Howard couldn't figure out which ones he needed to take. Meekly, he said, "Thank you, Emma."

Maybe the change to calling Emma by name had nothing to do with disowning her. Perhaps it was due to the change in her parents' relationship. He no longer was the provider and decision-making patriarch. He'd become dependent for his life on his wife. The realization of the truth of the situation was bittersweet.

Trudy spent Thanksgiving morning helping stuff the turkey, making cranberry-orange relish, and candying sweet potatoes. While Emma set a jar of pickles in the refrigerator to chill, Trudy lifted the turkey into the pre-heated oven. "This is a nice, fresh turkey."

"Yes, it is. The Osborne's decided to go away for the holiday at the last moment so they gave us their turkey."

"Didn't you already have one?"

"We couldn't afford a turkey because the house insurance came due. No matter. Your father wasn't up to having company, and it didn't make sense to make a big dinner for two. We planned on going into town to eat at Ruthie's Diner. You know they serve free meals to seniors and the indigent at noon every Thanksgiving. The turkey is a blessing from the Lord because you're here. It feels so much more festive being in my own kitchen."

"It's a blessing, all right. You and Dad can eat for a month off it."

The turkey and trimmings were delicious, as her mother's cooking always was. The day was dimmed only by her father's somber attitude, and her own sense of loss every time she caught herself about to say, "I'm going out to ride Skipper."

Trudy spent the rest of the weekend sorting bills and insurance papers. She deduced her dad had a second heart attack immediately after learning Phillip stole their money. In matching up the hospital bills with the admission papers, something didn't seem right. She read through them all again and realized there was a billing error, considering that he could not have had a miscarriage. She also discovered the hospital had duplicated part of the billing from the first heart attack which had included extra days in the hospital.

Saturday evening Trudy went over the list of whom her mother had to call and what to say to handle the various problems. It was a scary thought that her mother, a woman who had always let her husband handle the finances, was now in charge.

If it unnerved Emma, she never balked. She went over the various items until she was confident of what she needed to do. Meanwhile, Howard didn't seem to follow that there was a financial crisis. He didn't do much but sit in his recliner and watch football games, and occasionally take oxygen.

Sunday, after church, Trudy returned to Indianapolis. She dove into her work with a heart that was heavy at her parents' situation, yet a whole lot lighter because she'd reconciled with them. She called home every few days to keep in touch, and to answer her mother's many financial questions.

Mid-December, Trudy stomped the snow from her boots as she made her way through the entry, up the stairs to her apartment. The building manager, Brett, stood guard in front of her door with hands on hips, face like a bull dog that was defending its territory. He was almost snarling as he faced a man whose stance held a studied casualness she would know anywhere.

Brett said, "Trudy, this guy says he's your husband. I wouldn't let him into your apartment with you not home. Do you know him?"

Phillip turned and flashed Trudy one of his famous smiles. "Hi, Tru. I'm back. Tell this guy who I am."

# Chapter Thirteen

Trudy couldn't help it. Her heart pumped faster. She felt light-headed. Phillip always showed up when she was least prepared. She was furious with him, but in that moment everything she wanted to say, needed to say, seemed to slip her mind. Trudy heaved a sigh. She admitted, "Yes, he's my husband."

"Told you." Phillip smirked at the building manager.

"I'm sorry. You aren't wearing rings. I didn't know you were married. I didn't want a stranger hanging around bothering you."

"Thanks, Brett. It's okay. I'll handle it from here."

Brett didn't move. Trudy didn't want the building manager nosing about her business. The best thing was to take this out of his sight because the angry words she wanted to say were trying to surface. She slipped her key into the lock and swung the door open. Phillip sauntered into the apartment. Trudy closed the door on Brett, who was trying to peer past her.

Phillip said, "By the way, Trudy, why aren't you wearing your rings? You had them on last time I was here."

Trudy tossed her key in her purse which she then hung on a wall hook. She removed her coat and hung it on the same hook, covering the purse with it. She closed her eyes, and conjured up the list of offenses she needed to address with him. Ire surged, displacing her desire for him. Bracing herself for confrontation, she drew a deep breath and spun to face Phillip. Her hands mimicked Brett's bulldog stance. "I spent Thanksgiving with my parents."

A look of surprise crossed his face. "Huh. Didn't see that coming." He hastened to add, "I'm thrilled for you. If I'd been able to come sooner, we could've gone together to see the folks. I'm on my way back there now."

"No point. You cleaned them out. You took everything they had." All her practices in front of the mirror left her. Screaming, she rushed at him and pounded him on the chest. "You hurt them. You hurt me. You sold Skipper."

He grabbed her fists and held onto them. She struggled to pull away. He said, "I had to. They were in a terrible financial state after his heart attack, the roof was leaking, the furnace went out, and medical bills were stacking up. I knew you'd want me to take care of your parents. You did want me to take care of them, right?"

He released her and she hugged herself. The words sounded good. She couldn't quite place what was wrong with this logic. She punched him one more time in the chest, but not very hard. "Of course, but that was for me to decide. Me. You should have told me he was sick."

"I wanted to protect you, darling. I see now it was wrong. I should've told you. I simply wanted to be sure he was better first."

Feeling off balance and uncertain, she stalked to the other side of the room. "No. You were thinking of yourself. You've wanted their money ever since I let it slip they had some. You're a rat. You're a horrible, stinking con man. You left them high and dry. Dad had another heart attack over it. You nearly killed my dad."

Phillip pulled a sad face. "Another heart attack. Trudy, that's horrible. He's such a great guy. Is he okay?" He approached and tried to console her with an embrace.

Trudy pushed Phillip. "No. He's not okay. He didn't die, but he's not okay."

"Is Mom okay?"

Phillip's relief seemed genuine. This confused Trudy. "She's okay. Exhausted from taking care of Dad." Trudy brushed past him and positioned herself with the couch between them. She tapped her foot. "How much do you need this time?"

"Why do you always have to go there? Tru, I missed you. I came to see you."

"How much?"

"Nada. Nothing. Zippo. I'm rolling in dough. I'm doing great. That job out east is a winner." He pulled his wallet from his jacket's chest pocket. He spread a thick wad of large bills in front of her as if they were a deck of cards. The gesture, meant to impress her, only served as a reminder that it could be gone in a moment with one hand of poker or one throw of the dice.

She snorted. "Who do you owe that to?"

Phillip lay the cash against his chest. "Tru, you cut me. I don't owe anybody anything."

"You owe my parents."

"Of course. I know that. I meant I don't owe anyone else. I told your dad his investment would pay off. Here it is. All of it."

"All of their money?"

"Well, all of this goes to them. It's the first payment. It won't take me long to get the rest."

"Why are you giving it to me? Take it to them."

"All right." Phillip folded the money into a stack and started to tuck the wad in his pocket.

Trudy grabbed his wrist. "On second thought, I'll give it to them."

As she reached for the roll of cash, he pulled it back. "How do I know you'll give it to them?"

Trudy glared.

Phillip laughed and tossed his coat onto the couch. "Oh that's right. You're honest as the day is long. Okay, Honest Abe."

Turning her back to him and fanning the money, Trudy took a quick count. "Is it real?"

"I'm offended."

"Is it?" She looked over her shoulder at him.

"Of course it is. I'm not a criminal."

Trudy snorted softly, but relief was like a drink of water after a long, dry run. Phillip had come through. He was making it right. This was the Phillip she knew and loved. She sealed the money in an envelope, tucked it in her purse, and snapped the purse shut.

Phillip pressed in close behind her. Trudy startled. He slid his hands around her waist and cradled her. His arms felt strong and familiar. His face snuggled against her neck and the warm, layered scent of spices and citrus from his *Eternity*@ aftershave was familiar and masculine. She leaned into him. How could she resist him, when he was like this? When she thought it could only get worse, he showed up and made everything right again. Almost right again. Enough so her parents would be okay.

A kiss tickled her neck. Trudy closed her eyes, squeezing them shut to keep the tears in, but a couple spilled out anyway. Why did he have to feel so good, so right? She didn't want to want him. Phillip took her shoulders and turned her. He touched her cheek and smiled. "From now on, Tru, it's all going to be different."

"Shut up," she snapped.

Phillip grinned and kissed her. He kissed her again. Trudy was filled with hope and a fluttering of happiness that this time it could be different.

In the morning, Trudy took one look at the clock and extricated herself from the sleeping Phillip's arms. She rolled off the couch where they'd been locked together in sleep. "I didn't realize it was so late."

"It's Saturday. You don't work on Saturday, do you?" Phillip's voice was husky with sleep. He rolled over and braced himself on one elbow.

Trudy laughed. She leaned over and kissed him. "No. No, I don't. Not usually. I forgot what day it was."

"You look good, all tousled and glowing."

"I feel good, Phillip."

"I like to think I had something to do with that, Mrs. Bellafonte." He held her face in both of his hands and kissed her again. "I almost forgot. I have something for you." He reached over the side of the couch and retrieved his trousers. From the pocket he pulled a tiny, black velvet jewelry box. He opened it and turned it toward her. A pair of ruby earrings twinkled.

"They're lovely."

Phillip stood and pulled his pants on. "They're not exactly like the ones we were looking at in Las Vegas, but I thought you'd like them."

He always noticed the details. She had at first thought they were the same ones, but upon inspection, realized subtle differences. Still, they were beautiful.

"Put them on."

Trudy did and admired them in the bathroom mirror. She came back to model them for Phillip.

His appraisal held admiration. "Beautiful. They were meant for you. You make them look good. When you wear them, you can think of me and know I'm always near. I'll always love you, Tru."

"I love you too, Phillip. Thank you." She went to him and their embrace felt complete and whole and bright with promise.

"You know what I do, I do for you. I want you to have the best, dear heart."

"Phillip, I think you're the best. I want us to be like this always."

He let go of her and sat on the couch. "I'm hungry. What's for breakfast?"

"We'll have to go out."

He pulled a twenty dollar bill out of his wallet and handed it to her. "While I finish getting dressed, why don't you go get breakfast?"

Trudy took the bill and he pulled her to him for another kiss. She wiggled into skinny jeans and bent over to zip the ankle zippers. Phillip slapped her bottom. She giggled. "Stop it."

"Can't. You are irresistibly cute."

Trudy pulled on a scooped neck, pink 1989 DKNY shirt with cabbage trim sleeves. She'd gotten it on sale at a retail store, because of a small spot along the side seam that was hardly noticeable. She slipped on a winter jacket and picked up her purse. "Be back in thirty. Forty-five, if there's a line at the bank. I want to deposit that money right away so I can send it to my parents."

"Hold on. I'll go with you. You're too delicious to let out of my sight." Phillip pulled on a shirt, socks, shoes, and black cashmere pea coat. With his arm draped lightly over her shoulders, they moved along the narrow hall, down the steps, and past the apartment manager.

Trudy chirped, "Good morning, Brett."

Brett stuffed the last of a donut in his mouth and wiped powdered sugar from his chin. He mumbled, "Boy, Trudy, I don't think I've ever seen you so happy."

"Phillip brought good news."

Brett said, "Good for you. You could use some good news."

A knowing smile quirked Phillip's lips. He gave a jaunty wave to Brett and whispered in her ear. "Is that what you're calling it these days?"

Trudy dug her elbow playfully into his rib. "Hush. Where's the Town Car?"

"In for servicing. Let's take the Pinto."

Brett trailed them to the front door and watched as they drove past. They waved. Brett returned the wave.

Because he was so hungry they ate first. Over breakfast, Trudy suggested a couple places they could spend the day. Phillip ran a hand over his thick black hair. "You know, Tru, I'm still bushed from traveling. I'd prefer to spend the day in the apartment with you." He gave her that brilliant smile that sent shivers up her spine. So they went straight back to the apartment.

They sat on the couch and talked as they used to in the beginning. They laughed about the quirks of their bosses, spoke of the people they'd met, and the experiences they'd had. Later, they dined at a seafood place and laid plans for the future. Phillip said, "My job in Atlantic City is wrapping up. They want me to go to Palm Springs, but maybe I can interest them in opening a branch here in Indianapolis."

"I thought you found Indianapolis boring."

"Not if I'm starting up that franchise. That would be very interesting. The work is always changing and very lucrative. Besides, you're here, dear heart. You're the draw, Tru."

She snuggled in closer to him. Contentment like a quilt wrapped her soul.

In the morning, Trudy said, "I promised I'd help in the nursery during Sunday school, but then we could go to church together. You could meet my friends."

"Ah, Tru. What did I tell you about making friends? They tie you down."

Trudy chose a red velveteen dress with a scoop neck trimmed in lace. She accented it with a gold necklace that went well with the new earrings and laid them at the end of the couch. "That's good, Phillip, because I'm not going anywhere. I want you to meet Kathy. And Spider and Mike. They're the guys that fixed the Pinto for me. They've led very interesting lives. They're very friendly. Real people."

Phillip scratched his stubbly chin. "You're right. If you stay somewhere you make friends and put down roots. It'll take me awhile, old habits are hard to break, but I'll do it for you."

Trudy beamed at him. "Then you'll come with me?"

He smiled and shook his head. "No, Tru. I'll meet them another time. You go to church. It's important to you. I'll stay here, get cleaned up, and read yesterday's paper. I'll take a real soaker in that huge tub of yours."

"Okay." Progress, not perfection, Trudy thought. She bathed, dressed, and kissed him. She checked her purse before she left. The fat sealed envelope was still in place. "I'll bring Chinese back for lunch."

"Sounds good, Tru. General's Tso's Chicken for me. Don't forget the fortune cookies."

"I won't. Remember the early years? We spent many happy moments over those cute little sayings and making up fortunes of our own."

"I remember. Now we're doing it for real." He blew her a kiss. She blew one back and pulled the door shut behind her.

Four hours later, when Trudy returned, she kicked at the door with her toe. Using her best attempt at an Irish accent, she called, "Phillip, me love. Open up. Me hands are full."

The door remained closed. No sound came from the WC, not even the TV. Phillip had to be in the tub, or perhaps had fallen asleep again. She clasped both bags awkwardly in one arm and unlocked the door with the other hand. It swung open. Trudy gasped.

Everything had been turned upside down and inside out. The couch was up-turned. The pillow pulled open. Its stuffing spread on the floor. Her one potted shade-loving plant was uprooted. Soil spilled everywhere. Clothing that had been stacked on the shelves between the studs had been pulled down and tossed in a heap. Even the heating vent hung half-way off the wall.

Trudy's lungs were as starved for air as if she'd run a marathon. In a vain but subconscious effort to steady herself, she squeezed the bags she carried. They rustled and the smell of spices and chicken rose afresh as hot juice soaked through the unbuttoned coat into her dress. "Ow."

She dropped the bags on the heavy coffee table and sank beside them. Had he lied to her about owing no one money? Had debt-collecting thugs found him? No bloody red spots marked the floor or the walls. Maybe Phillip had escaped and afterward they had ripped the place up looking for money.

Trudy took a second, slower look around the room. Phillip's duffle bag was gone. Plastic shopping bags lay empty on the floor, and the new shirts she'd bought him were missing. "Phillip?"

She stepped through the mess to the bathroom. The medicine cabinet was empty, the jars opened and dumped alongside the lids into the sink. His razor and toothbrush were no longer on the washbasin. She shut the medicine chest door. The mirror held a message scrawled with one of her lipsticks.

"I got a call.
It's a sure thing!
I'll double the $$
You'll be proud of me."

# Chapter Fourteen

Trudy read the message again before it made sense. "Oh, Phillip. No. No. No." She rushed back into the main room and stumbled over to the coffee table. She snatched up her purse, fumbled to open it, and tore open the envelope. Sheets of folded newspaper fluttered to the floor.

Trudy roared. She swept up the soggy bags of food and threw them. General Tso's Chicken splattered down the wall and pooled around the plastic-wrapped fortune cookies. Trudy spun around the room shouting. "I'm so stupid. I can't believe I fell for it again."

After several minutes, she found her cell phone at the bottom of her purse. Between sobs, she squeaked out, "Kathy, he was here. Phillip was here."

"I'll be right there."

Trudy spent the moments rocking back and forth, getting herself under control so that the sobbing had quieted to mild hiccups by the time Kathy burst through the open door.

Kathy halted at the sight of the room. "Did he do this?"

"Yes."

Kathy plowed past the mess and sat beside where Trudy hunched on the couch. "Where does it hurt?"

"My heart."

"Come on. Let's go to the hospital."

"No," Trudy wailed. "I mean it hurts inside. My soul. He didn't hurt me physically. He'd never hurt me that way."

Kathy's round eyes studied Trudy. She sat on the couch. "What happened?"

"I came home from church and he was—gone." Trudy gestured around the room.

Kathy assessed the damage and rose to close the door. "Did you have an argument?"

"No. Everything was perfect."

"Then why did he trash the apartment?"

"He taught me to hide money for a fast get away. I guess he was looking for that, except after the last time he took my stash, I've kept everything in the bank."

"Do you think someone took him?"

"I did at first, but his stuff is gone, and he left a note in the bathroom."

Kathy stepped to the doorway and read the lipstick message. "What does it mean?"

She waved the envelope with the newspaper clippings. "He'd given me tens of thousands of dollars to pay toward what he took from my parents this year. I put it in my purse in an envelope. I hadn't had a chance to deposit it because we were together all day yesterday. He must've switched it when I was in the shower getting ready for church this morning. That means he planned this. He probably found some wager that he thinks will double the money so he can pay them back more quickly. He means well—"

"Stop it."

At the harsh tone in Kathy's voice, Trudy clamped her mouth shut.

"Stop making excuses for him. He didn't borrow from your parents, he STOLE. His addiction made him steal again what he'd just paid back. No matter what you say, it doesn't make it right, and I don't want to hear it."

Trudy opened and shut her mouth.

Kathy's voice softened. Her arm made a sweeping motion about the room. "Is this the action of a sane person?"

Trudy shook her head. She put her head in her hands.

"You keep expecting him to change. Are those the actions of a sane person?"

Trudy felt a defensive wall rise up in her. She lifted her face to her friend. Kathy simply didn't understand because she didn't know Phillip. "I love him. I gave him another chance. Isn't that what God wants me to do? Isn't God a God of love and forgiveness and hope and second chances?"

"Oh, God is love, and God loves Phillip, as much as he loves you. God also forgives, but doesn't exonerate indiscriminately. A person has to accept that forgiveness and change what he's doing. God says to hope, but that isn't wishing on a star, it's expecting Him to work good out in the end. It's a faith that for those who trust in him to do so, God is in control and is faithfully working to bring good out of the chaos. Phillip obviously isn't ready for that. What about you?"

"What do you mean?"

Kathy shook her head and heaved a long sigh, like Trudy's fourth grade teacher had done when her students didn't understand the math she'd spent an hour teaching. "It isn't love to let someone keep hurting you while wishing they'd change. Hope is good. Stupidity, no. If Phillip hasn't changed after all your attempts to get him to change, then it's insanity to keep doing the same thing. Only God can work real change in Phillip. Seems to me you keep getting in the way."

Trudy broke the gaze and stared instead at the mess the Chinese food made on the wall and the floor. Her words sounded familiar. There'd been much discussion at the Al-Anon meetings on this topic. Why did it always sound so good until she was with Phillip? Then, everything faded away except him.

Kathy's voice gentled. She hugged Trudy and didn't let go. "You waste time and energy trying to figure out why Phillip does the things he does. Even if you could figure it out, it wouldn't change him. When are you going to let go and let God do his thing?"

Trudy didn't know what to say. Was she getting in God's way? She wiped the last of the tears with a tissue. She set the wastepaper basket upright and tossed the tissue in. Her shoulders slumped.

Kathy gave Trudy another big squeeze and released her. "Come on. I'll help you clean this mess." She picked up one of the shopping bags and started filling it with pillow stuffing. She smiled at Trudy. "You can wash up that sticky chicken mess. That's on you."

Trudy cocked a half-smile. "Yes, Ma'am. How'd you know I did it?"

"It's exactly what I would've done."

By the week of Christmas, Trudy had more or less recovered from Phillip's visit. Kathy constantly reminded her that it was pointless to squirm over past mistakes, whether years ago or new ones. She could change none of it. She simply had to take one day at a time and live that. Like mining gold, she had to find the good in whatever happened each day.

Phillip's visit and her reaction to him did produce one nugget. Trudy finally admitted it would take God to bring sanity to her life. She prayed about her over-willingness to put herself at the mercy of Phillip's charms.

In front of the bathroom mirror, Trudy role-played scenarios with Phillip in which she'd respond more healthily to what he might say. Only this time, she didn't allow these to turn to daydreams or wishful thinking. She quit imagining her lectures or arguments. She simply thought of the things he might say and how she could better respond. The more she thought about it, the clearer her thoughts became and the more a little steel was injected into her soul.

## Chapter Fifteen

Sitting in the Pinto in front of her parents' house, Trudy rubbed her naked ring finger. Not wearing the rings had become the symbol of her dedication to respond to Phillip in a more healthy way. Whether she wore the rings or not, she was aware of them – and of Phillip. Someday when he returned, she would resist falling prey to his charms. And he would return. He always came back to her. That was her ace in the hole.

She unzipped the pocket in her purse and pulled out the rings. She slid them on and gazed at them. Someday, Phillip would want her more than he wanted to gamble. He'd commit to her and building a life together. Then, she'd put them on permanently. For the time being, there was no sense in inciting her dad's anger by letting him think she was divorced.

Trudy opened the car door. The rush of cold air swept around her as she swung her legs out and stood. She gathered her purse and hat and gloves. Her black wool skirt brushed the tops of her knee high boots as she leaned in to withdraw her travel case. She took a breath of frosty air and headed for the house.

Al-Anon was helping restore her confidence to handle her problems. One problem was how to help her mom. Her mom had handled the list of insurance problems with only a dozen calls to her daughter. Afterward, her mother seemed even more self-assured.

On the last night of Trudy's Christmas visit, they shared conversation over a cup of tea and apple pie. "You're doing really well, Mom. You've handled these problems like a pro. I'm proud of you."

"It gives me something to do while I sit here with your father. He's getting worse. I don't like leaving him. I don't dare go to midweek service because he seems more confused when evening comes on. I don't go to Sunday evening service anymore either, because one night I came home and he was gone. I found him standing in his slippers in the backyard without even a coat. It scares me."

"That's hard, Mom. What about the quilting circle and your Farm Women meetings?"

"It's too hard to get away. I've stopped cooking for funeral dinners at the church, and someone else is arranging flowers in the sanctuary. I worry about him the whole time. Sometimes he doesn't even feel strong enough to go to morning worship on Sundays."

"It sounds worse than I thought. I wish I was closer to help. It must be lonely for you, Mom."

"Oh, my friends stop by and sometimes bring their husbands to talk farming and machinery with Howard. Even so, everybody is so busy, it still leaves many hours in the day. We get by. It's okay."

Why was it that women of her mom's age never could be open? They always put on a bright face and swept reality under the rug. Trudy hugged her mom. "No, Mom. It's not okay. It's hard."

As if given permission to be real, Emma snuffled into a tissue. Trudy held her and let her cry as she murmured soothing words. "...I wish I didn't live so far away. If this wasn't such a good job—"

"Don't talk like that. You've been a big help. Your phone calls mean everything to me. They keep me going. I'm so glad to be a family again. You're all grown and have a life you've made for yourself. Don't feel badly, Trudy. Not even about Phillip." Emma squeezed Trudy. "You can't be blamed for what he's done."

"Mom," Trudy started to say that she'd seen Phillip, but as quickly realized mentioning this would only cause her mother more pain. "I love you."

"I love you, too." The crying jag over, Emma stood and cleared the dishes from the table, stacking them beside the sink. "These'll wait until morning. I'm going to bed. I'm so tired these days, I can hardly stay awake until eight. Good night."

"Good night, Mom."

"Lock the doors and turn off the lights, please." Emma padded out of the room, her fuzzy slip-on slippers whispering on the floor and up the steps.

Despite her mother's assurances, Trudy did feel badly. She sat in the kitchen a while longer, pondering, but coming up with no new options to the many problems she faced. She did up the dishes, locked the doors, and shut off the lights. Guilt made for a heavy partner that followed her into bed and kept her awake for a long time before she finally drifted asleep.

*Thump.*

Trudy jolted awake and sat up in bed, her heart pounding. The night was quiet. Her door didn't bust down. No rent was due. She was safe. It must've been another dream. She lay down and pulled the covers over her shoulders against the cool night air.

Soon, rustling and low voices in the hallway stirred her curiosity. The floor was cold as she moved barefoot to the door and peeked into the hall.

The night light on the wall socket revealed Emma bent over Howard who was on the floor. They both grunted with the strain as she pulled him to his feet. They stood in place a moment to steady themselves, then moved into the bathroom leaving a smelly mess on the floor.

"I'm so sorry Emma. I tried to get there." Howard choked out the words in a defeated tone.

Emma's voice was reassuring and patient. "Now, never you mind about that. Let's get you cleaned up."

Trudy shut the door on the private moment. Dad would be so embarrassed that she'd witnessed his shame. Should she go back to bed and pretend she'd seen nothing? She released the knob.

Could she do that? Maybe she should clean up the mess so her mom didn't have to. She gripped the door handle again. Cold crept up her legs as she stood there trying to decide what to do.

The shower started running and there was more indistinct talking. The bathroom door opened. Trudy released the knob and held her breath for fear of being discovered standing behind her bedroom door. Emma's light steps moved down the hall and passed into the master bedroom. A drawer opened and closed, but Emma didn't reappear.

Trudy strained to hear. The bed squeaked. She caught the sound of soft weeping, a restraining sob, and a few moments later the soft padding of feet returned to the bathroom.

As soon as the bathroom door shut, Trudy ran down the stairs for the bucket, soap, rubber gloves, and rags. She made quick work of it, and vowed never to say a word. Afterward, she lay in bed, unable to sleep. Now that she was attuned to the night sounds, she heard every time either one of them moved.

Howard was up twice more during the night, but had no more accidents. Emma walked with him each time to steady him. If this was the nightly norm, no wonder Emma had lost weight and they both looked so washed out and exhausted. It was a long night for everyone.

In the morning, Trudy sat at the kitchen table in a pair of blue velour sweatpants and sweatshirt, having the first cup of the day. Overhead, Emma was in the shower. Howard shuffled down the hall into the kitchen.

"Morning, Dad."

"Morning, Trudy. Are you having a good breakfast?"

"Drinking coffee, right now. Would you like some?"

He frowned as if he were going to launch into his usual lecture about the importance of eating breakfast. Trudy stood, and his expression changed as if he were surprised she was so tall. Then, he seemed to recognize her as she was, as an adult, not a child. He nodded and sank heavily into his chair. "Coffee would be great."

Trudy set a steaming mug in front of him and gave him a peck on the cheek.

"Thank you."

"You're welcome." Trudy wasn't certain if he meant the coffee or the kiss, and decided he meant both. They drank coffee together companionably while wind rattled the windows in their sashes and flung flurries against the glass. The fat, wet snowflakes clung to the pane a moment, then slid into a watery heap at the base of the sill.

Howard stared at his coffee mug. A frown creased his forehead, as if trying to figure out a complex problem. "You were right."

Unsure of what he meant, Trudy cocked her head to the side, waiting for him to finish the sentence. His gaze met hers. "About Phillip. I shouldn't have trusted him. I understand now how you were taken in. He's likeable and persuasive. I should've known you wouldn't have done the things he said you did. You were always a bit adventurous, but never foolish about money. I should've known you'd never sell Skipper, either."

Trudy didn't know what to say. She put her hand over her father's and felt his trembling. "No, I wouldn't have ever done that. I'm sorry, Dad."

With his free hand he patted her hand. Behind his glasses, his eyes were watery. "When you first left home, I was embarrassed. I thought it made me look bad. When Phillip came around helping us,

I believed him because I was still angry with you for disobeying me and running off with him."

It was as close to an apology as she'd ever heard the proud man make. The moment passed. He pulled his trembling hands back and sipped his coffee. Trudy moved to the refrigerator. "Would you like some eggs?"

"The doctor says I can't have them. I have to have oatmeal."

"Then, it's a good thing you like oatmeal. I'll make some. Do you want raisins in it?"

"That'd be nice, Trudy-girl."

She beamed at him. If he were using his pet name for her, all was truly forgiven. He smiled back, and the cold wintry morning became a whole lot warmer. She dumped the oatmeal into the boiling water and stirred.

Howard said. "Would you hand me some milk for my coffee?"

"It's all gone. I'll get more when I go to town."

"Guess I should go out and milk the cows."

Trudy stopped mid-stir and turned to him. His expression hadn't changed. Should she say they didn't have cows anymore? Should she say that she'd do it after breakfast, and hope he forgot?

Emma, fully dressed, entered. "No need, Howard, it's done."

The frail man visibly relaxed. "Thank you, Emma. I really didn't feel like doing that today."

"Yes, it's a nasty day out there. We have to thank the good Lord that we're safe inside." She set about putting bowls on the table. They ate breakfast as if nothing odd had happened.

That evening after supper, Trudy kissed each parent good-bye with promises to be back as soon as she could. She carried her weekend bag under her arm and went through the wet falling snow to the Pinto. Her parents stood in the door and waved until she was out of the driveway. On the six hours back to Indianapolis, her thoughts went round and round in an effort to work out how to best help her parents.

Trudy was still worrying over it Monday night when her cell phone played "Don't Be Cruel". She recognized the number and set down her purse and shucked off her coat before answering. "Hi, Mom. I'm getting home from work now. I was about to call you."

Her mother's voice was low and controlled. "Trudy, you're father passed away."

"Oh, Mom." Trudy dropped onto the dilapidated couch. She whispered, "What happened?"

"It was another heart attack. I was fixing lunch. He was watching the *Price is Right*. When I called him to the table, he'd already gone. God took him home."

God always seemed to be taking and never giving, but Trudy couldn't very well say that to her mother or she'd die on the spot, too. "I'm on my way." She bolted to her feet and then sank back onto the couch. "Oh, no. Peter wants me to meet with a new client tomorrow morning. He wants my opinion of this particular author and her book before he signs her. It's the first time he's asked me to make a preliminary assessment on a client. I need to get this right."

"Of course, Trudy. I understand."

"I'll come as soon as I can. I'll leave right after the meeting. I should be there tomorrow night. Will that be soon enough? Then, we'll take care of everything together."

"That's fine, Trudy. My friend Sarah is here with me. Come when you can." They talked a little longer, then hung up.

In the morning, Trudy entered Francie's pastry shop ten minutes early and claimed a table and ordered coffee. She envisioned an open, empty file cabinet and dumped in all thoughts of her dad, all the details of having a funeral and its cost, if she should move her Mom to Indianapolis, whether she should sell the farm, and all the imaginings of what she'd do to Phillip if she could get her hands on him for shortening her father's life. She mentally closed the drawer on all that mess.

She had to get into the game. Like barrel racing Skipper when she was a girl, she had to plan the maneuver, see herself marking the course, and feel the ride. She imagined a broad, clear desk in front of her. She placed on it the file marked 'Carol Streeter.'

The potential client was a first time author who had written a book about dealing with grief. A publisher had already sent her an advance to finish the book. That was a good sign that they thought the book could go somewhere. The woman was savvy enough to know how important publicity was to sales, and was asking for help. Trudy opened her eyes.

A petite, small-boned woman with blonde hair and blue eyes stood in front of her, waiting politely. She carried a purse as big as a backpack. She smiled and warmth radiated from her, drawing Trudy in. "Hi. Are you Trudy Bellafonte from Faulkinroy Publicists?"

Trudy nodded and gestured to the chair across from her. "Ms. Streeter, so nice to meet you. Can I offer you a coffee and a sweet roll?"

"Mrs. Streeter. I'm a widow. Sure, coffee would be great. I could use a coffee. I'll try not to spill it. I can get a little klutzy when I'm nervous."

The comment struck Trudy as odd. If it were a gimmick to be self-deprecating, what was the goal? It'd be more natural to hide faults to appear professional. She made herself smile.

Carol wasn't paying attention to her. She was busy setting the huge purse on the empty seat beside her. She slipped off her coat, hung it on the back of her chair, bumping the purse. She grasped it before the contents spilled. "Oh, sorry." She scooted her chair, and then had to stand to adjust her coat which had caught under the legs of the chair.

Goodness. The woman was simply being honest. She was a klutz. After Carol's coffee order was placed, Trudy smiled as disarmingly as she could. "Tell me a little about yourself, Mrs. Streeter."

"Please, call me Carol. I'm not a particularly formal person."

"Okay. Carol." Trudy, wanting to maintain formality, didn't suggest Carol use her first name.

Carol didn't seem to notice. She pulled a book about an inch and a half thick from her bag and shoved it across the table. "Here's the ARC."

"ARC?"

"Advanced Reviewer Copy. It's not fully ready for publication, but it gets bookstores and reviewers interested. I was widowed almost two years ago. To deal with my grief I wrote about it. It's a faith journey showing how God can walk us through tragedy.

"A writer friend, after reading it, sent it to her publisher. They liked it, and I signed a contract with them. They want me to establish a platform to sell the book at conferences, speaking engagements, and that type of thing. They want me to make a big push. I work full time. I thought I needed help putting that together."

"I see."

"Isn't this what a publicity agent does? How can you help me? What do you suggest I do first? Will you contact churches locally or around the country? How do I go about putting together a conference? I don't understand how we get people to want me to speak if the book isn't out yet. How much should I charge to speak? What do I do about travel expenses? It's all new to me. I definitely need help. How much is all this going to cost me?"

They worked through the questions one at a time so the meeting lasted longer than Trudy expected. Carol was open and friendly and unpretentious. After a third cup of coffee, Carol said, "Forgive me for mentioning it, but I sense something seems to be weighing you down. Can I be of help?"

Trudy was too surprised to put off the friendly overture. "My father died yesterday. I'm leaving from here to drive back to Iowa."

"I'm so sorry." Carol reached out to briefly touch Trudy's hand. She asked about the family, the circumstances, and listened as if she cared.

Trudy wanted to visit more with this disarming woman. She hoped Peter contracted with her. She scooted the chair back and stood. "I'll read the ARC and bring Mr. Faulkinroy up to speed on our meeting. He'll get back with you in a week or two to let you know if he'll be taking you on."

Carol stood as well. "Thank you for meeting with me. I do hope you can help me, Ms. Bellafonte."

"Thank you for listening, Carol."

Carol nodded. "I understand loss and grief."

"I'm sure you do. You did lose a husband."

"When I was a girl, I also lost my father and—"

Trudy had the idea she was going to say something else. Instead, Carol tapped the ARC and then touched Trudy's arm. "Perhaps this will help you. Perhaps it's God's timing. I'll be praying for you and your mother. I know this is hard, but you will get through it, Ms. Bellafonte."

"Trudy."

Carol's smile widened. "Drive safely, Trudy."

On the drive to her mother's, Trudy called Peter. "I think you should meet Carol Streeter. I have a feeling this book is going to go somewhere and you can make some money."

"Have you read it?"

"No."

"Read it. Call me when you're finished."

"You do remember I'm not on vacation. I'm here to bury my father and handle his affairs."

"Didn't you say it was a book on grief?"

"Yes, but—"

"Read the book, and I'll pay you for the days you're gone."

"Fine." Trudy closed the call. Even if it was generous of Peter, she resented having to take the deal. She wanted to focus on her mother, not read books, especially new ones by unknowns.

The viewing took place at Crombley's Funeral Home. It seemed as if almost all of the town turned out for it. That was only fitting to honor one of the oldest hometown boys who was so generous and community-minded.

From the obvious stolen looks at her and the whispers behind hands, several had come to glimpse the local runaway legend. How many knew of the shame she'd brought on the family when her husband conned her parents? Better to be bold, then try to hide. Trudy went up to each person and called them by name. Slowly she made her way toward the casket.

Potted plants and flower sprays arrayed around the room were dwarfed by one enormous arrangement. It commanded the attention of everyone. When she thought no one was looking, Trudy, on the pretext that she was adjusting the planter on the stand next to it, checked to see if Phillip had sent it. The card held her boss's name.

Peter could afford it, but it should've been Phillip. Of course, he probably didn't even know his father-in-law had died.

"That's a nice bunch of flowers."

Trudy straightened and looked into the sky-blue eyes of Beau Svenson. "Hey, Beau."

"Sorry about your dad, Trudy."

Trudy nodded. Beau continued, "Is your husband here?"

"No."

When she offered no further explanation, he said, "Lots of people were surprised to see you come back here, but not me. I remember how close you were with your dad. He used to take you fishing, and I remember when he bought you your horse.

"He was at every competition you ever did. He never showed much emotion, but I caught him letting out a whoop that time you won the barrel race by one second. He told everyone seated by him that you were his daughter."

Trudy cocked her head. "Really?"

"Oh, yeah. Always wished my pa had that kind of pride in me. I used to come by from time to time and go fishing with him." Beau shuffled his feet and cleared his throat. "I offered to buy Skipper when you sold him."

"I didn't sell him." Trudy almost shouted. People turned their heads. She caught herself and lowered her voice. "That was a big misunderstanding. He wasn't supposed to be sold."

Beau brushed loose blond hair out of his blue eyes. "I wondered. Of course, I was surprised, when you moved away and left him behind. I used to come over and ride him, to keep him exercised."

"I didn't know that." She reached out and laid a hand on his arm. "Thank you, Beau."

His lips formed a thin line. "When you, um, when he was sold, your dad wouldn't let me have Skipper. Said he didn't want the horse close by where he could see it. He had your husband drive it to over to a buyer in Albert City to a fellow named Cooper."

"I didn't know that, either. I couldn't find the bill of sale. Mom didn't remember who it was."

"Do you think you'll move back here, now?"

"No."

"Too bad." His voice dropped low. "You know, I've had a crush on you ever since we kissed. Remember? In the choir loft at church?"

"We were kids."

"Remember that time in our sophomore year? We snuck out and went skinny-dipping in Miller's Pond."

A mild heat burned her cheeks. "It wasn't skinny-dipping. We wore underwear, like a bathing suit."

Beau grinned and his blue eyes sparkled with amusement. "That's the same argument you gave Deputy Seagan, but whatever you were wearing, when it got wet, you could see through it."

"You're making things up. Anyway, it was night. You couldn't see a thing."

"I could when Deputy Seagan flashed that big old spotlight on us and ordered us out."

She remembered how boldly she had strode out of the pond and stood there arguing with the deputy that they were swimming to cool off and not doing anything wrong. She remembered how odd both males had acted. Beau had even moved away from her. At the time, she thought he was scared of the deputy. When he'd handed her his checkered shirt while facing the other way, she thought he was simply being a gentleman. The mild heat in her cheeks flared to a fire. Trudy smacked his arm with the back of her hand. "Liar."

He chuckled. "Don't worry. I never told anyone. Deputy Seagan never said a word either as long as he lived. He told me he never even wrote a report 'cause he knew it'd get around town if he did. It was obvious to both of us you had no clue what you were doing. You were feisty, though. I always admired that."

Trudy covered her eyes with her hand. "I'm so sorry, Beau. I didn't realize. I'm sorry. Boy, I seem to be saying that a lot lately."

Beau chuckled again as one of the old ladies from church came sidling up, head tilted toward them, trying to hear the conversation. His eyes shifted her way and back to Trudy. "Anyway, I thought you'd appreciate that fishing tale of your dad."

"I do. Thank you."

"He was a good man." As Beau made his way toward the door, Trudy wondered what would've happened if Phillip had never come. If she had stayed in Amesville, would she have made a life with someone stable and nice like Beau?

Trudy turned to greet the busybody and pretended she didn't notice the snooping.

The next morning, the flowers and the casket were moved to the church for the service. More people attended the pre-service viewing. While the organ groaned low and mournful, visitors paused at the open casket and then again at the monstrous arrangement, searching for the card which read, 'Peter Faulkinroy, Faulkinroy Publicists.'

Over and over, Trudy saw heads bob together and gossip whispered.

"...still married?"

"...always a wild one..."

Trudy didn't care for herself, but her mom had to live here, at least for a while. When she was younger, she would've tossed her hair and said, "Let 'em think what they want, the shameful gossips." Now, she couldn't abide talk that would shame Emma and add to her grief. Trudy wrote a note and handed it to the funeral director to give to the fat and balding Pastor Higgins.

After the eulogy and the sermon, the pastor thanked everyone on behalf of the family for the food that had been brought and for the flowers. He named each of the givers, including "the big city one from Trudy's boss, Peter Faulkinroy, and the entire staff at Faulkinroy Publicists, a premier publicity agency in Indianapolis."

Scattered whispering assured Trudy that assumptions about what that huge bouquet meant were being adjusted. No one needed to know "the entire staff" consisted of the woman seated in front of them. Trudy was grateful that Peter, never missing a chance to promote his business, had signed the card that way rather than more personally.

Like some subliminal message in an ad campaign, Pastor Higgins rubbed his stomach as he said, "After interment at the cemetery, Emma and Trudy invite you back here to the meeting hall for a luncheon provided by the women's auxiliary."

The long-speaking pastor was gratefully brief with his prayer at the wind and snow swept graveside. People hurried back to their warm cars and then to the church. Trudy, like Emma, visited with each person, accepting handshakes and hugs and vague offers of assistance while repeating the expected assurances that they were fine and needed nothing, thank you so much for coming.

The truth was her mom wasn't fine. Trudy offered a quick, but heartfelt thanks that the funeral was paid through a term life insurance policy her dad had purchased years before. Other than that, she wasn't sure how her mother was going to manage.

# Chapter Sixteen

They arrived home from the long ordeal as a rusty old van pulled up and delivered aluminum pans of leftovers from the funeral dinner. Trudy set them on the table because the counter was already lined with bags of bread, cakes, and pies. The refrigerator was full of Jell-O salads and casseroles and ham.

Hardworking as ever, Emma was already putting on an apron. Trudy followed her example and was surprised at the comfort she felt working side by side with her mom. A good part of the late afternoon slipped by as they portioned the bounty into meal-size packages for the freezer. They blanched trays of vegetables and fruits, and froze them.

"You should be able to eat for the next six months without buying groceries," Trudy said.

"Yes, indeed. Thank the good Lord." Emma poured the leftover coffee from the big urn into pint jars for freezing. Trudy thought that was taking thriftiness too far, but said nothing. When the job was completed, Emma crept up the stairs for a nap.

Trudy sank onto a kitchen chair. Whoever came up with the term 'I feel like a wet noodle' must have been feeling as limp and weak as she felt. A nap with a heating pad would probably set her right again. Using the bannister, Trudy pulled herself up the stairs. At the top, through the closed door, she heard Emma sobbing. Trudy's head began to throb. She crept to her own bed and fell into a deep sleep.

A raucous jangling penetrated like an electrical shock. It seemed to be everywhere. Trudy clutched her head to still it. It pierced again. She clambered up and groped about the room, trying to get away from it. What was that? She roused enough to realize it was the house phone, which had a ring as loud as a fire siren. Somehow she found the bedroom door, yanked it open, and stumbled into the hall.

A white robed specter was gliding down the staircase. Mom. The insistent noise stopped mid-ring. "Hello?"

Sunlight streamed in through the upper bathroom window. She'd slept through the evening and night. How could she still be groggy? Why did it feel as if she hadn't slept at all? She sat on the top step of the staircase, willing herself to come fully awake.

"Yes, Mr. Crombley, good morning...I don't understand. We've had that policy in place for years."

Trudy's head cleared like a mist at mid-day and her heart beat faster. She descended halfway down the stairs to hear the conversation better.

"Oh....Oh....Oh." With each word Emma seemed to shrink. "I'll talk with Trudy. I'll call you back...Yes. Thank you. Good-bye." The phone clicked into its cradle. Emma dropped into the little chair beside the tiny old-fashioned phone table.

"What is it, Mom?"

Emma lifted her face toward Trudy, but her eyes were scrunched shut, her face screwed up, and her hands pressed against her lips.

Trudy held her breath and waited to hear what new disaster had befallen them.

Emma opened pale blue eyes and met Trudy's stare. "Your father cashed in the insurance policy. The funeral wasn't covered after all. I owe them six thousand and fifty-four dollars."

"That's crazy. Daddy wouldn't have done that. There must be some mistake."

"No mistake. They checked it twice. He sent a letter. How am I ever going to pay that?" Emma pulled a tissue from the pocket of her robe. She spread it wide and pressed it to her lips.

That familiar elephant plunked down on Trudy's chest again preventing her from inhaling. The room grew fuzzy for a moment, then she breathed. "Phillip did this."

"What am I going to do?"

Trudy knelt in front of Emma and hugged her grief-convulsed body. "Don't worry Mom, we'll think of something. We'll take care of it."

"This is our punishment for judging you, for turning you out. I should've stood up for you. I'd done it before and when I did he listened. Instead, I let it happen."

"Don't say that. It's my fault for running away with Phillip. I'm so sorry Phillip hurt you."

"If we hadn't been so heavy-handed, you might've listened to our concerns."

"Mom, I'm sorry I didn't listen. When I first met him, he was so exciting and I was so bored with small town life in Amesville."

"Lamesville."

Trudy gasped. "You knew about that?"

Emma gave a weak smile. "We knew about most of your antics. Gladys Elling saw somebody in blue jeans and a rival high school cap climb the water tower with a can of paint. I found the cap at the bottom of our trash when the dog knocked it over."

Trudy shook her head. "I was young and dumb."

"You were never dumb. Not by any definition. I thought you were amazingly brave. It did take some talking to convince your father not to tan your hide on that account. That's why he offered to paint over it. We hoped you'd get past it and settle down. The same way I did. Yes, indeed. " Emma nodded.

Trudy stared at Emma, trying to take in the meaning, trying to imagine her mother as a wild teen. She gave up and focused on what she did know. "I wanted wealth and glamor. I didn't realize it was so ugly and rotten on the underside."

"It probably isn't all like that. Some wealthy people do incredibly good things and serve the Lord."

There was a shift in her mother's mood Trudy couldn't quite follow.

Emma lifted her head. "Is this what he put you through?"

"Yes. We lived like royalty for a couple of years until he lost everything in a poker game. Then, we had to pay by the night to stay in a motel with bugs and no hot water. I went to work to help clear up the debt and get us back on our feet. He got on a winning streak and everything was fine. Until he lost big again.

"It was up and down like that. The last time, in Las Vegas, he held a fine job. One he liked. Life was grand. I thought the worst was behind us. I don't know when he started gambling again. I didn't know anything until he left me with nothing. He signed the house over to pay the biggest part of his debt, emptied our accounts, and disappeared. I didn't even know where he was."

"He abandoned you. That's why you wanted to divorce him," she stated.

"Yes, but I also didn't like who I was becoming. I didn't divorce him though. Part of me hopes he'll get well so that we can be together again. The worst was when he turned you and Dad against me."

Emma pulled Trudy into her arms and rocked her sideways. "I'm so sorry. I know your dad was sorry, too."

Trudy gripped her mother tightly for several moments. "Well, we're together now."

"Yes. We're together now." Emma stood and moved into the kitchen. She tied on an apron. After starting coffee she sat across the table from Trudy. Her lips drew into a line. "I hate what he did to my girl. If that Phillip ever shows up here again, I'll, well, I'll put a bee in his lemonade."

Trudy snorted. "He won't get that far. I'll slam the door in his face."

Emma grinned. "And I'll drop a potted plant on his head from the upstairs window."

"I'll take scissors and cut his favorite Italian tie." They took turns shouting out vindictive plans until the personal revenge on Phillip became so ludicrous they howled with laughter.

When they grew quiet, Trudy's arms hung limp as a rag doll by her side. Across the table, Emma drooped in her chair, mirroring Trudy's posture. Trudy slid onto the floor and put her head in Emma's lap, something she hadn't done since she was five. "Oh, Momma, I love you. I'm sorry about all of this. We'll get through it. I know we will."

Emma patted Trudy's back. Her voice was hoarse. "Of course we will. The Lord will guide us. He's always there. And Trudy, remember you don't have to make Phillip pay for the wrong he's done. God will do that in time."

Trudy had her doubts, but didn't argue. "Let's sort through all of Daddy's papers. Maybe we'll find something that will help."

"Okay. First we need some coffee and something to eat."

Trudy opened the refrigerator. "Let's see. Cherry Pie. Blueberry Pie. Coffee cake."

"I think we need something more substantial for the task ahead." Emma reached for the iron skillet.

"Right, Mom. Here's a scrambled egg casserole. It's got ham and eggs with cheese."

"Flora Jean made that. It's always a hit at church breakfasts."

"Okay, egg casserole it is. And here's a bowl of fruit salad to go with it. We'll save the pie as a reward after the job is done."

The meal boosted their energy and their outlook. By lunchtime they'd gone through almost every scrap of paper in her dad's tidy desk, but nothing that indicated immediate income except for Emma's own Social Security check.

Other than the funeral, there were a few outstanding bills due, such as the electric and telephone. They wrote a check to return the amount for the month that Social Security had paid.

Trudy didn't count as income the handwritten I.O.U.s from Phillip or the additional notes of how much her dad had "invested" with Phillip, because the returns on those were a fantasy. She held up an old real estate sales contract. "What's this? It says Dad sold some prime acreage."

Emma looked over her shoulder. "Oh, that's when we bought Skipper. We had a few hard years then, but your Dad wouldn't touch our savings. We had to sell to get the purchase price for Skipper. He wanted to be sure we could afford his upkeep."

"I never knew that. Why'd Dad do it?"

"He loved you, honey, and you had your heart set on that horse."

"But it's so much."

"It was worth it. You rode that horse every day. Even in winter, we could hardly get you out of the barn. You treated him like a person." Emma put her hand to Trudy's cheek. "My, you loved that horse."

"I still do Mom, wherever he is. And I love you so much."

A knock on the door interrupted them. Emma rose to answer it. Trudy didn't recognize the voices and couldn't understand what was being said.

She was on her feet by the time her mom came back into the room with a thick, manila envelope. "Mr. Crombley said people left cards for us at the funeral home. He sent his head man over with them." They turned the large envelope upside down and let the smaller envelopes it held pile up on the table. They each opened an envelope, taking turns reading the sentiments aloud. The condolences bolstered their spirits and the gifts of cash warmed them against the cold financial reality.

"It's providence. This will cover the mortgage due at the end of the month." Emma tapped a pad of paper with her pencil. She stopped tapping and rested her hands in her apron. Pretty soon she started wadding her apron. Her face crumpled. "After that, how am I going to manage? I'll never be able to pay Mr. Crombley for the funeral.

"I know it's hard to have to deal with all of this on top of Dad's passing, and everyone says not to make any decisions for the first year, but you can't afford to wait a month or two."

"What do you suggest?"

"You do understand I have to go back to work in a few days. Why don't you come live with me?"

"That's a nice offer, but Amesville is my home. What about my friends? My church? The farm?"

"You and Daddy haven't worked the full farm for a few years. You could sell it."

"Sell it? Your Dad would never agree to—oh." Tears welled in Emma's eyes. She bowed her home-permed head, stood up and walked out of the kitchen.

Trudy heard the stairs creak and the door to the bedroom click shut. She massaged the taut muscles in her neck. Why did everything have to be so difficult?

That afternoon while Trudy was washing dishes, she startled at a touch on her shoulder. "Mom, I didn't hear you come in."

Emma's face was filled with resignation, but her voice was resolute. "Evan Biers has wanted to buy the farm for years. I'll give him a call. He's wanted this house for himself so he can move out of the old farmstead they've been sharing with his parents. His wife is expecting again, you know. I'm sure he'll snap it up. That will solve a big problem."

"Then you'll come live with me?"

"I love you, honey, but I don't want to move. My life is here. I don't want to start over."

"Okay. We'll find you an apartment in town. "

"Actually, my friend Sarah is having health problems since her husband passed. I can stay with her. We can help each other."

Trudy patted her mother's hand. "That's a big decision, Mom. I'm glad you have a plan."

"Your father's gone. I have to make decisions now. And I don't want to be a burden to you, Trudy."

"You're not a burden."

"There may be a time in the future I'll have to depend on you, but not now."

"You're brave. It's a side of you I've never seen before."

"I've had to work hard at being a submissive wife. It didn't come naturally to me. I was more like you than you know."

Trudy wondered if she'd ever known her mother at all. She set that thought aside to think on later. While she used her cell phone to learn the going rate for farms, her mom used the house phone to call Evan Biers.

Evan Biers agreed to come that night. He was a broad shouldered, big boned man of Swedish descent with hair so blond it was almost white. Six or seven years older than Trudy, she remembered seeing him play high school football, but had never known him personally.

Evan had a gentle, quiet attitude about him as the three of them sat around the table in the kitchen, drinking coffee and discussing the sale of the property. He agreed with hardly a quibble over the asking price. It was enough to pay off the mortgage and to partially clear the debt to the funeral home. At the end of the discussion, he rose and shook hands with Emma and Trudy.

After he left, Emma folded her hands on the table. "This is really going to happen."

"I'm afraid so."

Emma waved her hand in a vague manner. "What am I going to do? It's a life-time of building a home. I can't take it all to Sarah's."

"We'll rent a storage unit over in the city."

Emma stared straight ahead. In a few minutes she said, "That's silly. I'll never move into a bigger house, I'll only need smaller spaces. We'll let Evan's wife have first pick. Then, we'll have a big sale. Whatever is left we'll take to Salvation Army and Goodwill and drop supplies to the church for the indigent."

Trudy stared at her Mom. Who knew that under that mousy, honor-thy-husband exterior was a woman with such a strong will of her own?

"Whatever you want to do, Mom."

The cell phone played that Elvis song. Trudy checked the number and for a moment considered not answering. "Hi, Peter."

"What'd you think of the book?"

"Give me a break. I buried my father yesterday. It's pandemonium here. Unexpectedly, the funeral is going to be out of pocket and we have to sell the farm which means my mom has to move."

Emma's chair scraped the floor as she rose. "Trudy. Don't flaunt our business in public."

Trudy moved the phone away from her mouth. "Peter's my boss. He needs to know why I'm staying. He's very discreet, Mom, or he wouldn't stay in business."

Emma continued to frown. Trudy moved away from her mother. "Anyway, Peter, I'm going to need a few more days here. Maybe a week more."

"That can't all happen in a week."

"Sure it will. This is Amesville, Iowa. A burg. We have a buyer. He banks at the same bank. We both know the banker personally. The time-consuming problem is we still have to empty the house and move my mom."

"I need to know about that book. What's your impression so far?"

Trudy couldn't even remember where she'd laid the ARC. Probably still in her suitcase or maybe by the chair in the living room or on the bedside table. She hadn't seen it since the day she arrived. "I'd prefer to finish it before I give you my report. I'll call you tomorrow."

"Make it in the morning. I meet with her for lunch. She already had a local church group ask her to come talk with them in anticipation of the book's release. A friend of hers arranged it. I need to know if I'm getting on board with this."

"Sure. Not a problem. In the morning then." Trudy looked heavenward as she disconnected the call. "Mom, I have some work to do. I have to read a book by an author Peter's thinking of representing. He needs the information by morning. I better go find it and start reading."

"Is that the one you brought titled, *Life after Death - Beginning Again After the Loss of a Loved One?*"

"Yes."

"I read most of it. It was very helpful. Very comforting. It gave me real strength."

"Really?"

"Oh, yes. It's beside my rocker in the bedroom. I couldn't sleep with your Dad gone. The bed seems so empty. Let me know when you've read it. I'd like to finish it."

"Okay, then." Trudy went up the stairs into her parents' bedroom. She found it where her mother had said. She picked it up and read the blurb on the back cover. What was in it that encouraged her mom?

Trudy carried the book back to her childhood bedroom and lay down to read. She read through most of the day. Her mom poked her head in after the ten o'clock news to say goodnight. Trudy said, "This woman really went through some hard times."

"Yes, she did. God was so faithful to her and brought her through all of those trials. I'm sure I'd have turned up my toes and died."

"I'd never have thought it. When I met her, she was so lively and bubbly."

"You met Carol Streeter?" Emma came into the room and sat on the bed.

"Yes. I had coffee with her the morning I left. My boss wanted me to give him a heads-up on the project. She seemed to have a good head for business. She's already lined up some churches to speak at."

"What's she like?"

"She's easy to talk to. The kind of person that after a few moments, you feel as if you've known her forever and are best friends."

"That's how the book reads, too. I hope she will be your best friend. You always seemed to have trouble having girl friends in school."

"I didn't think you even noticed. All the girls from church were so strait-laced, no fun at all. They were afraid to do anything. The girls in 4-H were somewhat better, riding horses, taking care of animals. That's why I hung out mostly with boys. They did fun things."

"Is that why you'd sneak off with that heathen bunch?"

"Yes, but they weren't bad. They weren't druggies. A little drinking, maybe. Mostly posturing, flaunting authority. I wanted to do something besides sit, sit, sit."

"With all the farm work you had to help your dad with, I'd have thought you'd be happy to sit."

"I wanted to do something fun and daring. Swimming in the river at night. Racing trucks or motorcycles. Climbing the water tower."

"You were like that even when you were little. You never saw anything as impossible, always swinging the highest, walking the fence rail, climbing trees or the silo. My heart nearly stopped when I caught you swinging on the loft pulley. You said you were trying to swing on top of the barn roof."

Trudy laughed. "I don't remember that. I must've been a real handful."

Emma smiled. "You kept us busy, that's for sure. Always doing something."

"That's why I liked riding. It was the only time I felt free."

"We thought we were doing what was best." Emma cupped her hand to Trudy's cheek. "You are so beautiful. We were too strict about letting you go out. Your father was afraid you'd sneak out and get involved with boys."

"Which is exactly what I did with Phillip."

"I'm sorry you were so unhappy."

"It wasn't your fault. I don't know why I wasn't content. I had a great life growing up. I didn't appreciate it, though. I wanted glamour and glitz, long dresses and high heels, not calico and work boots. Except for riding, Dad wouldn't even let me wear jeans, for Pete's sake."

"Our church teaches a lady doesn't wear pants."

"I know, Mom, I know. I'm sorry I was such a disappointment to you and Dad."

Emma bent her white head. After a moment she said, "I never understood what was wrong with jeans, as long as they aren't skin tight. They're easier to work in. When we were building the barn, I nearly fell from the second story when my dress got caught. Like to scared me to death. That'd never have happened if I was in jeans. I convinced your father to let you wear jeans for riding."

"I never knew that. I always thought you believed exactly what the church taught."

Emma stood. "While we're clearing up misconceptions. Follow me." Trudy trailed her mother back to the kitchen. Emma opened a drawer and handed Trudy a stack of letters bound by a ribbon. "Here."

Trudy said, "What's this?"

# Chapter Seventeen

"These are the letters we sent you whenever you let us know where you were. You did move around a lot. You were so angry with us that you sent them back. I thought maybe you'd like to read them now."

Puzzled, Trudy shook her head. "No. I mailed two or three letters to you, but I never got a reply. I gave up."

Emma gestured toward the letters.

Trudy sorted through them. "Return to Sender" had been written across each unopened envelope. An angry scream tore at Trudy's throat, but her vocal cords didn't cooperate, the scream stuck in her throat with no breath to push it out. Her mouth worked silently.

A great sadness pulled at Emma's face. "Oh. I understand now. This was Phillip's doing, not yours. Read them. Maybe they'll help you heal some of the hurts your dad and I caused."

Trudy nodded. She held the letters as if they were priceless. She choked out, "I can't just now. I'll read them when I'm feeling a little stronger, back in Indiana."

Her mother didn't answer. When she looked up Emma had turned away, her fists pressed against her lips. Trudy placed a hand on her Mom's heaving shoulder.

"I miss your Dad. I wish he were here to see this."

"So do I, Mom, so do I."

"It's going to be hard to go to church without him. Everyone will be so kind. They'll say I'm strong and that I should call if they can help, but there's nothing any of them can do to bring him back or change what I'm going through." She drew a few deep breaths and the tears that threatened were once again under control. Emma's lips went into a single flat line. A moment later, in a muffled, cracked voice she said, "You tell that author lady that I'll be praying for her speaking engagements."

"I will, Mom."

Back in Indiana, the thought of the years of unnecessary absence from her parents was too much for Trudy to bear. She moved the letters into the bottom of a suitcase and focused on work.

On the merits of her detailed report, Peter signed the author. After that, Carol Streeter was in and out of the office frequently. Prompted by her boss to assist Carol with presentations, Trudy invited Carol to lunch. This also provided a good excuse to take Emma's advice and see for herself if Carol was a good person to befriend or if all that sunshine and sweetness was hype.

At a trendy little diner, over pulled pork sandwiches and a cup of tomato basil soup, Trudy said, "My mother said your book is amazingly helpful. She said she'd be praying for you and the women at your conferences."

"That's so sweet of her. Tell her thanks. I covet her prayers."

Trudy shifted in her seat. She smoothed her hands over her tan suede pantsuit. She pumped her straw up and down a couple of times in her iced tea, thinking of all the church people she knew who would say something like that. It sounded good, then they'd gossip, stretch the truth, and judge others for every little thing that was different.

"That's the kind of thing people in the congregation I grew up in said all the time."

Carol finished chewing her mouthful and swallowed. "Oh, you're saying when I say 'covet' I'm using Christianese. Good point. When I address an audience many might not be churched people. How about if instead I say, 'Your prayers are an encouragement to me.' Is that better?"

Trudy nodded. "More specific. Easily understood by anyone."

"Okay, I'll try to listen for other phrases I say that might be like that."

The woman was eager to learn and do well, but this wasn't the point. Trudy blurted, "What I really meant was, did you really go through all that?"

Carol blinked in surprise. "I see. You're wondering if I embellished for the sake of the book."

"To be blunt, yes." Trudy lifted her chin a tiny bit, a throwback to the childhood defiance she'd often felt.

"No, I didn't embellish. Every bit is true. I lost my parents, three of my five children, and my husband. I have the obituaries and the death certificates to prove it." Carol swallowed her final bite.

A heaviness invaded the atmosphere. Trudy knew she should apologize. She didn't. It was important to know this for Peter's promotion, as well as her own curiosity. She picked up the check. "I've enjoyed lunch. Thanks for meeting me."

"Thanks for inviting me. It doesn't always have to be business. Next time, we'll go double-dutch, like friends do. How about next Thursday?"

"Speaking of business, Peter would like me to discuss your attire."

"What's wrong with the way I dress?"

"As a speaker, you need to emphasize friendliness and approachability. This you ooze, by the way. He also wants people to see you as a professional. He wants me to help maximize your professional look. Together, we'll work with your wardrobe and I'll give you hints on which outfits present well, how to accessorize, and how to mix and match so you won't have to pack so many clothes when you travel."

"I don't want to look like those models in my daughter's fashion magazines with pouty faces or haughty attitudes."

Trudy laughed. "No. That wouldn't suit you at all. On the other hand, you don't want to look like a soccer mom or a tired grandma."

"Definitely not a tired grandma. I'm too young for that." Carol's attitude turned upbeat again.

Despite the disclaimer, Trudy was sure, when the time came, Carol would think she was the perfect age to be a grandparent. She exuded the *joi de vivre* of someone who embraced life, wherever she was in life. Where exactly did that confidence come from? Could it really be from the God she so openly gave credit to in the book?

"We'll touch up your make-up, too."

Carol groaned. "My daughter's going to love this."

Carol showed up for Thursday lunch with a beautiful, perky girl in tow. Unlike Carol who dressed nicely, but was more concerned with comfort than style, Kim had a flair for fashion. Her long dark tresses shone and the word lustrous popped into Trudy's mind.

"Trudy, this is my daughter Kim."

Trudy greeted her. "Aren't you still in high school? Are you skipping school?"

"We have a day off for teacher conferences. If I were skipping, I don't think I'd be doing it with my mom, as much as I love her." Kim threw a sweet smile at her mom.

Trudy laughed. "Truth."

"Mom's been telling me how beautifully you dress, but wow. That fawn colored blazer is gorgeous. I love your nails."

"Thanks. I did them myself."

"Really? I thought you'd been to a professional."

"I'm not quite in that financial position, yet."

"Would you do mine sometime?"

"Um, Sure. I'll do both yours and your mom's."

"Come over tonight. We'll feed you Chinese take-out and chocolate éclairs. I'm warning you, you'll have to guard the éclairs. Our beagle, Minnie, loves éclairs. She'll slip them right off your plate, if you don't watch her."

Trudy laughed, but that night Minnie proved her reputation as an elite éclair thief. The three chased the beagle around the kitchen table and down the hall, but the dog gulped her prize before they caught her.

"That's bad," Carol scolded the dog. Minnie licked her chops and gloated as if to say evidence to the contrary. Carol released the dog's collar and straightened. "I'm sorry Trudy. You can have mine."

"No way," Trudy responded. She patted her flat tummy. "I'm having a hard time staying trim with all this dining out I'm doing. I don't have a kitchen in my apartment."

After the remnants of supper had been cleared away, they clustered at the kitchen table working on their nails and leafing through style magazines. Kim said, "I'm sorry. It's not the latest issue, but Mom and I are saving money for my college. We borrowed these from the library."

"I think that is admirable."

Kim huffed a bit, but seemed mollified.

"If you want something, you have to make sacrifices," Carol said.

"True enough," Trudy said.

"I bet you don't have to do that," Kim said. "Your handbag is a real Chanel."

"I bought that before I came here. I lived a different lifestyle back then." For a moment, Trudy considered revealing her past, but resisted the urge. "And before that time in my life, I was raised on a farm where everything was down-home. Since coming here, I've learned to shop bargains and second hand stores again, and to mix a few stylish accents with my more classic items of clothing. I buy things that fit easily with one another by layering or varying the accessories. I need less that way."

"Huh," Kim said as if this was a revolutionary thought. "Do you find name brand clothing in second hand shops?"

"Sometimes. Less than you'd like, but probably more often than you'd expect."

"Could I go shopping with you?"

Trudy studied the girl's face for signs of teasing. There was only eagerness. "Sure."

The conversation drifted from topic to topic, setting an easy mood, until it was time for Trudy to leave. On the way home she realized she was relaxed.

Thoughts about her father, her mother's financial problems, and Phillip had moved into the background most of the evening. She could've talked about her situation if she wanted to, but anonymity felt good. For a while she'd been a normal person, not one that was broken by her love of a faithless gambler who'd left her and her parents in ruin.

After that, she fell easily into spending time with the Streeters. Some nights they watched movies like "Ghost" and "Pretty Woman" which led to discussions of what made a man attractive, a particularly favorite topic of Kim as she dated a wide range of boys from high school.

Where once she would've listed wealth and adventure, Trudy now held the opinion that faithfulness, honesty, kindness, and being a hard worker were essential. While she expressed these thoughts, she steered the conversation into the hypothetical, in case she let something personal slip.

As Peter had predicted, even with a ready buyer, everything was taking longer than a week to process. Months longer. Her new reality became driving to Iowa every weekend to help Emma dismantle the accumulation of a lifetime.

Estimation of her mother grew as Emma tackled each day with a stoicism and strength that contradicted Trudy's long held belief that her mother was weak and ineffectual. Many times she expected Emma to break down and cry, but she never did. The lack of tears baffled Trudy until she was dressing one Monday morning at 3:00 a.m. for the long drive back to Indianapolis. Soft, weeping issued from behind her mother's bedroom door.

Trudy refrained from disturbing her privacy and opted to leave a note on the kitchen table promising to call later that day. The drive gave her plenty of time to contemplate the complexities of grief. She found it rather like trying to unroll a tangled ball of yarn. Her mind went round and round with the regret, pain, loss, anger, and weariness of it all.

She thought of the letters of reconciliation her parents had sent, which still laid stored and unread. They were evidence of the lost years because her parents thought she had rejected them, and she had thought the same, all because of the faithlessness and narcissism of Phillip.

How her father must have hurt thinking she'd turned her back on him. How he must have felt betrayed when he thought his sacrifices and that special gift of Skipper had been rejected. She longed to re-do her life. To have a second chance at all those faded dreams.

One Friday night, Trudy attended Kim's high school choir concert with Carol. Leaving the event after nine, she drove to visit her mother. Somewhere in Illinois the blaring of a car horn roused her. The front end of a semi loomed ahead. She jerked the wheel and the Pinto veered into its proper lane. Heart pounding and fully awake, Trudy pulled off at the first exit. In a convenience store/gas station parking lot, she walked around the building a couple of times until the shaking stopped.

Between work, karate, Al-Anon, and her time with the Streeters, her weekday schedule was taxing enough, but the long trips every weekend were brutal. Still, the end of the selling, packing, moving, and cleaning was in sight. The big sale was scheduled for the following weekend. If she could only last a few more weeks, she could take a rest.

Until then, Trudy knew she had to be more careful. She couldn't explain how the collision had been avoided, but was very grateful it had.

Shored up by a large Styrofoam cup of coffee, Trudy headed back to her car. She noticed a young couple standing at the back of their vehicle. A couple of kids in booster seats snoozed in the back seat. The couple argued as he filled the tank. They didn't seem angry, only distraught.

The woman said, "They have to eat."

"I know, but they'll have to wait. If I don't fill the tank we won't make it to your mom's and then none of us will eat," he replied.

With a defeated attitude, the woman sank onto the bumper and lifted her head to the sky.

Trudy set her cup of coffee in the car and returned to the convenience store. She carried a box of cereal, a jar of peanut butter, and one of jam, a loaf of bread, milk, a 2-liter of pop, and a hot pizza to the check out. She added several cups, plastic spoons, and numerous napkins to the bag. She paid and said, "When that young couple comes in to pay for their gas, give them the food. Also, tell them to pay it forward someday."

She waited and watched through her rearview mirror long enough to be sure they got her gift. Smiling at their joy, Trudy pulled onto the highway again, fully revived and her mood improved.

She turned on the radio. Once again it refused to work. Trudy gave the dashboard a thump to no avail. She pressed buttons and thumped it a final time. Conceding defeat, Trudy pulled out a tape of the book of Matthew from the audio Bible Kathy lent her for the drives.

The words of the Bible did the trick to keep her weariness from turning to brooding over the regrettable consequences of her own poor choices and of Phillip's betrayal. At least nothing she heard reminded her of Phillip the way emotional country songs sometimes did.

The week after the big sale, Trudy cleared out all signs of their life in the farmhouse and hauled them away in a borrowed truck. Meanwhile Emma and Sarah scrubbed and dusted and sanitized every inch of the place because Emma declared, "We can't have the Biers moving into a dirty house, now can we? Always leave a place better than you found it."

That weekend, Emma settled in with Sarah, a pudgy, grey-haired woman with a pug nose and a ready smile. The two friends enjoyed each other's company so much that any remaining reservations Trudy had dissolved. Sarah also assured Trudy that an extra bedroom was hers to use, whenever she visited.

The day they agreed Evan would assume ownership of the farm, Trudy performed a final walk-through. Childhood memories echoed throughout the empty rooms, like an old family video flickering to life: hiding in the stairwell closet during hide and seek at her sixth birthday party, fixing supper in the kitchen with her mother while a pie sat cooling near the open window, helping her father set up the Christmas tree in the living room.

At the top of the stairs, Trudy turned away from the room that had been her parents and entered her old bedroom. More memories crowded her, including the time Skipper was sick and she'd slept in the barn with him even though she was told to go to bed. Early in the morning Trudy had sneaked in through the window before her mother came to wake her. Emma had closed the window and with an odd smile on her face told Trudy to wake up.

Now Trudy knew that her mother had pretended not to notice fresh mud tracked the floor and that under the covers her daughter still wore clothes and smelled strongly of horse.

Trudy ran her hand over the bed that the Biers were going to keep. It had been a good home to grow up in. She wished things could have been different in her teen years, but the past is in the past and today is all anybody has. If Kathy, Carol, and her mother were right, then God would use this pain for good.

Her teen years, so filled with restlessness and a sense of not measuring up, were tempered by a better understanding that fear and over protectiveness, motivated by love, instead of judgment, had driven her father to harshness. Trudy chose to let it all go.

"Hello?" The words echoed up the stairwell.

"Hi, Evan. I'll be right down," Trudy said. "I was giving the place a final check to make sure everything was in order."

The big, burly man said, "And saying good-bye?"

Trudy flashed him a weak smile. "I'd hardly thought I'd be so nostalgic."

"It was your home."

"Well, not anymore. Now it's ready for someone else to make a home." She handed Evan the keys. "I hope your family will be happy here."

They talked a few more moments, then Trudy walked out to the Pinto. She stood a moment looking at the barn and corral, so obviously empty of Skipper, and murmured, "Okay, then."

As she drove home toward Indianapolis, the heavy weight of unfinished tasks lifted. She offered a spontaneous and heartfelt, "Thank you, Lord Jesus." However, the release from it all finally broke her. She powered through the work week, but the following Friday night Trudy's exhaustion edged on illness. She placed a call to Iowa. "Mom, I won't make it this weekend."

"That's okay. In fact, it's good. You need a rest after all your work. Sarah was saying how washed out you were looking. I'll see you next weekend."

"Mom, I won't be back until next month."

There was no response.

"Mom? Are you there?"

"But you will be back?"

The uncharacteristic querulous note in Emma's voice tugged at her heart. "Yes, Mom. I'll be back. It won't be like before. I won't disappear on you. I promise."

Even after promising to phone often, the call left her smothered in guilt and more exhausted than ever. Trudy holed up in the WC and slept while videos or TV ran. It was soothing to have the background sound of human voices, especially ones who required nothing of her, not even her attention.

By 9:00 a.m. Sunday morning further sleep became impossible. Trudy's overworked mind still wanted the world to go away, yet her body wanted to get up and get going. As she sat on the edge of the couch and sucked down the cold remnants of a cup of day-old coffee, Trudy considered running or working out. On TV, Joyce Meyers preached God was faithful to a filled auditorium.

Had God been faithful in the midst of her circumstances? Well, he hadn't struck her dead. Did that mean he was giving her a second chance? She hadn't had a head-on crash when it seemed unavoidable. Was that God's faithfulness at work? Could he be with her?

If so, maybe life would be a little easier if she weren't fighting God at every turn. It made sense, but what would he ask her to do, go back to Phillip? No, a life of deceit was a despicable lifestyle. It wasn't healthy. It wasn't godly. All the signs of God's faithfulness had happened after she quit lying to cover for Phillip, after she quit skirting the edges of his cons.

Would God point out his own faithfulness if he didn't mean it? That would be the biggest scam of all and if she knew one thing, it was that God didn't lie.

Maybe God pitied her because she was alone. There was that verse about God being a husband to widows. She felt as lonely as a widow. What if she wasn't alone? Would God love her any less if she divorced and remarried?

Her father's church taught divorce was a sin except in cases of adultery. Even though she suspected Phillip hadn't always been faithful, she had. If God was now blessing her, she didn't want to do anything to mess that up, even if it meant she'd always be alone and never have a family of her own.

Anyway, she couldn't divorce Phillip. What if he ever did kick the gambling habit and came back to her? Surely that would please God.

Many minutes slipped by with Trudy daydreaming of Phillip's return. He'd ask forgiveness and really mean it. He'd prove he wouldn't leave her in the lurch. He would hold a job. He'd pay back all that he had taken. They'd have a nice little house, nothing fancy, an average middle class home on the edge of the city with plenty of land for a horse or two. They'd have a dog. Maybe kids.

An image of a wide field filled with golden sunshine and hemmed in by mountains surged to the forefront as vivid as a picture on TV. Horses grazed and a couple of laughing children burst onto the scene, followed by a frisky dog.

Trudy bolted off the couch. What a fantasy. Even if Phillip ever did quit gambling, he'd never wanted kids. He never liked dogs or horses, except when they were running at the tracks. He absolutely hated ordinary houses. He insisted on huge impressive mansions in fancy neighborhoods with people he could schmooze and wheel and deal.

They were so different. Had she ever loved him, or had she jumped at the first chance to leave the small town she thought of as Lamesville? Perhaps she didn't miss Phillip as much as the idea of him being rich and adventurous.

This was a depressing thought. She ached deep inside and tried to sort out if the ache was for Phillip or for the wealth she'd tasted.

Was it for the loss of her innocence? Her joy? Her dreams? Her faith?

Her stomach growled. Maybe it was simply hunger. The morning had slipped away. No use going to church, it was nearly over. Trudy stretched her arms overhead. Ugh. She could definitely use a bath.

She hauled herself off to the bathroom and soaked in the hottest water she could stand. She slathered lotion all over her still-damp body. While it dried, she picked up the litter of almost two days spent on the couch ordering take-out and eating crackers between naps. She needed a real meal.

It was impossible to tell from the WC, whether it was raining or sunny, but it didn't matter. In April, the weather was often still cold. She dressed in a brown cashmere sweater, jeans, and high heels and slipped into her coat. Trudy claimed her purse and car keys, eager to be on her way. Flinging the front door open, she faced an upraised fist.

Trudy yelped and ducked.

# Chapter Eighteen

A feminine voice said, "Good grief."

Trudy opened her eyes. Carol's hand dropped to her side.

Trudy pressed her hand to her heart and straightened. "You scared me."

"I'm sorry. Maybe I should've called. Peter gave me your address. I hope that was okay." Uncertainty clouded Carol's features.

Trudy pulled the door shut behind her to hide how tiny and awful the WC was. "I was heading out to eat. Want to come?"

"Sure. I'm always up for a good meal. Where to?"

"Nowhere fancy. How about Cowboys Chuck Wagon? I'm having a juicy steak and a big baked potato, and they have a tremendous salad bar."

Carol's face brightened. "I like the way you plan to eat. I can drive. My car is already warm."

Trudy followed the diminutive woman to her car. She pushed aside thoughts that Carol probably was embarrassed to ride in the decrepit Pinto. She'd have to get a better vehicle as soon as she possibly could.

At Cowboys Chuck Wagon with the steak half finished, Trudy said, "Do you think God is more faithful to those who are faithful to him?"

"Interesting question. Yes and no. God is God. He is faithful all the time. He can't change that. It's who he is. I do think God is able to show his faithfulness more to those who are obedient."

"Why?"

"His blessings aren't interrupted by having to give correction. Obedient people are more open to his will. Therefore, they experience a lot less angst than those who are bucking his plan all the time, trying to do it their own way. Even in adversity, they have more peace because they know ultimately God's got them in his hands. They know he's faithful. They accept it."

Trudy thought about that as she poked a fork in her baked potato. "Like training a horse. You can do more when the horse is trusting you than when it's wild. It's a two-way street. A working partnership."

Carol nodded. "Doesn't mean he loves the unfaithful any less."

"Like you can love a wild horse, but there's no bond, no partnership."

"Exactly. I wish more people would partner with God. This world would be a better place. Yet, most people go off on their own, hurting themselves and others. They'll have to pay for it."

"I've certainly had to pay for—"

When Trudy didn't finish, Carol set her drink down. "For what?"

"For being wild. Giving my parents grief when I was a teen. Disobeying them. Sneaking around. Getting into trouble. Leaving them."

"Did you get pregnant?"

Trudy wiped her fingers in her napkin. "No. That's one thing I didn't do. Although I'm sure they feared that I was."

"What'd you do that was so bad?"

"There was a guy."

"At that age, there's always a guy," Carol said out of the corner of her mouth. Her blue eyes twinkled.

Trudy snorted. "Yeah. I guess so."

"And they're always incredibly handsome and so much smarter than parents."

"You got that right." Trudy sipped her iced tea. "I hated small town life. I couldn't wait to get away. Or, maybe the small town only seemed stifling because everyone seemed to think alike. My father was strict. What he said was law, and my mother did whatever he said. The more rebellious I got, the more he clamped down on me. They were God-fearing but rigidly religious. To me, it all seemed so joyless and mundane. I missed the whole point.

"I wanted adventure. It really hurt my parents when I left. Every time I called them we had the same arguments, so I stopped calling. For years."

"Peter said you go visit your mother almost every weekend, and I know you went home when your father died. You must be reconciled. Right?"

"Yes, but it was my fault my dad died from a heart attack."

"I thought he had heart disease. That's not your fault."

"It kind of is. The stress is what did him in. It was his second one and I didn't even know he'd had a first one. Things happened that would never have happened, if I'd been a better daughter, if I hadn't left.

"What things?"

"Financial ruin."

Carol leaned back in her chair. "Yes, that's stressful all right."

Trudy exhaled making a sharp little *pshaw* sound. "What can you know about financial ruin? You live in a nice, comfortable house. You and your daughter dress well enough. You eat out and don't have to think twice about it."

Carol twirled her straw in her lemonade. The ice made a clinking sound as it swirled against the glass. "Sure, we're doing better now. I don't have to fast suppers anymore so that my daughter will have enough to eat. The bills are paid. I can even eat out a couple times a month if I'm careful. The IRS is still breathing heavily down my neck for business taxes, but I'm on a payment plan. Sure, some things are better. Thanks to God's faithfulness through this book deal, we're coming out the other side, bit by bit.

"However, Kim had to give up a special summer program in Boston she'd earned and a senior trip to Paris with her friends. She nearly had to give up plans of attending college, but we're working it out. She's learning to be frugal. She's stepped up. Between the receptionist job and the dog-walking gig, she's saving money. It hasn't been easy."

Trudy stared at Carol. "I had no idea. I thought your husband left you well off."

"Andy had a policy that paid off the house at his death, but his business partner embezzled, defaulted on bills, and left the country. I was left holding the bag on the tax debt. We weren't incorporated, so it all comes back on me. I'm responsible."

They ate in silence for a while, picking at their salads and baked potatoes. Trudy picked up her knife and sawed viciously through her steak. "Men. Cheats and liars. It's better to be single forever than deal with men."

"Trudy, not all men are cheats and liars. It wasn't A.J.'s fault I'm in this mess. He was always good about paying bills. It was his partner."

"Exactly. A man. An unscrupulous man. Andy sounds like my dad. My dad got taken in by a lying, cheating man. That man would never have even met my father if it weren't for me. So I'm to blame. How can I live with knowing it's what killed my dad?"

Trudy chewed her steak vigorously and swallowed. Knife in her right hand and fork in her left, the butts of the silverware clicked on the table as she leaned forward. "What do we need men for, anyway? They preen and strut around like roosters crowing to the whole world that they are better than the rest of the flock."

Carol gave a half-smile. "Um, I can think of a few things."

Trudy snorted. "Sure, but they're argumentative and proud and self-absorbed and know-it-alls. Even when they're wrong, they always think they're right."

Carol held Trudy's fixed look. "I haven't known you really long, but Trudy, you always think you're right."

Trudy set back and glowered at her dinner companion for a long moment. Carol opened her eyes wide and stared right back. Trudy was the first to look away.

As Carol took a long drink of lemonade through her straw, Trudy said, "Well, that's different. I am always right." Carol choked and shoved a napkin up to her face. She laughed.

The knife and fork clattered against the plate as Trudy put her hands to her mouth and tried to smooth her own laugh into a stern line. She only succeeded in laughing harder. She gasped. "No hypocrisy here."

People at a nearby table turned to eye them. Trudy waved at them. Carol took a deep breath and wiped her mouth a last time. She grinned at Trudy. Trudy grinned back. It was a silly thing, but in that moment an unspoken contract was drawn up and sealed. A pact of friendship bound them.

Trudy's second weekend without a road trip left her feeling at odds with unscheduled leisure time. The CMA wasn't meeting. Her work was caught up. She'd regained her energy. She had no desire to sit alone in her apartment where thoughts of Phillip were always waiting to waylay her. Saturday morning she drove by the Streeter house.

Carol and Kim were heading to their car when she pulled into the drive and parked behind them. Kim carried a gym bag. Beneath the open flap of her school jacket, she wore leotards, tights and tennis shoes. Carol dressed in a sporty, green pea-jacket, jeans, and scuffed and worn tennis shoes.

Trudy rolled down her window and stuck her head out. "Hi."

"Sorry we can't visit," Carol called. She opened the driver's side door of her car. "We're heading out to Kim's balance beam competition."

"Say, I'd like to go see that. Do you mind if I tag along?"

"Really?" Carol sounded surprised.

"Really?" Kim echoed. "That's so cool. I can't wait to show you this routine. I do this back flip. It's hard, but I do it really well."

"I can't wait to see it."

Carol called. "Great. Park in the street and come on. Kim get in the backseat."

They made one stop on the way. They pulled up to a huge stone house with turrets and bay windows and an enormous round porch with wide steps. Trudy gaped at it in wonder. She opened her mouth to say, "This would be Phillip's absolute dream home." She snapped her mouth shut.

Carol honked the horn. Moments later a young girl dressed like Kim skipped down the steps. She slipped into the backseat, "Hello everyone."

Kim said, "Ruby this is Trudy."

"Ms. Bellafonte," Carol corrected in the motherly tone Trudy had heard all mothers use.

"Trudy," Trudy said, smiling at the carrot-colored redhead.

Ruby's smile wrinkled her freckled nose. In fact, she had a surprising amount of freckles crowding her face and spilling down her neck.

Kim said, "Trudy's my mom's friend. She's cool. She's coming to watch us perform."

Trudy screwed her face up with pleasure and moved her shoulders back and forth. She nodded at Carol and gave a thumbs-up toward herself. Carol grinned back at her.

The competition was noisy and fun. Kim scored a nine on her back flip dismount and the team ranked well. The girls were jubilant on the ride home. They chattered as they relived every successful moment and rendered opinions on the other competitors. It all felt familiar, like the rides home from Trudy's horse competitions.

She arrived at the door of the WC aglow with a sense of satisfaction. As she unlocked the door thoughts of Phillip crowded out the good feelings of the day. She often expected to find him on her doorstep. Even though he'd only lived in the WC a matter of weeks, memories of him plagued her. She missed his playfulness and laughter.

Phillip was always eager to race motorcycles on the winding roads in the mountains of Nevada or motorboats in the Pacific. They'd explored coral reefs and swam with dolphins in the Florida Keys. Once he'd grabbed the mike and joined a jazz band onstage in New Orleans at Mardi Gras to sing to her. He'd even taken her paragliding, in tandem, off The Point of the Mountain in Utah. Phillip made her think she could truly fly.

Her disappointment each time he failed to appear was confused by an equal amount of relief for he brought heartache each time he showed up. With each appearance, they could only fly for a brief moment, then like mythical Icarus, who flew too close to the sun, they'd crash and burn. The crash was inevitable, if they continued as they were. She understood that, but the disappointment wasn't a mystery, either. She still hoped he'd change.

If she ever accepted her marriage wasn't going to work out, would she stop missing him? At times, the sense of him was so strong Trudy swore she caught a whiff of his aftershave. It drove her crazy. Perhaps this was God's way of keeping his presence alive to her, telling her to give him another chance.

Trudy held her breath and pushed the apartment door open and switched on the light. The room was empty. Phillip wasn't there. She was alone.

A few weeks later, the CMA gathered after church for lunch and a ride south to Spring Mill Park. As she often did these days, Kathy rode with Mike. Those two seemed to be becoming an item. It was a kick watching the romance blossom. Mike was such a nice guy that it was hard not to root for him to win a great girl like Kathy.

Sometimes Trudy drove Kathy's bike. This time she'd lent it to a new couple trying to decide if they wanted to join the group. So, Trudy rode behind Spider whose wife, Denise, had a baby shower to attend.

Once they were at Spring Mill Park, the women formed one loose group and the men another. The two groups merged and separated, depending on the conversations. The constant chatter as they explored trails and the waterfall made it easier to push aside thoughts about Phillip, money and the long hours she'd been working for a boss who expected perfection. That last didn't bother her so much because her own expectations usually were even higher than his.

They found a picnic table and ate the bag lunches they brought. Mike read some verses from the Bible and the group discussed them. This led to testimonies of what God was doing.

Hearing about how God worked in the lives of people she personally knew caused hope to flutter like a butterfly emerging from a cocoon. Perhaps God was doing something for her, too. Maybe even making Phillip quit gambling. Making him responsible. Restoring her marriage.

The sun sank low in the west and the group headed back to the aptly nicknamed Circle City. When they reached Indianapolis, the riders split up to go to their respective homes. Spider dropped Trudy back at the church to pick up the Pinto.

"Thanks, Spider. Tell Denise I said hi. It was a good day, like a vacation for my brain."

"Yeah, it was a hoot." Being the tattooed, pierced, black leather and boots gentleman he was, Spider waited until Trudy was in the car and had it started. She waved. He gave her a salute and rumbled off.

She shifted into drive, nothing happened. Reverse. No movement. The vacation was over. Trudy pounded the wheel and used some very unladylike language. She rested her head on the steering wheel and groaned. The roar of a bike, kept her from giving in to tears of frustration. Spider pulled along the driver's window. "What's wrong?"

"I think the transmission is shot. It won't budge." She shoved it from gear to gear to prove her point.

"That's bad."

"You don't know the half of it." Trudy closed her eyes and concentrated on maintaining composure.

Spider took a walk around the rusted, dented vehicle. He ran his hand over his head. "Well, I don't want to discourage you, but if it were mine, I wouldn't put any more money into repairing it. It's worth more as scrap metal and spare parts."

Trudy couldn't help being discouraged. "How much are tow trucks charging these days?"

Spider rubbed his jaw and quoted a price.

Against her will, Trudy felt her face pucker and her eyes tear up. She turned her head away and pretended to search for something in the glove compartment.

"Hey, don't worry about it Trudy. Mike and I will tow it for nothing. Say, I know a guy who is selling an older bike. It's cheaper than a car. It's not a hog or anything, but it'd be a perfect size for you to use until you get another car. Hop on. I'll take you over to him now."

"Okay. Sounds good." When Spider wasn't looking, Trudy swiped her tears with the sleeve of her jacket.

The man's bike rode well and the engine practically purred. It cost more than she had, but with Spider vouching for her, the seller agreed to let her pay it off in three installments.

Spider promised he and Mike would haul the junk Pinto to the dump in the morning so the events of the day came to an acceptable conclusion.

Trudy parked her new acquisition at the curb in front of her apartment building and checked her watch. She had enough time to change before stopping by the office for materials and picking up burgers. She was scheduled to help train Carol for her first major presentation. Trudy's footsteps echoed in the bare stairwell of the entry. On the first floor, someone called her name. She paused to identify the caller. "How are you doing, Brett?"

"Fine," he said.

"I can't stop to talk or I'll be late for a meeting." She ran up the steps.

Panting, he lumbered down the hallway after her. "We'll miss you around here."

# Chapter Nineteen

Trudy slowed, stopped, and swung around to face him. "What do you mean?"

Confusion stiffened the apartment manager's face. "Uh, Phillip said you'd be out by the end of the month. That's today. I'm glad you came by because I need to collect your key."

"Phillip? You must have misunderstood. I'm not going anywhere."

"Um, your husband said you and he were moving."

"Phillip isn't here, anymore. I'm not going anywhere."

Brett shifted from foot to foot and stammered. "But, you have to. I've already rented the place."

"You can't rent my room. I paid you on time. Even if I hadn't, the security deposit and extra month's rent would allow me to stay through June."

The big man tugged at his ear and shuffled his feet. "Phillip took the deposit and the last month's rent."

Trudy closed the distance between them until her nose was almost touched his. "Why would you give my money to Phillip? He isn't on the contract."

"But you looked so happy about your good news. He said the good news was his new job. You were gone so often setting up your new house. I was trying to be helpful."

"Brett, there is no new house. I've been visiting my mom in Iowa most weekends since my dad died."

A sweat broke out over Brett's upper lip. He tugged his ear again. "I'm really sorry, Trudy. But you and he were always here."

"What do you mean? I haven't seen Phillip for two months."

"But he was here almost every day."

"He was in my apartment?" Trudy pointed to her door.

"You were on day shift, and he was on night shift."

She kicked the door. "That rat scum. No wonder. No wonder."

Brett's face was beet red and wet with sweat. He wrung his hands in obvious distress. He stuttered, "I thought you knew."

Trudy whirled away from him and unlocked her door. She swung it open. The room was empty. She shouted. "My stuff? Did that scum of the earth steal my stuff, too?"

"No. No. Today when we came to clean the carpet, I saw you still had clothes here. It wasn't much. I stored it in a locker downstairs, Trudy. Your husband said you'd take care of anything that was left."

"I bet he did." Trudy made fists. She wanted to bash in the walls of the crappy WC. She wanted to pummel Phillip to a pulp. She spun on Brett. "How could you do this to me?"

Brett stepped backward. "I'm so sorry. I wanted to help you."

Trudy wanted to kick the stupid out of Brett. She did none of the things she felt like doing. Instead, she made a quick tour of the room to be sure nothing was left.

Brett swayed from foot to foot. "You have to sign to get your belongings from the office. After you drop off the room key, of course. You aren't going to press charges, are you, Trudy?"

She was too angry to speak. She faced him. He backed up, spun, and lumbered toward the office. Fuming, she followed Brett. She wanted to punch his puffy face, but that was out of the question. The karate discipline kicked in and she controlled herself before punching a hole in the wall, which she'd then have to pay for.

In the office, she signed the paperwork. Then, Trudy pulled the apartment key off her key ring and tossed it on the desk. It pinged against a cup that was sitting there. She stuffed a suitcase under each arm, stuck the strap of another between her teeth.

"Do you want help with that, Trudy?"

"Argh." She looked daggers at him. With adrenaline coursing through her body, Trudy lifted the final two large pieces of luggage and left a distraught Brett to stew in his own juices.

Outside, Trudy realized she had no way to carry her possessions. Chewing on the strap in her mouth, she traipsed back to the office, and swallowed her pride. Her voice quavered. "Brett, I need a favor. My car broke down. I traded it for a motorcycle. I have no way to carry this luggage. I'll have to come back for them. Will you hold them here and not let anyone else take them?"

"Sure, Trudy," Brett stammered. "I won't let anyone else take them. Just you. I won't even make you pay for the storage. When do you think you'll get them?"

"I don't know. I have to find a place to stay. Do you have any other rooms?"

He shook his head vigorously. "Sorry."

Trudy tried calling Kathy. No answer. She checked her watch. 6:00 p.m. As Trudy roared away on her motorcycle, she recognized the cramping in her stomach as hunger pangs.

First, she purchased bungee straps at a big chain supply store. Then, stopped at the office for equipment and Carol's files. She barely had time before the appointment to swing through the drive-through at Bubby's for burgers.

Trudy dismounted at Carol's and removed her helmet a few moments before the appointed time. She breathed deeply several times focusing on switching off her personal worries and assuming a professional persona. She tucked a folder under one arm and a carried the bag of burgers in her other hand.

In response to the doorbell, Carol flung the door open wide. "Welcome food-bearing friend."

Trudy felt an easing within and grinned. Carol liked people in general, but when she called you friend, it was genuine. Like when Mr. Rogers had seemed to look through the TV screen right into her eyes as he declared, "I like you, just the way you are." It was nice to know somebody still did.

She handed the bag of burgers to Carol. They wasted no time eating the burgers hot and washing them down with cans of cola. Afterward she made a second trip to the motorcycle and set up a video recorder and a short tripod in the living room. "Now, go ahead and give your speech. Pay no attention to the video."

When Carol concluded her talk she said, "How did I do?"

"You did great. The information you have is sure to help people. You come across as caring and friendly. Your personal story is compelling. There won't be a dry eye in the place. I know it certainly choked me up."

Carol smiled and heaved a relieved sigh. "Great."

Trudy had spent a lot of time at the library researching what made a speaker good. She had lots of advice to give Carol, but didn't want Carol to know she'd only learned some of these elements of presentation this week. Speaking with authority, she spread a short stack of cards onto the table. "Now, let's make it better. Read over these do's and don'ts."

Carol sorted through the stack. "Is this really necessary? I thought I'd just be myself."

"Being yourself is great. You have a lot to bring to the table. It's also good to be as professional as you can be. That might make the difference between getting more speaking engagements and a one-off. That all translates into book sales.

"Okay."

"Let's take a look at your video, compare it to the cards, and see if there's anything we need to change."

Together they worked out the kinks in the presentation. When they finished, Carol felt confident and fairly shone with excitement. "I think this is going to be really, really good."

"Absolutely. Word will spread fast that you're an excellent speaker with a powerful message. Your schedule will fill up even more quickly now that we're moving out of the local area. Peter is sending professional photographers to this conference and has lined up interviews for you at the radio station. They'll also do attendee interviews for future promotional campaigns."

The front door opened and closed. Kim entered the living room. "I wondered who was here when I saw the motorcycle. I thought maybe my mother was entertaining a man."

"Oh good grief," Carol exclaimed, and rolled her eyes.

Trudy chortled. "Nope. It's mine. I'm in the Christian Motorcycle Association. We drove down to Spring Mill Park today."

"You do the coolest things. How'd the speech prep go?" Kim leaned against the arm of the sofa.

"It was a good first try. I've got some things to learn," Carol admitted.

"You'll get it Mom. You'll be terrific. Night. Night, Trudy." Carol and Trudy called goodnight as Kim disappeared up the stairs.

"I'm cool," Trudy murmured.

The friends chatted as she packed everything away and stacked them near the front door. After a couple more unanswered calls to Kathy, she said. "Carol, I have a favor to ask of you."

"What is it?"

"There's a problem at my apartment. I need a place to stay tonight. Could I stay here?"

Carol was taken aback. She blinked a few times. "Sure. No problem."

"Thanks. That's a big relief."

It was evident Carol was curious, but since she didn't ask, Trudy didn't offer an explanation. Instead she said, "Could you drive me over to my apartment building so I can get my clothes? I can't carry them on the bike."

"What happened to your car?"

"It died." Trudy shrugged. "Can't say it was a premature death."

Carol smiled at the joke. "I'll get my keys."

The car seemed filled with the awkward silence of unasked questions. Trudy didn't want to talk about Phillip for fear that Carol would no longer see her as a competent professional. It was hard enough to admit she needed a place to stay. She certainly didn't want to reveal the details. The silence stretched out until Trudy said, "There was a misunderstanding. I lost the lease to my apartment. They've already rented it out."

"What kind of misunderstanding?"

"It wasn't lack of payment, if that's what you're thinking."

"I wasn't. You seem very responsible to me."

"It was miscommunication. Part of it was because I was gone so much visiting my Mom. Somehow they got the idea I was moving out."

If Carol doubted her explanation, Brett's constant apologies brushed them away.

Back home, Carol helped Trudy haul the luggage into the house and up the stairs into a guest room. She set out fresh towels. "Feel free to help yourself to anything in the kitchen. Do you need anything?"

"No. I'm set. Thank you."

"Okay, well, if there is anything you need, ask. You're looking tired, so I'll let you be. Good night."

Trudy readily admitted she was ready to drop, but feared that all she would think about was Phillip. While her anger at him continued to simmer, thanks to Al-Anon, she reminded herself to put first things, first. She put aside what he had done and focused instead on what she needed to do in the morning for damage control. She'd already sold everything she considered expendable, but she had kept one special item in reserve. Perhaps it was time to let it go.

# Chapter Twenty

During her lunch hour the next day, Trudy set her jaw and entered the pawn shop. The brawny shop owner looked up from bracelets he was arranging on a tray. "Hey, Trudy."

Trudy forced a smile. "Hi, Branson. How have you been?"

"Great. Got a new tat." He pushed back his white T-shirt sleeve to reveal a Cheshire cat.

"Nice. That's some good detail."

"Thanks. Been a while since you were here. Figured things were going good for you."

"Things were going pretty well 'til my husband showed up."

Branson snorted. "Don't get me started on exes. They can be a bear. So you're not looking to buy, you're looking to sell. Whaddya got?"

Trudy didn't bother to correct Branson about her marital status. She placed the ruby earrings on the countertop. "These."

Branson examined them. "New, a few hundred. Used, I can give you $50."

Trudy had known they weren't the high end jewelry she'd looked at in Las Vegas. Phillip had admitted that much himself. Still, this was a blow. It wasn't enough. After a moment's deliberation she said, "Okay. I've got something else."

She slipped her wedding band and diamond ring out of the zippered pocket of her purse. She put the band on her finger and handed him the diamond. With a determined sigh she said, "And this. Of course, I'll be buying it back in a couple of months or so, if you'll give me a little extra time."

He looked at it, grunted, and picked up a jeweler's loupe. He put the magnifying glass to his eye and bent his head over the ring. His coarse brown hair smelled of dandruff shampoo, but his white T-shirt hid any evidence of a problem. Branson straightened. He set down the loupe and handed the ring back. "Trudy, I'm sorry to tell you, but this is a piece of glass."

"Oh, no. It can't be. We went to the jeweler's together."

Branson gave an exaggerated shrug. "Don't know what to tell you. It's not worth much at all."

Trudy bent over the glass case and put her head in both her hands. Sometimes she simply wanted the world to stop spinning so she could get off. She lifted her head and straightened. She pulled the wedding ring off. "What about this?"

Branson inspected it. "It's real. 18 karat gold. I can give you a decent price for it, if you want to sell it outright."

Trudy handed both rings to him. "I don't want either anymore. Give me whatever you can for both. How much for the man who gave them to me?"

Branson's grin held no real humor. "I think I'm better off with the rings."

"You've got that right," Trudy said.

On the way back to work, Trudy called Kathy. "Where were you? I needed you. I tried calling and calling." Trudy gave Kathy the entire story of what Phillip had done to make her homeless. Again.

At the end of the tirade, Kathy said, "I'm in Phoenix. When Mike dropped me off last night I had a call. My twin sister is in the hospital with MRSA. I drove straight here."

Stunned, Trudy murmured, "That's awful. I'm sorry. Here I was only thinking of myself. How is she?"

"It's touch and go. We'll see. Pray for her. Anyway, it sounds as if your crisis is handled. God provided protection. You didn't have to sleep on your motorcycle."

This brought a grudging smile to Trudy's lips. "Yeah."

"Trudy, I don't mind you calling me, but like last night, there are going to be times when I'm not there. In fact, I won't be there for long. Mike proposed. We're getting married later this summer and we're moving here to Phoenix."

A ton of bricks couldn't have knocked Trudy any more senseless. She needed Kathy. What would she do without her confidante, her support? What was the point of making friends if they left? Why did God do this to her?

"Trudy, are you there?"

Trudy forced her voice to sound light-hearted. "I'm speechless. Congratulations. Mike's a great guy, but he's really getting the better part of the deal."

"Thanks. Let's talk about this more when I get back. In the meantime, I want you to think about something. People are an important part of your healing process, but God is the healer. People can fail or be unavailable. God is always there. Do you understand?"

It was uncanny how Kathy seemed to know what she was thinking. "I guess so."

"I'm telling you, don't go back to the way you were. Make God your first go-to person, then you can have others to talk to. Isolation is dangerous and unhealthy. Call me when you've worked out where you'll be staying."

Despite Kathy's words, Trudy felt anger bubbling up inside. Why would God give her Kathy for a friend and then take her away when she was needed so badly? It wasn't a very nice thing to do. "Please God, make Kathy and Mike decide to live here. Make her sister well again so Kathy's not needed there."

That night Trudy returned to the Streeter home. Carol was at one end of the couch. Trudy sat at the other end. She smoothed her gray wool slacks, then dropped folded hands into her lap. "Thanks for letting me stay last night."

"No problem. Any time."

"Really? Because I wanted to talk with you about that. Could I stay here for a while? I'll pay rent."

In slow motion, Carol shook her head. Her face bore an expression of incredulity.

Trudy's heart sank. It had been out of line to ask this of someone who was a business acquaintance, even if she was friendly. "Forget I asked."

Carol grabbed Trudy's arm and shook it gently. "You misunderstand. It's only that I can't believe it. I should though. This is a blessing straight from God. I've been worried about leaving Kim alone while I'm traveling to conferences. Who would've thought he'd solve it this way? Of course, you can stay."

"Woo. Thanks." Trudy melted into the couch with relief.

"I don't want your money as long as you help pay for food. I want something else. I'll be gone often on weekends starting next week. Most of the time, I'll have the car. If you'd drive Kim to balance beam competitions and stay there to cheer for her, and then be here at night while I'm gone, well, it'd be a big load off my mind."

"Sure I can do that," Trudy said. "Only—"

"I know, I know what you're thinking. She's heading off to college. She's eighteen. She's an adult. I shouldn't be worrying."

"No, I'm not judging."

Carol continued, as if Trudy had put up an argument. "It's so hard to let go. This makes a nice transition over the summer. It'll give me a chance to get used to the idea of her being all grown up. If you're still here in three months, then we'll talk rent."

"Agreed, but what I was going to say was, I visit my mom monthly."

"That's not a problem."

"Also, I don't have a car anymore, only the motorcycle."

"Well, if God is working out all the other details, he'll work that out, too."

He did. One of Carol's in-laws lent Trudy an old Chevy Cavalier wagon. It was a secondhand car they used infrequently.

Easy to handle, comfortable to drive, it was big enough to fit the teens. Trudy loved it.

Carol's first full weekend away was at a women's retreat in Pennsylvania. She left before noon on Thursday and drove straight through.

Keeping her side of the bargain, Trudy drove Kim to balance beam regional competition that Saturday. The team placed well. When the scores were announced they all shrieked and bounced around hugging each other.

Her face aglow with excitement, Kim's ponytail swished as she bounded up to Trudy. The freckled Ruby and a pimply-faced, impossibly young looking senior named Eric followed close behind her. She pointed to the boy. "I'm going to ride home with Eric and Ruby."

"No drinking, right?"

"No, Ma'am," said Eric.

"No extra stops."

Kim, bouncing up and down on her toes, her lustrous ponytail swinging behind her, said, "Of course not. We only want to enjoy our big win."

Ruby said, "You know, relive the glories of our triumph."

Eric added, "The thrill of victory, instead of the agony of defeat."

Trudy laughed. "Okay. Okay. I see you've been watching old sports shows with your dad, Eric. Go. Relive the glory. I'll be right behind you."

Kim said to her friends, "I told you she'd be cool with it."

Ruby's cute, freckled face lit up. Eric grinned and gave Ruby a side-ways hug. He said, "Come on, ladies."

The wipers cleared huge droplets off the Cavalier's windshield as she waited for her turn in the exodus of cars. Despite the sweatshirt and the jacket she wore, Trudy found the car interior to be damp. She turned the heat on for a few minutes to take the chill out of the air.

She followed Eric and the girls out of the slowly emptying parking lot. The setting sun broke through the clouds causing the wet two-lane roads to shine.

The hour-long drive home maneuvering his 1985 tan pickup truck through moderate traffic was enough to prove Eric was a cautious and alert driver. Trudy's thoughts turned to her mother, her job, and wondering where that swindling ratbag, her errant husband, could be.

Eric turned down a narrow street that lead in the direction of Ruby's subdivision. Victorian homes crowded close to the curbs on both sides in an area dotted with mini-strip malls and houses converted to businesses. He stopped at a red light.

Lights from a gas station across the road created silhouettes of the heads of the three friends, turning one way, then the other, talking, being teens. Trudy doubted any of them had done some of the mischief she'd done at that age. They were good kids who channeled their energies into gymnastics instead of hijinks.

The light turned green. Eric entered the intersection. Trudy glimpsed a dark flash. Eric's pickup lifted sideways off the pavement while the charging vehicle bucked like a bronc kicking its hind legs. The heads of the teens snapped sideways and back like boxer speed-training bags. The sound of crunching metal rolled past. Both vehicles rocked then came to a rest in tangle of metal in the middle of the intersection. The front of a black truck protruded from the smashed side of Eric's cab.

"Oh my—" Trudy snapped her mouth shut. She snatched her phone from her purse and dialed 9-1-1. She rattled off information to the dispatcher, adding, "And hurry." Leaving the door of the Cavalier hanging open, she sprinted toward the passenger side of the car and Kim.

Trudy jerked the door open. The overhead light revealed fear, shock, and tears distorting Kim's lovely face. Blood spurted from her nose, flowed down her chin onto her chest. "Trudy," she said and started to lunge forward.

Trudy put both palms out. "Don't move. Stay where you are."

Kim pressed her hands to her head. Her eyes became unfocused. Suddenly she hunched over, held her hand over her mouth, but vomited anyway. Beside her a low wail burst from Ruby. Tiny shards of glass oozed droplets of blood among the freckles. Her round blue eyes were wide with fright.

Trudy said, "Ruby are you hurt badly?"

"No, I don't think so," she sobbed. "Help Eric. Eric's hurt."

On the side of the impact, Eric leaned toward the bloody, steering wheel, resting his head, groaning. His door was caved inward, crowding into the driver's area. Pieces of glass covered him and more shimmered throughout the truck cabin.

Trudy said, "Eric is anything broken?"

He groaned in response.

"Everyone stay still. Help is on the way. Eric, can you turn the car off?"

Eric didn't respond. With a shaking hand, Ruby reached to turn the key. Trudy kept talking to the teens, keeping them quiet, reassuring them. Eric's body went limp. Ruby sobbed harder. Kim clasped Trudy's hand until it felt crushed. She winced, but didn't pull away.

Trudy couldn't see the driver who had run the red light. Men stood around the other vehicle peering inside. More people gathered, streaming from vehicles which couldn't pass through the blocked intersection. They came running across the street from the filling station.

Sirens. Flashing lights. Police cars. "Ma'am, step away, please," a deep voice said behind her. Trudy stepped back to allow the uniformed officer to lean into the truck cab.

More uniforms were at the other vehicle. Others directed traffic. What seemed like a century later, but was only minutes, sirens wailed again as emergency vehicles arrived. EMS in light blue jackets scurried about transferring the teens into ambulances. Trudy called out, "Kim, Ruby, Eric, I'll be right behind you."

"Call my mom," Kim wailed.

"I'll call all your parents."

Feeling that her knees would buckle if she didn't sit, Trudy made it back to her car. She placed her hand on her heart and felt it racing. She was grateful she wasn't wearing high heels because she would've toppled for sure. It was an odd thought to be bouncing around her brain, but she thanked God anyway and also that at least she could breathe. Oddly, no elephants were crushing her in spite of the crisis.

An officer asked her for a statement. From him she learned which hospital the ambulances were headed. Trudy called Ruby's parents and with measured calmness passed on the information. They put Trudy on speaker phone so Eric's parents, who were with them, could also hear the details.

The deafening shriek of another siren announced the arrival of a large red firetruck. It inched as close as possible and firemen leaped out carrying the Jaws of Life to extricate the other driver. Police moved about the congested scene gathering statements from other witnesses. Slowly, the traffic jam untangled. As soon as she could, Trudy followed the teens to the hospital.

# Chapter Twenty-one

Trudy hunched in the emergency waiting room. She was miserable that the nurse wouldn't give her an update because she wasn't Kim's mother. Why did she let Kim go with friends instead of taking her home? Not that it was Eric's fault. The driver had run a red light. An interminable time later, the nurse motioned for her. "Kim's asking for you."

Trudy crowded into the already congested ER room. The area around both eyes was a darkening red making Kim's pale face and bandaged head appear serious. A nurse was taking blood pressure. A doctor said, "Ms. Bellafonte, Kim is eighteen, but has given me permission to talk with you."

"Good. How bad is it?"

"Not as bad as it looks. In a car accident, the car stops almost immediately, but the passengers don't. Her body was thrust into the seat belt strap which caused severe bruising on the torso. This is very common, but far less severe than if she hadn't been wearing a seatbelt."

"Thank God."

"Because it was a sideways collision, she hit the side window. Her nose is broken. She lost consciousness at the scene briefly and seemed mildly disoriented so we'll do a CT scan to make sure she doesn't have any brain damage. We'll keep her overnight for observation. She'll need surgery to set the broken nose once the swelling goes down. She should see an Ear-Nose-Throat specialist, in a few days. We're moving her to a room soon. A nurse will come down to the waiting room and get you so that you can be with her."

Trudy nodded. "Thank you, doctor. How are Eric and Ruby?"

He shook his head and began to recite the standard disclaimer, then his face softened. "You'll find their parents down the hall in the waiting room."

She thanked him and sank with relief onto the green plastic seat, drawing several calming breaths.

The nurse finished taking the blood pressure. Kim asked, "Did you call my mom?"

"Not yet."

"When you do, tell her to stay and speak."

"Are you sure?"

Kim nodded. It was easy to see she was trying to do the grown-up thing while wanting her mama. "Tell her I'm fine. You're here." Aides stepped into the room and prepared the bed to move it. Kim tried to smile. She gave a tiny wave.

"Okay. I'll see you in the room in a little bit." Trudy located the waiting room after asking directions twice.

Ruby sat between a heavy-set woman and a heavily freckled red-headed man. Her hands were interlocked with theirs on both sides.

Trudy smiled. "Ruby, how are you doing?"

"Turns out the middle of the truck was the safest place. My friends cushioned me from getting hurt. I'm bruised and scratched. They had to dig some glass out of me, but that's all. How's Kim?"

"She'll be okay."

Ruby didn't release her parents' hands but nodded with her head first one way, then the other. "This is my dad, Culcallen, and my mom, Opal. Eric's in a lot worse shape." She dipped her head toward another couple in the room. "This is his Mom and Dad, Mr. and Mrs. Farnsworth."

The couple Ruby nodded at were a few chairs away. They introduced themselves. Trudy touched the woman's shoulder briefly. Her voice quavered, as she said, "Mrs. Farnsworth, how serious is it?"

Eric's mother spoke so low it was almost a whisper. "Eric has several broken ribs, whiplash, and needs stitches. His lung isn't punctured."

"No puncture. That's good. I'm glad," Trudy said.

The worry that had gathered across Mr. Farnsworth's forehead never left. He said, "His legs are messed up. They're going to admit him for surgery."

Mrs. Farnsworth's lips trembled and she pressed them together. Her husband patted her hand. She smiled wanly and seemed to draw strength from his touch. Her voice grew louder as she said, "They said it could've been so much worse. How is Kim?"

"Broken nose, cuts and bruises. They're keeping her overnight for observation, but only because the EMTs said she blacked out. They're sure it's nothing."

Opal said, "Trudy."

Trudy turned toward Ruby and her parents.

"Ruby told us how you kept them all calm. We're so glad you were there. Carol must be going out of her mind," Opal said, giving Ruby's hand a squeeze.

"I haven't called her yet."

The two sets of parents frowned and exchanged glances. Trudy felt compelled to explain in the face of their disapproval. "They wouldn't talk to me until Kim okayed it. I only finished getting the update before I came here. I knew Carol would want to know everyone's status because she loves your kids. No point in worrying her with half-information."

The group nodded their understanding.

Trudy chatted a few more minutes and excused herself to make the call. She stepped out of the hospital and moved down the sidewalk to where it was permissible to use cell phones. Security lights, like stage spot lights, cast white pools onto the concrete. Trudy felt the pressure of being on stage in a performance for which she didn't know her lines and would have to improvise.

Carol was appalled. "I'll leave the car here and fly home tonight."

"Carol, Kim is fine. They're only keeping her overnight as a precaution. They'll release her in the morning. Call and talk with her yourself. You'll see."

"I'm going back in there and tell the women. They'll understand. They'll all pray."

"You're being paid for this gig. You're a professional. You can't up and leave. It's not life-threatening. There's nothing you can do. Besides, Kim told me to tell you not to come. She knows what you're doing is important." Trudy took a breath and plunged in. "Remember how you said Satan might try to keep you from speaking to women? I think this is one of those times. You're there. I'm here. I'll stay here with Kim all night. I won't leave her side."

"What about Minnie?"

"I'll slip over to the house long enough to take care of her. Then, I'll come right back here. God has everything under control."

After much consoling and assurances, Carol agreed to stay. "You're using my own words against me, you know that, don't you?"

"Truth is truth, as you like to say."

Even though she had spoken Carol's words without believing them herself, she found that once spoken, a seedling of faith sprouted.

A prayer welled up from somewhere inside. "Dear God, I know I haven't been talking to you lately. I've been mad about Kathy leaving, but I'm not asking for me this time. I'm asking for Carol and Kim and you know how they love you. Heal her. Heal all of them. Don't let there be any permanent damage. They haven't done anything to deserve this. Please hear me, for Kim sake. For Carol's. Don't let Carol be angry with me, either."

Next, Trudy called Peter and told him what had happened and that Carol was finishing the two day speaking gig. He commended her for talking Carol out of flying home. As an after-thought, he asked about Kim.

Later that night as Trudy wriggled about trying to find a comfortable position in the hospital room's one reclining chair, the full weight of responsibility hit her. This was a taste of parenthood. She shuddered to think what she'd have felt if Kim had been permanently injured or killed.

The next evening as Trudy settled Kim onto the Streeter living room couch with a blanket, pillow, and a cup of cocoa, Kim said. "I'm okay. You don't have to hover."

"I don't know what else to do."

"If I need anything, I'll let you know." Kim pointed to a bouquet of flowers with a Get Well balloon attached. "Who sent the flowers?"

"Peter Faulkinroy."

"Except for the balloon, they look like funeral flowers. They're huge. He must be trying to impress Mom."

Trudy giggled. "You're right."

Carol burst into the house calling their names. She rushed to the couch, barely giving Kim time to sit up before embracing her.

"Ouch. Not so tight, Mom."

"Oh, sorry. I'm so glad you're safe." Carol released her, leaned back, and eyed her face. "Boy, are you swollen."

"Eric was hurt the worst. He's still in the hospital. His knees are all jammed up. He's out of the gymnastics competition and might not be walking by graduation. At least there's no permanent damage."

"We'll go visit him tomorrow."

Carol gave Trudy a big hug. "Thanks."

"You're not mad at me?" Trudy said.

"Of course not. Why would I be mad?"

"It's my fault. I shouldn't have let Kim ride with her friends."

"I'd have done the same thing. That didn't cause the accident. You didn't know some guy was going to run the red light. I don't know what I'd have done if you hadn't been here to fill in for me. I'd have hopped on a plane and flown straight home. Your words encouraged me. What Satan meant for evil, God used for good.

Trudy wrinkled her nose. "What do you mean?"

"Those ladies at the conference rallied around me. It bound us together spiritually in a way mere words could never do. In fact, if it weren't such a serious accident, I'd accuse Peter of orchestrating it as a promotional stunt." Carol laughed.

Relief flooded Trudy. She snickered. "I don't think even Peter would plan an accident."

"Maybe that's why he sent such a large bunch of flowers," Kim said, rolling her one good eye towards the arrangement.

Carol also eyed the bouquet. "That is a big bunch of flowers."

"He can afford it," Trudy said.

"Trudy did a great job, Mom." Kim laid on the couch and pulled the covers over her shoulders. "She's been like helicopter aunt, hovering over me."

Carol said, "Helicopter aunt. Guess that means you're family now."

The thought warmed Trudy in a way that nothing else had in a long time. Could it be that God brought Carol as a friend because Kathy was leaving? She smiled without reservation at both of the Streeters.

# Chapter Twenty-two

Carol, Kim, and Trudy visited Eric the next evening at his home, which was a sprawling ranch, more upscale than Kim's home, but not nearly as posh as Ruby's. His spacious bedroom was full of visitors, who had followed him in as he arrived home.

Ruby sat on his bed signing his leg cast with fluorescent pink ink. Culcallen and Opal, stood on the other side of the bed in conversation with Eric's parents. Despite the bruises and bumps, he laughed at what Ruby wrote and read it aloud, "There's better ways to get a newer truck." Everyone chuckled.

Eric answered Carol's inquiries about his condition and added, "This is a disaster. Ruby and her parents are leaving for a Hawaiian vacation next week. I was supposed to house sit. Now I'll be sitting, but not at their house."

Culcallen said, "Don't worry about it, Eric. The main thing is that you'll be well enough to attend commencement."

Ruby's mother heartily agreed, and added. "Although I don't know what we're going to do with Finn McCool. He hates going to the kennel."

"Finn McCool is an Irish Wolfhound. He's enormous," Kim explained.

"He's enormously spoiled," Culcallen added.

"He's my baby." Opal lifted her hand to eye-height.

Kim clapped her hands together. "Say, I bet Trudy would house- and-dog sit for you. It's perfect. She's really good with animals. She owned horses. Finn McCool is as big a horse. Isn't that right, Trudy?"

"You're the dog walker, Kim," Trudy responded.

"I've already got my hands full. I have several other families who are going on vacation and I've picked up more hours at the Talent Agency."

Trudy didn't protest any further once she learned what the job paid for two weeks.

When she arrived at the sprawling brick house with small turrets, stone pillars, and bay windows, it seemed as if she'd walked into a fairy tale. She parked her motorcycle next to a gently splashing fountain and set her helmet on the seat. The large manicured yard was bordered with rhododendron and boxwood. The estate was as impressive as the first time she'd seen it.

Who would've thought Ruby, who only ever appeared in everyday jeans and T-shirts with fun sayings, came from money like this? It certainly blew the common conception of prissy well-to-do princesses. She mounted the rounded three-tiered porch and rang the bell. While waiting for the butler, she admired the elaborately carved door.

Opal herself opened the door. Dressed as down-to-earth as her daughter, Opal sported blue jeans and a cotton eyelet shirt that would look in place with anyone else at a ball field or soccer game. Trudy felt completely comfortable in her own jeans and red pullover.

"Trudy, come in. Come in."

Trudy stepped into a spacious foyer and paused to let her eyes adjust after the bright sunlight. Another step brought her nose to nose with a monstrous furry face. "Oh, my," she exclaimed. Big brown eyes evaluated her through a thatch of brown hair.

Opal made a tiny gesture toward the shaggy dog. "This is Finn McCool. He's named after an Irish hero who was a great defender of his country."

Trudy greeted Finn McCool. The dog accepted her with a nod and the quiet calm of the lord of the manor.

Opal reached up to give a hearty scratch to the floppy ears. Her voice raised a few notes. "He's a sweetheart. He's the best dog ever." Accustomed to being lauded, the massive dog smiled indulgently. Trudy had never seen a dog smile, but that's definitely what he did.

Opal led Trudy into the formal sitting room. Finn McCool followed. He stood with utter patience as if overseeing his owner's rather long, detailed list of dog care. He padded companionably alongside Trudy during a house tour that ended in the kitchen. Then as if willing to turn the more domestic part of host duties over to Opal, he settled into a huge dog bed as Opal poured two glasses of lemonade.

Trudy sipped the chilled, not-too-sweet-not-too-tart fluid. Tiny bits of lemon pulp teased her tongue. "Where will I stay?"

Opal waved like a magician performing a trick. "Any room you like. As long as everything is in order when we return. I know the house can seem intimidating when you're alone, but you don't need to worry. We've got timed lights, surveillance cameras, high security locks, and the police patrol regularly. The main thing is taking care of Finn McCool. You take care of him and he'll take care of you."

The big dog's ears flicked and his tail thumped once, as if to affirm Opal's words.

Finn McCool proved to be no trouble at all. The long early morning walks invigorated Trudy. She enjoyed his company in the evenings outside on the back lawn or watching TV in the living room or cooking supper in the big kitchen. His soulful eyes pleaded with her until she scratched the sweet spot behind his ears. His tail thumped. "You miss your family, don't you? This big old house gets lonely."

The middle of the second week Trudy settled into the living room on the computer Peter had provided. She worked late into the evening, researching and fine-tuning details of a particularly big campaign for one of Peter's clients.

Finn McCool stayed close so that every time she took a moment to stretch or stopped to think through a problem, her hand automatically set to petting him. "Don't worry big guy, they'll be home in a few days."

Finn McCool leapt to his feet. A low rumble vibrated in his broad chest. Trudy cocked her head and listened. Nothing. He growled again. Trudy held her breath. Afraid to disturb anything, she rose, glided to the window and peered into the night.

Motion sensors had activated, flooding the wide porch in yellow light. A single figure stood half-turned away from her. A hand reached out to the lion's head door knocker. Even so, when it sounded, she jumped. Three knocks total. Trudy moved to the door and opened it, counting the murmured *beep, beep, beep* of the alarm system.

"Hi Tru,"

"What are you doing here? I thought Atlantic City had called."

"I was worried about you. Guess I shouldn't have been. From the looks of this place, you're doing well. I'm surprised you're answering your own door."

"You can beat that green-eyed monster back into the dark cave of your soul. I'm house-sitting."

"Well invite me in."

"No. The owner doesn't care for snakes."

"You cut me." Phillip placed a hand on his chest.

"I'd like to after that stunt you pulled last time. You left me homeless. Again. And when did you steal my diamond?" Phillip feinted to her left. When she moved to block him, he moved right and strode into the foyer. She whirled around. "No. Get out."

Finn McCool's growl exploded into a bark that reverberated off the high ceiling of the foyer. Phillip emitted a terse exclamation and stepped backwards. The enormous beast advanced stiff-legged. Phillip held his palms up. "Easy dog. Good boy. Nice dog."

Finn McCool was having none of it, he snapped and snarled.

Phillip sidled toward the door. "Call him off. Call him off or—" Phillip snatched up a small bronze statue from the side table and raised it overhead, ready to strike. Finn McCool pounced. He covered a five foot distance in the blink of an eye. Phillip dropped the statue and slipped through the open door. He raced down the drive with the dog after him. Finn McCool stopped at the edge of the property, barking into the night. Trudy was sure the message was clear, "and don't come back."

She leaned face first against the doorframe, clutching it with both hands. *Beeeeep.* The alarm blared. With shaky hands she punched in the code and silence folded over her, but only for a moment. Two patrol cars arrived with sirens chirping and lights flashing. Finn McCool ignored them. He continued to pace back and forth across the end of the drive.

Trudy called, "Good boy. Heel, Finn McCool."

The dog silenced and returned to her side. He stayed next to her, remaining alert. She stroked him to soothe herself as she related the event to the police. With great embarrassment, she admitted the intruder was her own husband. For the first time she used the term estranged. The police statement took forever and some of the questions left her unsettled.

One officer said, "Has he ever hurt you?"

Trudy frowned. "You mean physically? No. Never. I don't think he meant to hurt anyone this time, either."

"You said he raised the statue."

"Finn McCool frightened him, that's why he grabbed the statue. It was a defensive move."

The officers exchanged looks.

"Finn McCool didn't think he meant harm. He could have attacked, instead he simply chased him off the property."

"What did he want?"

"I have no idea, we didn't get that far."

"Have you talked with him recently?"

"No. I haven't heard from him in weeks. I thought he went east. I don't know how he even knew I was here. He knows where I work. He must've followed me from there. He doesn't like dogs. I don't think he'll come back as long as Finn McCool is here."

"Keep the doors locked and the alarm set. We'll step up the patrol." His parting words were, "Don't worry Ma'am."

Trudy did nothing but worry. Whenever she was in the house she went from window to window peering out. She checked the alarm repeatedly to be sure it was active. What if Phillip hurt Finn McCool? What if he came back and stole something? Would Culcallen and Opal blame her for this?

Trudy felt tremendous relief when the family returned. She mentioned the incident and was astonished that Culcallen's anger wasn't directed at her. He said, "That's a regrettable experience. I guess nowhere is safe these days, no matter what precautions you take. You handled the situation well, though."

Guilt nudged Trudy. She had left out the part that Phillip was her husband. She told herself it had nothing to do with them and everything to do with Phillip being Phillip, out to annoy and take advantage of her. "I'm glad nothing was taken and no damage was done to your property."

Opal wrung her hands. "This simply shouldn't have happened. We're so sorry. You had to have been scared out of your wits. We're so glad you weren't hurt. We'll double your wages to make up for it."

"No. No. No. It's not your fault. Good grief, no." The suggestion upset her so much that Opal relented. Trudy added, "Anyway, Finn McCool lived up to his name. He's my hero. He'll always have a place in my heart."

Finn McCool's tail thumped. Ruby sank to her knees and fondled the enormous head. Opal cooed her praise and Culcallen added a gruff, "Good dog."

The big dog, thrilled to have his family where they belonged, lapped up the attention. He smiled. Trudy wouldn't miss the beautiful, lavish house, but she would miss Finn McCool. She administered an extra good scratch behind his ears and said good bye.

Trudy wished Finn McCool could accompany her everywhere as a Phillip-locating warning system. She kept looking over her shoulder to see if he was nearby. She didn't see him hanging around the city street where she worked, nor did he show himself at Carol's house. Still, she checked before she answered the door. Day after day passed and the breath she'd been holding released.

By commencement, a minimum of make-up was needed to hide the discoloration of Kim's broken and re-set nose. Trudy assured her that even in a photograph, no one would notice it among the sea of other faces all dressed in cap and gowns. This seemed to satisfy

Kim, especially after Carol agreed to postpone the graduation party until the middle of July.

Despite the pale undertones of Ruby's skin, the effusive freckles hid evidence of remaining bruises and red marks left by tiny scabs from the flying glass. Eric attended commencement in a wheel chair and compensated for walking by enthusiastically waving a school pennant. The gymnastics team gathered around him making sure he wanted for nothing. His parents left him in the care of his friends and mounted the risers to sit with Carol, Trudy, Culcallen, and Opal.

Peter Faulkinroy joined them, talking with Eric's father. Soon he turned toward Carol, but addressed the group at large and passed out tickets. "I've been nominated for The Year's Most Successful New Businessman in Indianapolis. I'm inviting all of you to join me at my table for the banquet a week from Thursday."

Congratulations were extended all around and even some people nearby acknowledged Peter. He preened a little, loving the attention.

Carol smiled at Peter. "Trudy told me you had been nominated. What a great honor. I know how much work she's done, so I have a good idea the effort you've put in. Congratulations. And, thank you for the invitation. I haven't had a chance to go to something this fancy since my husband died. I'll plan on being there."

"May I give you a ride, Carol?"

"Peter, how thoughtful. However, Trudy and I have a thing to do with Kim beforehand. After we're done, we'll attend together and meet you there."

"Good," he said as the opening chords to "Pomp and Circumstance" rolled over the stadium. The graduating class was large and the day was quite warm under a brilliant sun, but the crowd remained jolly as the high school band repeated the song until every graduate was in place.

Carol pulled a camera out of her oversized straw purse. "I'm going down to snap photos."

Opal said, "I'll go, too."

"Count me in," Eric's mom said and nudged her husband, "Come on."

Culcallen and Trudy remained in their seats, exchanging friendly chatter while Peter was engaged in conversation with someone beside him. Without a change in tone, Culcallen said, "Have you seen your husband since that night at my house?"

"No. Thank God. Yet, other times it drives me nuts not knowing where he is." One of Peter's clients waved at her. Trudy returned the gesture. She dropped her hand and cast a sidelong glance at the man beside her. "You know Phillip's my husband?"

Culcallen chuckled. "You don't know who I am, do you? I'm a lawyer. My uncle is the police chief. My nephew is one of the policemen who came to the house that night. Of course, I know."

"Oh." Trudy closed her eyes and wished that would make her disappear. "I didn't mean to deceive you. It didn't seem important since I didn't think he'd come back. He didn't come back, did he?"

"No, but I watched the security videos of that night. You obviously knew each other, so I asked my nephew about the report and I had my uncle do some checking. Your husband is in deep to lots of people. Some with mob connections. Also, certain government agencies are looking into him for racketeering. What I learned had me concerned for Carol and Kim, so I checked into you."

Trudy opened her eyes and tried to ferret out veiled threats. His face remained pleasant, if serious.

"I found you have a history of clearing up his messes. I also know what you're doing for your mother. Although you have been good to them, I suspect you've not been candid with Carol and Kim."

Trudy breathed shallow and fast. She didn't deny it.

He nodded. "Still, I think you're someone trying to do the right thing in a difficult situation. So, I'm offering a word of advice. Cut ties with your husband, or by helping him you may find yourself in so deep with the law you can't get out."

Culcallen continued, "I'm not saying this for their sakes alone, but for you. You've been a friend to Ruby and to Eric. Be careful. Some of those people after him can be unforgiving. Understand?"

She nodded. The rest of the group were climbing the bleachers toward them. As they filed into their seats, he said, "If you ever need help, call me. No strings attached. A friend helping a friend."

Trudy released a very long breath and mumbled, "Thanks."

Opal sat beside her husband. "Oh, is he telling you about our friends that need a house and pet-sitter next week? I told them how wonderful you were with Finn McCool. They want you to help them, too."

# Chapter Twenty-three

Opal's friends lived in a grand house, too. This house was in the Victorian style with lots of plush draperies and intricate wood paneling. The job included giving care and attention to six demanding, yappy, and surprisingly obnoxious Pekingese, in addition to three neurotic birds, two aloof Siamese cats, and various goldfish in bowls on pedestals throughout the house.

There also were exotic plants in the conservatory that needed attending. The man of the house would be home, but was in and out at odd hours with his work and refused to care for his wife's menagerie.

The owners were more reserved than Opal and Culcallen. They insisted Trudy keep to a small maid's apartment at the side of the house once her various duties were complete. The plant and animal routine took longer and wasn't as companionable as caring for Finn McCool, but Trudy wasn't complaining. She planned to use the extra money to pay off another old debt.

The maid's apartment was appointed with pieces of furniture that had been cast-off from the main house because they were damaged or stained. The spacious room sported an uncomfortable, high-back maroon velvet sofa. Bricks had been used to replace a missing leg on it. Beside it a round rosewood table, with scratch marks hidden beneath a lace doily, held a hurricane lamp and a statue of courting Victorian lovers.

Near the kitchenette entrance, there was also a rosewood desk. A Tiffany lamp cast light upon a huge overstuffed wing-backed chair that was the most comfortable thing Trudy had ever curled up in to read a book.

Though the pink floral room was not to her taste, it was cozy. She found it to be a good place to concentrate on work. Peter provided a copy/FAX machine in addition to the computer and cell phone so she could keep up with the increase of business.

She would've insisted Peter hire more help, if she didn't need the overtime money so badly. She liked the Cavalier she used on the weekends Carol was gone and intended to buy it as soon as she had the asking price.

The day of the New Businessman of the Year banquet, Trudy left work early and rushed through her care-taking duties. She drove her motorcycle to the Streeter home where the preparation became a party in itself. Kim fussed over them, doing their nails and choosing jewelry and purses before she sent them to their rooms to dress.

Carol reappeared in the cream colored dress from her 20th wedding anniversary. Trudy wowed both her friends with her blue satin Chanel, one of two dresses she'd kept from her Las Vegas days.

"I don't know what you did before you moved here, but you sure dressed fabulous. You both look great." Kim crossed her arms in satisfaction and nodded at the women.

"Everybody should get the chance to dress up every once in a while," Carol said as she picked up her purse and coat.

Trudy agreed. She reveled in the luxury of dressing in her finest. The pleasure of the evening would only be increased if Peter would take the award and the title.

The banquet was held at a downtown hotel. The finest businesses in the city attended. For once, Trudy didn't feel like a fake. She was simply herself. She felt comfortable around Peter's high-class clients, whom she knew on a first name basis.

She was at ease conversing with Culcallen and Opal. They in turn introduced her to many of their friends, including the mayor. Her status with Peter raised a few notches when he saw her chatting like old friends with Culcallen's cousin, the district judge.

Peter in white tie and tails, found excuses to be near Carol whenever he wasn't schmoozing with the mayor or the police chief or some other important businessman. He introduced her as a successful author and one of his clients.

When they went to freshen their lipstick, Carol said, "Does it seem odd to you that he's escorting me around?"

"Well, your name is going around the country. It's good advertisement for Faulkinroy Publicists. I'd be surprised if he didn't. You know he never misses a chance to promote himself."

"I guess not. I'm probably not used to having a man around since my husband. It feels odd. Stay close by me, huh, Trudy?"

"Sure. I'll run interference if you need it. I'm having a great time. I hear the band is good and when they start playing I intend to dance with anyone who asks and by myself if no one does. You should, too."

Carol nodded. "I think that's sound advice."

"Come on. The hall is quieting. I think they're about to announce the winner." They hurried back to their seats.

The normal speeches about how the program started and why and who benefited drew to a close. The mayor stood ready to present the certificate. The committeewoman announced, "And this year's Best New Businessman of 1991 is Peter Faulkinroy, Faulkinroy Publicists."

A low roar swept through the crowd accompanied by applause. Peter, look regal as he climbed the stage to accept his honor and took the podium. "Thank you for this acknowledgement… I've worked hard this year, but behind every businessman's achievement is a team. My secretary and personal assistant shares in this honor tonight."

Carol whispered in Trudy's ear. "I notice he didn't bother to say your name."

"Progress, not perfection," Trudy said, clapping with enthusiasm. "This was a big step for him. He's probably afraid someone will want to steal me."

The band played and the party ramped up and continued past midnight. Peter said, "Trudy, I've been invited to a late private party with some clients here in the hotel. Will you drive Honey home and bring her in to the office tomorrow?"

"Sure," Trudy said, accepting the keys to his beloved yellow Porsche.

"Be careful."

"I've driven a Porsche before. I'll treat her as if she were my own."

His eyebrows lifted. "No. Treat her as if she's mine and you're liable for anything that happens to her."

"Gotcha," Trudy flicked her pointer finger at him. "No worries. The racetrack is closed tonight."

Peter gave her a black look, shook his head, and returned to his group. Trudy chuckled. Carol said, "That's humorous. You love riling him up, don't you?

"He makes it easy. Besides, it's good for him."

The two friends left the hotel together and parted in the parking garage.

Peter's Porsche purred to life. Trudy maneuvered the car out onto the street. How she wanted to take Honey out on some dark road for a real test run. Trudy resisted the urge and before long pulled into the lengthy drive and parked next to the huge Victorian house. "You're one sweet ride, Honey." She patted the hood. "Good-night."

Her high heels clacked pleasantly along the path that lead to the rear apartment. Oversized rhododendrons and leafy maples cast eerie shadows from security lights tucked high up under the eaves. She rounded the hulking house and spotted the welcoming glow of the table light she'd left burning in the window. A motion detector created another spotlight of yellow as she approached the door. She punched in the security code and heard a click as the door unlocked.

"You're looking good, Tru."

Trudy clutched her purse to her chest and spun around. Fear. Relief. Anger. Hope. Wariness. All hit so fast she wasn't sure which emotion was first or strongest. She gathered her wits and kept her voice calm. "Hello, Phillip."

With one leap he covered the two steps and pressed in close. "Hey, dear heart. Aren't you going to ask me in?"

"No. I don't think so."

"Don't be like that, Trudy. We've got history." He placed his hand on her waist. She brushed it off.

"Yes, and that's what it is. History."

"Not exactly. We're still married."

Trudy paused a moment, thinking hard, then pushed the door open. He gave her a triumphant smile, self-assured that he still had her charmed. He sauntered past, taking in the apartment in the soft light of the single table lamp. He gestured toward her and himself. "Cozy. Room for two."

Trudy flicked the overhead switch. The room flooded with light. He scrutinized her. She shivered and looked away.

"You look fantastic, Tru. Truly delectable, but then you always could make an appearance. Chanel. Oh-la-la. Coming back in style."

"It's an old dress, but good enough for here. No royalty to impress, although I hope you realize we never did fool anybody. Old money always can spot new money and pretenders. It's the little things that give it away. The subtleties." She tossed her purse on a table and moved about the room turning on all the table lights.

"Maybe that was true for you, but I was one of them. People always loved me. Even hard sells, like your parents."

"Dad died from a heart attack after you cheated him out of everything."

"Now, Trudy, that isn't true. His heart was already weak. I'm sorry he passed, but it was way after that investment didn't pan out. It wasn't my fault. Besides, I have every intention of paying that back."

She ignored the fact he seemed to have known about her dad's passing, yet hadn't offered condolences. She snorted. "Yeah. I remember how that went last time."

"You can't fault me for that. I had a really good chance to double the money, to pay them back everything in one fell swoop."

"Where is it?"

Phillip shrugged. "I'll get it back. Don't you fear."

Trudy snorted again.

"You don't believe me?"

"I'll tell you what I don't believe. I don't believe for one minute that Dad cashed in his life insurance policy. You forged his name, you slimy double-crossing swindler."

Phillip bristled. "Hey. Hey. Hey. Stop. Don't call me that."

"Mom got stiffed with over six grand to bury him. She had to sell the farm, which was already mortgaged to the hilt."

"That's a real shame, but, honestly, Tru, she couldn't have taken care of the farm, anyway."

"I suppose in your depraved mind you think you did her a favor by cheating them."

"I didn't cheat them. They were generous to me. I appreciated that." He walked about the room, surveying everything. He stopped in front of the rosewood desk. "By the looks of things you can afford to help her. Fancy car. Fancy dress. Late night out at what, a two hundred dollar a plate banquet?

"Are you stalking me?"

He continued as if she hadn't spoken. "This place is great. And look at all these top notch gadgets. A FAX and a computer."

"They're for work."

"You must be working a lot if you take them home with you. Does your boss work here? You're my wife. You haven't forgotten that, have you?"

"I'm always painfully aware of it, no matter how I wish to erase the past. That's not why you're here. You need money. How much this time?"

He studied her, visibly deliberating whether he should ask outright or butter her up. "Eight grand."

Trudy laughed bitterly. "Eight grand? Is that all?"

"Sarcasm doesn't become you. From the looks of things you can afford it, even if all you are is a bit of fluff to the silver-haired man of the house."

Trudy tromped over to the desk, opened her work bag and withdrew a set of papers. "Fine, Phillip. Fill in the information and sign this, and I'll give you what I have."

Phillip took the papers and read them. "These are separation papers."

"That's right."

He tossed them on the rosewood table. "So you're moving on, huh? Which guy is it?"

"There's no one else. There's unlikely to be anyone else ever, because being married to you left such a bad taste in my mouth I want to retch."

"Come on, Trudy. Don't be catty. We had some good times. We'll have good times again. I love you." He gifted her with one of his famous smiles that had never before failed to melt her heart.

She turned away to ward off the magic. He put his arms around her and tried to draw her to him. Trudy dipped out of his grip and hoofed it a safe distance across the room. She kept her voice calm, cool. "Sure, at first, when you weren't gambling everything away, which for the past four years has happened more than not. I know you cheated on me, as well. Plenty of grounds for divorce even by church standards."

He stepped forward, his head shaking almost imperceptibly, a frown darkening his features. "No, no, no, Tru. I never did. You're my one and only."

She almost believed him. She faced the desk so he wouldn't see her press a hand to her heart. "This is merely a legal separation, so I don't keep paying for any debt you rack up. If you give up gambling and get your life straightened around within a year, I'll reconsider. Otherwise, I'm filing for divorce. Do you want the money? Sign it."

Phillip didn't move. "What about divvying up our assets?"

She scoffed, "What assets? I don't have any assets. As far as I know, you don't have any assets. Even if you do, I don't want them."

Phillip pursed his lips and rubbed his chin, "You're not hiding anything?"

"I drive a second hand motorcycle because that piece of junk you left me died. You can have it too, if you'll leave me alone."

"Nah. You keep it." Again, he rubbed his chin where the shadow of a day's beard grew. His blue eyes glinted. He was in expensive jeans and a taut black T-shirt. Sleek.

She smoothed the papers on the desk and laid a pen on them. "Come on. I promise to give you every penny I have."

He traced some scratches on the table, then bent to sign both sets of papers where she indicated. She verified the signatures and faxed a copy to Culcallen. She handed him one set. "Here. Unless you get straight, we're through, Phillip. Don't come back until you're serious."

"My money?"

"Wait on the sofa." Phillip acted as if she didn't mean it. When she didn't move, he snorted and went to sit on the sofa. Trudy opened her purse and pulled out the checkbook. She sat at the desk and opened the computer. Pulling up her savings account she transferred money to her checking account. Then she wrote him a check. "This is the last time, Phillip. I'll close this account as soon as your check clears. This drains both accounts."

Phillip licked his lips. "Transferring money on line. You've come a long way from hiding it in your room. You always were resourceful. It's too bad you were as rebellious as your father said. It's why our marriage failed. We could've been a great team, but you never wanted to work with me."

She handed him the check. "I never wanted to be a con artist. Take it and get out."

"This is only $500. You promised me eight thousand."

"I promised you all I had. $500 is all I have."

Phillip glanced about the room.

"Go ahead. Tear the place apart. You won't find anything. That's it. Everything. Every dime I've saved. It's yours. It's a good deal. My mother and I won't press charges for forgery nor for involuntary manslaughter in causing Dad's death. It's a very good deal. Now, leave me alone."

Phillip's jaw hardened. "You lied. You tricked me."

"I didn't lie, but you certainly taught me a few tricks. And Phillip, if you ever forge my name again or if you change the amount on this check, I will press charges for everything to the full extent of the law."

The hit was unexpected. Trudy reeled into the wingback chair. Enraged, she sprang up and karate-chopped him a couple of times.

"Whoa." He grabbed her wrists, overpowered her, and threw her to the floor. He pounced on her. The full weight of his body crushing into her ribs as she fought him. He laughed. "You surprised me. I guess there still is a fire-ball in there somewhere."

"Let me up."

"We sure had some good times before you got boring."

"Before I came to my senses," she gasped, bucking against him.

Phillip pressed his mouth over hers. Trudy tried to bite him. Phillip laughed again, bounced on her, expelling her breath. He leapt to his feet. Trudy lay panting on the floor. The room whirled, then righted again.

Phillip stuffed the check into his jeans. Grabbing her purse, he pawed through all the pockets to make sure nothing was tucked away. He took the twenty dollar bill he found. "So long, Trudy. You'll never be sophisticated or the woman of adventure you dreamed of being. You can dress in a classy evening gown, but you'll always be that back-forty farm hick."

He strode over to the FAX machine, set it on top of the laptop computer. He pulled both plugs. "For my inconvenience." He picked them up and stood still, looking at her. The harshness of his face softened into regret, or sorrow, or longing. She couldn't be sure what it was. It was a momentary flash, then he was gone, leaving the door wide open.

He'd actually hit her. It was proof of the progression of his addiction and his desperation. Kathy had tried to tell her. Trudy pulled herself onto the couch. The pain in her cheek radiated into her eye and down her jawline. Crying made it hurt more, but the angry tears kept falling.

Anger at him. Anger at his sickness. Anger at herself for still having feelings for him, for being so tied to him. She punched the couch, grunting with each thrust until she was too exhausted to continue. She collapsed into a heap. After a while, the huge, convulsing sobs subsided into hiccups.

Trudy closed the outside door and made her way to the refrigerator. She pulled ice cubes from the freezer section, wrapped them in a towel, and pressed them against her cheek. She wished she'd worked harder at karate. If he ever came back she'd be much more effective, because this was never going to happen to her again. He would never hurt her physically again. He wouldn't steal from her. She wouldn't let him. It was over. Of course, Phillip might never come back for her. She missed him already.

Trudy dialed Kathy. The call went to voice mail, but she left no message. She called Carol. "I've had an intruder. I need to make a report. Can you drive me to the police station?"

# Chapter Twenty-four

Next morning, in the office, Trudy was typing a steady fifty-six words a minute when Peter entered, looking a little worse for the wear from his after-party party. She greeted him and let him settle at his desk before she approached him. She sent up a little prayer that he wouldn't fire her over this. "I have some bad news."

He paled, set down his pen and leaned back in his chair. "Is Honey hurt?"

"No, your precious Porsche is in fine shape. By the way, she is one honey of a ride."

He relaxed and then stiffened again. "Did a client back out of a contract?"

She shook her head. "Last night my estranged husband came by. He stole your FAX machine."

Peter frowned.

Trudy really didn't want to say the next part. "And the computer."

Peter's frown deepened. His eyes flashed. "What do you think he'll do with it?"

"Knowing Phillip, he needs the money. He'll sell. Probably wipe everything off of it first. Hopefully."

"How much damage can he do?"

"If he's feeling vindictive, he could try to sabotage you. He'd only try once or twice, out of fear they'd track him down. You haven't lost anything. It was all backed up. I've made up a list of the clients that were on that computer. I wanted you to know before I called them. I'll explain the computer was stolen and tell them not to talk to anyone, including vendors and suppliers, only to you or me personally."

"Do it. Then call all the vendors and suppliers, too. Did you report this to the police?"

Trudy felt the heat climb her neck and nest in her cheeks at the humiliating memory. She nodded and pointed at her bruised cheek that make-up didn't quite hide. "Last night. They said even though I let him in the apartment, it's aggravated robbery because he hit me and took property against my will. That's a felony. If they catch him, it's three to sixteen years in prison."

"When they catch him, Trudy. Nobody steals from me and gets away with it."

"When they catch him," Trudy repeated. She thought the likelihood remote until she noticed Peter's set jaw. Besides, Phillip was desperate and desperation breeds mistakes. That's what the cop who took the report said, but it seemed a small crime in a very big city.

Even though she tried to keep the theft quiet, Trudy noticed she no longer was asked to house sit. This suited Carol fine. She had wanted Trudy to stay with her and Kim throughout the summer.

Without house-sitting duties, Trudy put more overtime into her work to make it up to Peter. Any spare time she did take, she helped Carol co-ordinate Kim's graduation party.

This close interaction afforded Trudy's first glimpse into how perfectionistic Carol could be. The day of the party, Carol spent twenty minutes arranging and rearranging the same flowers and photos on the mantel.

Trudy said, "Enough already. It's lovely."

Carol kneaded her hands together. "I want everything to be perfect. My baby girl will only graduate high school once."

"At this rate, you'll still be arranging them when she graduates college." Trudy laughed to take the edge out of her voice.

"I've seen you work. You're a perfectionist, too."

"Maybe, but I'm not compulsive. I roll with the flow. There's a beginning, a middle, an end. All done. On to the next thing."

"I wish I could be like that. I always say I won't, but every special occasion I get like this. Keep me in check, will you?"

Trudy stood. She adjusted the reddish orange bolero over her yellow-gold sundress. "Sure. I've got it handled. After all, I work for Peter. Whatever monkey wrench Peter or his clients throw in the works, I always twist it to our advantage."

Carol put her hands on her hips. "Don't compare me to him."

Trudy raised her eyebrows. "That got a rise out of you. What's going on?"

Carol waved the question away. "Later. Come on, Ms. Twister, let's get those sandwiches set out. Thanks for helping Kim and me make them up last night."

Carol and Trudy entered the kitchen as Kim wrestled Franz the huge greyhound she was dog-sitting through the back door.

Minnie skittered between Kim and Carol, leaping high in her excitement at greeting all of the people she loved as if they'd been away a month. In mere seconds, she wrapped her leash around Franz's back leg and was firmly lashed to his undercarriage. Franz's face was even with the counter top. He peered up at them with a puzzled expression and stood still, panting. The beagle let loose with a bellow to call attention to the urgency of the situation.

The women laughed. Kim disentangled Minnie. No longer distracted, Franz's eyes scanned with interest the top of the island where Carol was removing cellophane from platters of sandwiches.

"Oh, no you don't." Carol said. "You better crate him before he gets into trouble."

Kim urged him into his crate, and then settled Minnie in hers. She wound up the leashes. "The platters of sandwiches look attractive, Trudy. The garnish is a nice touch. Did you serve sandwiches at your graduation?"

"No. Family and friends all brought potluck. It was the same as for every other graduation, wedding, anniversary, or funeral in our small community. Everybody knew what everybody else would bring. It rarely varied. Good down home food from the breadbasket of America. Not cuisine, but do those farmers' wives know how to cook. Fried chicken, potato salad, ham, casseroles, I could go on."

Kim laughed. "I'm getting stuffed thinking about it."

Carol eyed the sandwich platter. "Do you think this is okay?"

Kim rolled her eyes. "Mom, it's great. I didn't want a sit-down meal. This is perfect. And I licked each of the mixing bowls clean last night. Everything was delicious."

Trudy nodded. "This will be grand. I'll set them out. People will be coming soon."

Carol continued to stare uncertainly at the platters.

Kim waved a hand in front of her mother's face. "I better go wash my hands and change clothes."

"Phew. That stinks of dog." Carol turned her face away. Kim laughed and kissed Carol's cheek.

Trudy admired the affectionate display. She promised herself if she ever had a daughter, it would be like this, more spontaneity, more moments of rejoicing and laughter and fun.

Carol touched her daughter's arms when Kim started to leave. "Oh. Kim, I laid a dress out on your bed for you to wear today."

The happy smile dissolved into a pout. "Mom, I'm not a kid. I have an outfit all picked out."

"Are you sure? Because Trudy and I thought you might like to wear that pink and red sundress you were admiring at the mall last week."

Kim squealed. She hugged Carol and drew Trudy in, too. "You both are the best. Thank you. Thank you." She dashed up the stairs. Carol beamed after her disappearing form. "That was worth it."

Trudy blinked the mist from her eyes and cleared her throat. "I better get to it. Oh, don't worry about the food. I'll keep everything stocked. Your only job is to visit with guests."

The bright sunshiny day brought out loads of family and friends, who also brought friends, far more than Carol had planned to entertain at the open house. They crowded in the door right at the start of the party and no one seemed eager to leave.

Still, Trudy was confident they would have plenty to eat. Carol's worry-wort zealousness had caused them to prepare far more food than could possibly be consumed in one afternoon. She picked up an empty platter from the serving table and set one full of tuna sandwiches in its place. Trudy measured fresh ingredients into the punch bowl.

Another group of friends arrived and Carol brought them over to introduce to Trudy. When they drifted off, Trudy headed into the kitchen for another platter of chicken salad sandwiches.

The counter was empty. Every sandwich and even the wad of cellophane was gone. Empty platters and a few crumbs remained on the floor. Of the two cakes that had rested on the huge island one remained. The other was on the floor in a half-eaten smear. Franz the huge greyhound straddled the pan. His paws and snout a gloopy mess. Past him, Minnie, the beagle stood on top of the table working her way through one of the cakes on the table.

Trudy shrieked, "Minnie."

Franz leaped backward guiltily, splattering hunks of cake and frosting across the cupboards, but the beagle braced herself and went into hyper-drive wolfing down cake.

Carol appeared. "What happened? No. No. No."

"Get Franz. He's getting it everywhere," Trudy shouted as she latched onto Minnie's collar. Minnie yanked away, scrambling across the table, gulping cake as she went. Trudy renewed her grip and pulled Minnie back across the table.

"I'll get him all right. Come here, Franz." Carol spoke through gritted teeth. The usually compliant Franz must've heard the murderous tone. He took one look at Carol and darted around the table, trying to escape into the pantry. Franz crashed into Trudy, who lost her footing. She released Minnie's collar and grabbed the table. Immediately, Minnie leaped from the table toward the island and dove head first into the last cake with mouth open wide, gobbling as she went.

Trudy steadied herself. Wrapping the beagle's wriggling body in a bear hug she lifted her off the table. "How much did you eat? You're twice your size."

Trudy carried Minnie to the dog crate, launched her inside, and closed the door. Minnie bayed once in protest at being removed before she'd finished her snack, but was quickly distracted by the frosting on her feet and set to licking herself clean.

Franz gave up his temporary rebellion either because he saw his partner in crime had been put in the pokey or perhaps he simply thought he'd be safer in the crate from the crazy woman chasing him, despite slip-sliding through the mess. Franz avoided Carol's clutch and meekly walked into his crate. Trudy secured the latch.

Carol collapsed against the counter. "How'd they get out?"

"I don't know. Probably one of the kids wandered in here."

The kitchen floor, walls, tables, and chairs were covered in greasy white frosting. "Oh, no. Look at this." Carol started to put her hands to her head. They were only half-way up when Trudy grasped them. "Don't. You'll get frosting all over yourself."

Carol looked at her hands and groaned. She went to the sink and washed in hot water and soap while Trudy used a clean dish cloth to scrub the places where frosting clung to Carol's dress. Carol gestured to the kitchen and her voice cracked. "It's everywhere. It'll take hours to clean."

"It only seems like it. The bad thing is they ate all the sandwiches, and you have about a quarter of a cake left. That's already out there.

"It's not enough. That'll be gone in no time. We're barely halfway through the party."

"Carol, I know you made extra food, do you really need more?"

"Andy's whole family is due in about an hour. Only half of Kim's friends are here. We've got church people and teachers and co-workers and 4-H'rs, and—"

"I get it. I'll get more sandwich stuff."

"And more cake."

"Right. No problem. What about this mess? Maybe we should let the dogs finish cleaning it up."

"Ha-ha. I'd consider it if Minnie didn't already look as if she's about to explode." Carol bent down and pulled out a bucket and grease-cutting dish soap from under the sink.

"You can't do that. You'll get all messy. You have guests. Go take care of them. I'll handle it. Why don't you go find Eric and Ruby? They'll give me a hand."

"Right." Carol stepped over the mess. She wiped her shoes with paper towels so as not to track it into the rest of the house.

Trudy found a phone book and called bakeries. Most were closed on Sunday. She tried the nearest big grocery store. No cakes were available.

"How is that possible?" Trudy demanded into the phone as Eric and Ruby entered the kitchen. She pointed to the mess and they smirked. She pointed at the bucket and they looked at each other and glanced back towards the door. She frowned and pointed harder. They exchanged looks again and nodded. "Well, when will the next batch be done? Forget it. I'll try someplace else."

Trudy disconnected the call. She handed Ruby a plastic trash bag and a wide dustpan. She put a dish cloth in Eric's hands.

Eric said, "What happened in here?"

"Franz and Minnie."

As if to confirm it, Minnie started heaving. "I ain't cleaning that up," Eric said, shaking his head vigourously.

Trudy raised her eyebrows. "You 'ain't' college boy?"

"I don't go 'til the fall."

"Ah. Well, don't worry about what's happening in the dog crates, unless you hear one of them having difficulty breathing. One or both ate plastic wrap. My bet is on Minnie." She started filling the sink with hot, soapy water. "Can you two handle cleaning up this mess? I've got to buy a cake and some more food to replace what the dogs ate."

Ruby and Eric exchanged glances a third time. Trudy said. "I know your knees still bother you, Eric. Ruby can handle the floor and you can handle the counters and table. Come on, you like to call Carol 'Mom Streeter'. She'd do it for you if this disaster were your graduation party."

Eric shrugged. "Yeah, sure. Come on, Ruby."

Aprons and rubber gloves were distributed. Once they were into the task, Trudy found her boss in the living room. She pulled Peter aside. "Remember the promo work for that hoity-toity patisserie?"

"Yes."

"Would you call the man to see if he'll open up and give us a cake? Carol doesn't have anything left to serve. The dogs ate everything and what they didn't is smeared all over the kitchen."

Peter looked as if he not only found the suggestion outrageous, but cheeky. Glancing over at Carol a look of calculation replaced the annoyed one. "Absolutely."

By the time Trudy got to the patisserie, the master chef was putting the finishing touches on the cake. "Thanks a million for doing this," she said.

"No problem. Anything for Peter Faulkinroy."

Trudy looked at two huge sheets of decorated cake. "How'd you do it?"

"I scraped off the other party's name and put in 'Congratulations Kim'. I'll get another ready before my other clients come tomorrow morning. Don't forget this one." He pointed to an elaborate small three-tiered cake, beautifully decorated.

"It's gorgeous. How am I going to transport it?"

"No problem." He showed her how to dismantle and reassemble it. They loaded the car.

Trudy said. "How much do I owe you?"

"Peter's taking care of it. He said I could use it for promotional purposes." He placed an inch deep pile of cards in her hands. "Now, if you'll put my cards on the table and talk me up a bit."

"Sure. Not a problem. You're a lifesaver."

He grinned. "If you're really grateful, you'll go out with me."

Startled, she regarded him for the first time. He was good looking and well-built as if lifting large sacks of flour and sugar was better exercise than working out in the gym. Except for a powdery sugar glistening on his shirt sleeves and hands, he was clean and his black hair was trimmed.

Trudy panicked. "Sure, can I bring my six kids?"

His brown eyes seemed to bulge. "Six kids?"

"It's hard to find a sitter. They're all hyperactive like their dad was. Hey, do you think they can visit here in the bakery? I'm sure they'd love to help decorate a cake. We could all do it together. Kind of like a family thing."

"Uh—"

"Hey, we can talk about this later. I gotta fly."

He looked relieved. "Sure, later."

Trudy ran around Carol's car and got in the driver's seat. She shifted into drive and then pushed it back into park. Shaking her head, she went back in the store.

The baker was already mixing up a new batch of cake. "Did you forget something?"

Trudy said, "Yes. My manners. I don't have six kids."

He dusted his hands, folded his muscular arms, and cocked his handsome head.

"I don't have any kids, but I am married. Legally separated. I don't talk about it. It's why I don't date. You seem nice. Your offer scared me, but it kind of made my day as well. Thanks."

He gave a tiny shrug and nodded. His voice was kind. "If you're ever single…"

Her throat tightened and tears seemed imminent. She aimed her thumb at the door. "I better go."

She drove back to the party looking twice at every intersection to prevent any further cake mishaps. When she reached the kitchen, Eric was putting a bucket away while Opal wrung out sponges. Ruby was on her knees drying the inside of Minnie's dog crate. Culcallen dressed in damp jogging shorts and T-shirt, sat on the floor. He toweled the beagle's ears. The pleasant scent of oatmeal shampoo almost erased the smell of wet dog. Trudy said, "I see that reinforcements arrived. That's great. Thanks."

Culcallen gathered up the towels and stood. "We know what it's like to have dogs. We thought we'd lend a hand."

Opal laughed. "Dogs. Can't live with them. Can't live without them. Luckily, Culcallen had his gym bag in the car with a change of clothes. The neighbor let us use his yard and hose so we didn't disturb the party."

Carol flitted into the room. She oohed and aahed over the cakes and hugged Trudy. "I was getting panicky, the table is almost bare. You're a life saver."

Trudy said, "No worries. It was a piece of cake."

"Oh, you." Carol jostled her arm. "These are beautiful. I don't know where you found them at this late date."

The front doorbell sounded. Trudy handed Carol one tier and led the way to the serving table in the dining room. "Peter arranged it. I only picked them up. Although I had a close call of the dating kind."

"What was wrong with that? Was he ugly?"

Trudy realized her mistake at once. Why'd she ever say anything? She pointed to the cakes. "No, he's good looking and clean and very talented. I don't date."

"Why don't you date?"

"I'll tell you about it sometime."

Kim said, "I've been wondering about that, Trudy. Why don't you date?"

Trudy glanced up from setting the top tier on the cake. "What's got you all aglow? Did you find the man of your dreams?"

"Kind of." Kim waved her hands to draw attention to a delivery man with a tray of three-foot party sub sandwiches. "These subs are popular now. Mom this is great. I didn't think we could afford all this. Very cool. Thank you so much."

"This must be Peter's doing," Carol said. "Be sure to thank him."

At six thirty, only a few friends remained, hanging out or playing volleyball in the backyard while Carol's out of town in-laws lounged throughout the house, gathering in small groups for discussion. The red-haired cousin, Jasmine, about eight or nine years old, trailed after Kim asking a million questions. It was a relaxed, homey scene.

Trudy picked up her purse and spoke to the group at large. "It was fun meeting all of you, but I've got somewhere else I need to be."

"Like where?" Kim asked.

Carol said, "Kim, if she wanted us to know, she'd tell us. Trudy, Thanks a million. You've already done so much. I couldn't have done it without you."

"Don't go. You said you were going to tell us why you don't date. You can tell us while we all clean up from the party," Kim said.

"There's plenty of family around to help." Carol turned to the in-laws. "Right?"

Various family members assured her that was the case. Jasmine, the young red-headed cousin piped up. "I'll help."

"If you stay," Kim said. "You might get to meet Larry Dare. I met him at the agency and he said he might come by."

"I'll meet him another time."

"Besides, if you stay, then I can leave sooner. Some of the gang is getting together at the pool."

"You really are a pampered princess, aren't you?" Trudy gave her a hug.

Kim bestowed a beatific smile. "Yes. Yes I am."

Trudy laughed. "You may find college a bit more challenging."

Carol nudged Kim's shoulder. "You're not going anywhere, princess, until this mess is cleared. Start gathering glasses and plates and get the dishwasher going. Pronto."

"All right," Kim readily agreed. "Come on, Jasmine. It's time to play Cinder-girl." The little girl followed Kim about the room, picking up dirty dishes. As if by prearranged signal the women relatives pitched in to clear up party litter. Some of the men took their cue and rose to help.

Carol lowered her voice and leaned toward Trudy. "However, if you wanted to stay I could use some help rousting Peter out of here. He seems to think that providing the cake and sandwiches entitles him to play host. He's cozying up to Andy's family like they hold the key to the city."

"You're on your own there. It's my day off. I only deal with Peter at work."

"Oh, boogers and snot-balls, as Jasmine says." Carol followed Trudy to the front door. She whispered, "In that case you do owe me an explanation about why you don't date."

"Ta-ta." Trudy sashayed down the walk, away from the party, away from questions about Phillip. She recalled that odd look of regret on his face before he walked out the door with Peter's equipment. Then she remembered that he'd hit her. She brightened remembering the time before that when he high-tailed it down the drive with Finn McCool close behind. By the time Trudy reached her motorcycle, a smile tugged at her face.

During the Al-Anon meeting that night she shared how Phillip was out of sight, but not entirely out of mind. She wavered between being glad he was gone and wondering if some of the more unsavory creditors had extracted their due on him permanently. She feared she'd never know. She feared she would.

After the meeting, she told Kathy about how she'd dreamed he'd come to her with his black wavy hair and blue eyes, melting her heart by singing "My Wild Irish Rose" as if she were the love of his life. "I hate that I still love that man."

Kathy said, "God will help you. We'll have to keep praying."

Trudy honestly didn't know how to keep praying to God when she was still mad at him for taking her father and for going to move Kathy away. If she admitted it, she was mad at him for her disillusionments, even if they were of her own making, because if God was so powerful, why didn't he change Phillip? It would be for Phillip's own good and for hers as well, not to mention in God's best interests. The best she could muster was gratitude that Kathy was praying for her. She gripped Kathy's arm where the snake tattoo was.

Kathy turned her head, a questioning look on her face. "Thanks. You're a good friend."

# Chapter Twenty-five

On movie night, Carol popped the popcorn while Trudy set up the DVD. "I think Kim is going to like this movie."

"She's late," Carol said.

"How's she getting home from work?"

"I'm not sure. She said she had a ride."

"Let's go ahead and start the movie, then we'll replay it when she gets here," Trudy said and picked up the remote control.

The credits at the end of the movie were playing before they heard a motorcycle pull into the driveway. Kim entered the house arm-in-arm with a tall, stick-thin, young man, who walked with a swagger. When he caught sight of himself in the wall mirror, he ran a hand over his thick blond thatch to insure not a hair was out of place. Trudy almost rolled her eyes when he gave his reflection a self-satisfied smile.

After introducing Larry Dare, Kim said, "Larry has been offered a part in a movie they're shooting in L.A. He's really going places. He's going to make a big name for himself."

Carol made all the appropriate congratulatory sounds.

Larry said, "It's about time. They've been promising me a role for a year."

Carol said, "What type of role is it?"

"I'll be the older brother in a teen chick flick. It's not the role I was wanting. Unfortunately, I'm too mature to play the fifteen-year-old lead, but it's Hollywood. Once I get out there, get noticed, they'll snap me up like that." Larry snapped his fingers. "At least, that's what my agent says."

Kim eyed him adoringly. "I know they will. Don't you think so, Mom?"

Carol said, "I'm sure the agent knows what he's talking about."

Everything about the kid made Trudy's hair stand on end. He looked nothing like Phillip, yet the swagger, the way he held his head, and the way he talked was straight out of Phillip 101. The kid was an actor and one step away from being a con man, if he wasn't already. She said, "Is Larry Dare your given name?"

He smirked. "Yeah. My agent gave it to me. Pretty cool, huh?" He gave Kim a gentle hip bump. "Hey, go get changed."

Kim pulled her eyes away from him long enough to dash up the stairs.

Trudy said, "When do you leave for California?"

"Filming starts in a three weeks, so I leave in two. I figure I can drive it in a few days."

"Does the studio put you up out there?"

"Naw, but the weather is good. It's not going to be a problem. There's lots of cheap places to stay."

Trudy snorted. "Who told you that?"

He looked at her as if she were a moron. "Everybody knows that."

"That's not the experience I had out there. You need a plan."

"I got a plan. A buddy of mine got hired and moved out there. I hear he's staying in housing for actors and models. Once I find him,

I'll probably stay on his sofa for the first week or two until I find my own place."

Kim rushed down the stairs and again had eyes only for Larry. "I'm ready." She had brushed her hair into a ponytail and wore jeans and a peasant blouse. "I don't know when we'll be back. We're going to a party."

Carol said, "Who's giving a party this late at night?"

"Some people from the talent agency and it's not late because everybody works. We can't do it earlier."

Larry took her hand to lead her out the door, but somehow still managed to hang back long enough to check his image in the mirror.

Carol pulled the front curtain aside and peered out the window. The motorcycle roared away. She let the curtain drop. "I don't like him."

Trudy tipped her head back and stared at the ceiling. "He's trouble all right. Did you see the way she looked at him?"

"I'm going to have to tell her to stay away from him."

Trudy groaned. "Don't do that. That'll only drive her straight into his arms."

"You want me to act like this is okay?"

"I want you to play it cool. Don't get flustered. Only if she asks can you express your concerns. This kid will be gone in a couple of weeks. Wait it out."

Carol seemed to weigh her words. "You're probably right."

What do you want to watch next?"

"I don't care. You pick."

Much later that night, Trudy and Carol were watching *To Kill a Mockingbird* when Larry Dare's motorcycle pulled into the drive. Trudy picked the last pieces from a bowl of popcorn as Kim bounded through the door and raced up the stairs in a blur.

"Kim," Carol called. "Come in here a minute."

"Play it cool," Trudy warned.

"I will. I will."

Kim descended the stairs with a great show of reluctance. When she entered, her face was tight and her hands were on her hips. "I know I'm past curfew, but I'm eighteen now. I should come and go when I want."

Carol paused the movie. "I was going to ask if you had a good time."

Confusion crossed Kim's face. "Oh. Yes. The party was up near Carmel. We were riding around. I like riding bikes."

"I like it, too," Trudy said. "There's an unofficial race place up that way. Is that where you were?"

Kim considered the question. "Oh, uh, yes."

"Did you get to race?"

Carol's eyes widened at the thought. Kim took in her mother's expression. Her long pause before choosing her words spoke volumes. "Oh, you know, Larry would never let me drive his motorcycle. He loves that bike more than life itself." Kim shifted from one foot to the other. She lifted her thumb like a hitchhiker and aimed toward the stairs. "Well, then, I guess I'll head up to bed."

Trudy called out, "See you in the morning."

"Love you," Carol said.

Once Kim had ascended the stairs, Carol whipped around to Trudy. "That boy is racing motorcycles with my daughter on the back. She could get hurt."

"Sure she could. She could also get hurt when someone T-bones an old truck she's riding in. You can't keep her completely safe. She's testing the bounds. So what? Didn't you ever do that?"

"No, not really."

"If you don't let the reins out a little she'll try something riskier."

Carol hissed, "Like what?"

"She could decide to go to California with Larry Dare."

Carol reared back and stared at Trudy. "What do you know that I don't know?"

"I've seen the looks she's giving him. The looks he's giving her. The whispers. I suspect she'll tell you soon. She's putting it off because she expects you to blow up about it."

"She's got that right. I'll take care of this right now." Carol sprang to her feet.

Trudy stood and blocked Carol's way. "That's exactly what you don't want to do. Please don't do that."

"You think it's a good idea to let my eighteen-year-old daughter go roaring off across the continent with some star-wannabe biker dude?"

Trudy's ginger locks brushed her face as she shook her head. She hooked her hair behind her ears. "No. Of course not. He's a loser. She'd probably end up waiting tables to keep them in a room while he's playing fast and loose with starlets. He won't stay the course. She'd be very lonely and very unhappy."

Carol squeezed her hands to her head and sank onto the couch. "I'm confused. You said—"

"I'm saying don't do what she expects. Tell her you don't like him or act like you do, but either way tell her she has the freedom to make her own choice and that you'll support her. Then, tell her that she and Larry have an obligation to attend the family function."

"What family function?"

"Call your in-laws and make one up. Let it come from them. Isn't there a birthday or anniversary or reunion you can have? After that, invite him to dinner and to movie night and get her friends involved. Immerse Kim and Larry in as many social functions as you can with people she loves and respects. He's not educated. He's not socially adept. Help her see that without being obvious."

Carol locked gazes with Trudy and shook her head. "Why?"

"Oh, for Pete's sake, do I have to spell it out? Right now everything is on Larry's terms. What they do, whom they see, where they go. They're spending a lot of time alone, too.

"She's got to see for herself what kind of guy he is when he's interacting with others. She needs to see who he is while engaging in the give and take of ordinary life, the kind of life she likes to lead. We can't open her eyes for her, but we can certainly give her some opportunities to wipe the stardust from her own eyes and see him for what he is."

"What if he doesn't come to any of these things?"

"Then, she'll see him ignore all the people and things she loves. It'll draw a line."

"It's risky."

"Riskier than getting into a big argument in which you tell her no way and she says she can make up her own mind and leaves?"

"What if we do this and she still goes?"

"Then, it's no worse than what it was and at least you won't have cut communication."

Carol nodded slowly.

Trudy said, "There's another option. Perhaps we're wrong and we'll see Larry Dare is a stand-up guy after all."

Carol snorted.

"Yeah. That's the way I feel, Carol, but Kim has to discover that for herself. Better she has opportunities to find out now than if she's a thousand miles away and all alone."

Carol looked panicky as she mouthed, "a thousand miles away."

"Look, Carol. You've raised her well. She's made good choices up to now, hasn't she?"

"Pretty much."

"She's a smart girl. Trust her and, as you keep telling me, trust God to watch out for her."

Carol swallowed hard. "Okay. Let's do this."

Trudy grabbed a tablet of paper and together they sketched out plans. When they were done, Carol ran her finger down the to-do outline. "Trudy, did anyone ever tell you that you're devious?"

"No. They tell me I'm a remarkable organizer."

"Well, now you can add delightfully devious to your resume."

# Chapter Twenty-six

That Sunday, the four of them sat down at the kitchen table for lasagna and salad. Kim said to Larry, "I thought you were meeting me at church."

"Oh, yeah. I was, but my agent called. I couldn't get him off the phone until it was too late. Was it good?"

"Yes," Kim said, "It was about conquering complaining."

"Interesting," he said. "Useful, I'm sure. I know girls complain a lot."

Kim shot him a look and was about to protest when Trudy spoke up. "Let's thank God for this food."

They bowed their heads and prayed. Larry didn't join in, but he did bow his head. As soon as they finished, Carol added, "I'm glad you could join us for lunch, Larry."

The ladies spread white cloth napkins across their laps. Larry Dare left his on the table. Carol passed him a bowl of green beans.

Larry heaped some on his plate. "Thanks for the invitation. Every meal I don't have to buy is more money to take with me to L.A."

"Very practical," Trudy said as she cut the lasagna. "Would you like a piece?"

"Does it have meat in it?"

"Yes, of course."

"I'm vegan."

Carol apologized for not knowing.

Kim said, "You ate a burger and fries the other night."

"Yeah," Larry said, "That was before I talked with my agent. He said I have to be really thin to play this part."

Trudy said, "The things they make actors do."

"You're telling me. It's always some ridiculous demand, but it'll be worth it when I'm a star."

Trudy held the bowl of greens out to him. "Salad?"

"You bet, Trudy. Hand me that Italian dressing."

Carol took a bite of lasagna and said, "So tell us about this great part you have. What's the name of the movie? We'll be sure to watch it."

"It doesn't work that way. What the production goes by now isn't usually what the movie will end up being called."

"I didn't know that," Carol said. "Have you seen the script yet?"

"Enough to know I can be that character. My agent said they're still making changes. I'll get the full script when I get out there."

They continued to talk about Larry's past, present, and future through the rest of the meal. He seemed happiest with that subject. "Hey, Kim, I gotta go. I've got plans with the guys."

Kim waved him off from the front yard. Trudy joined her there. "Biking is a rush, isn't it?"

Kim smiled a dreamy smile and sighed. "Yes. And so is Larry Dare."

A desire to protect Kim raised a deeper understanding of what drove her parents to behave as they did. She knew she had to tread carefully. "I dated someone like Larry when I was your age. He was hot. I was the envy of all the girls."

Kim smiled a knowing smile. "Oh, yeah?"

Trudy smiled back. "Oh, yes. He had everything. Good looks. Loads of charm. A big appetite for life. He had big, big dreams and always wanted everything all at once. He planned that we'd be the wealthiest, grandest, most stylish couple in the big city. It was thrilling for a while. He was a real ball of fire."

"What happened?"

Trudy crossed her arms. A long, staggered sigh escaped her. "I got burned."

Kim looked down at her feet. "I'm sorry."

"So am I." Trudy turned to go back in the house. She paused, and added, "Kim, be sure you see the man and not just the magic."

On Saturday, Kim's aunt and uncle called. "Jasmine's birthday party for her friends is this afternoon. We've been called away. We can't cancel. Everything's here. I know your mom's at a speaking engagement, but you're an adult now. Would you mind supervising the party?"

Kim heard Jasmine in the background. "Please. Please. Please."

She held a brief conversation with Larry. "Sure. Larry and I can come over and take care of that."

"Great. We have to leave here about twelve, the party starts at two. You'll have to do set up, run games, serve food, and do the cleanup. Parents will pick the kids up between four and five. We should be back about eight or nine."

Kim and Larry arrived at Jasmine's house at noon. Kim's aunt shoved a party-planner list into Kim's hands while her uncle pumped Larry's hand and thanked him.

Kim looked over the list. "It doesn't look as if she's missed anything. This should be easy. The first thing is to decorate. Larry, would you please blow up these balloons while I hang streamers in the dining room?"

Jasmine, eager to help, pulled strips of tape for Kim to secure the streamers. When they were finished, Larry had only blown up half the balloons. "I've only got so much air, Kim."

Jasmine pointed to a box sitting beside the bags of party supplies. "Why don't you use the helium balloon inflator?"

"Because I didn't know there was one, smarty-pants. Why didn't you say so sooner?"

"It was sitting right there. I didn't think I had to."

Larry finished inflating the balloons while Kim set the table with paper plates, cups, and plastic silverware. Jasmine followed behind her placing a colorful party napkin at each setting.

Everything was in place by the time two boys and seven girls arrived. The noise level raised even as they stacked gifts on a table. Kim started the relay races, hide-and-seek, and pin-the-tail-on-the-donkey. When the girls found out Larry was an actor, they gathered around him.

Larry breathed some helium and chased Jasmine and the girls around the house squeaking like Mickey Mouse while acting like

Frankenstein. The girls laughed themselves silly. Kim smiled approvingly at Larry. He was such fun.

The little boys decided it was fun, too. They found a pair of scissors to clip the balloon tips so they could do the same. The ten kids running, screaming, and pulling to get control of the balloons seemed more like thirty. Kim could hardly hear herself yell above the din. She grabbed Larry's arm and spoke close to his ear. "Go cook the hot dogs."

Larry headed to the backyard. Kim opened up the packages of buns and broke up an argument between two girls. After what seemed like forever, Larry announced, "Hot dogs are done."

The news was passed around. Kids scrambled to the table and the bedlam finally quieted. He placed the plate of dogs in front of Jasmine. Some were twice the size, some had split open, and others looked as if they were still raw. Jasmine screwed her face up. "What are those?"

Larry shrugged. "Hot dogs."

Kim said, "What happened?"

Larry shrugged again. "Hey, what did you expect? I'm vegan. Anyway, I think something was wrong with that gas grill. I couldn't get it to work so I put them in the microwave."

"What'd you do? Cook the whole package at once?"

"It was faster that way."

Jasmine said, "We can't eat that. They look funny."

"Try it," Kim snapped. "I'm sure they taste fine."

Larry disappeared during the meal, but Kim was kept busy keeping cups and plates filled and didn't have time to find him. Then she snapped pictures for her aunt's scrap book while Jasmine opened presents. After cake and ice cream, most of the little girls settled in to look over and play with Jasmine's new gifts.

Kim sent the boys off to play video games. Kim helped herself to a piece of cake and a few moments of relative quiet. She took the first bite, closed her eyes, and savored the sweetness. When she opened her eyes, one of the boys stared at her from across the table.

She said, "Is there a problem?"

"That big kid won't let me have a turn."

"What big kid?"

"In there." Kim followed him to the TV room where the other boy and Larry were engaged in a video battle on the gaming device. "That big kid."

Kim put her hands on her hips. "Larry, what are you doing?"

"I'm winning."

"Why can't this kid have a turn?"

"He will. Neither of us have died yet."

"It's a kid's party. He's a guest. Get off and let him play."

Larry paused the game. He shot Kim a look of disgust. "Come here, kid. It's all yours."

When the last guest had been waved off from the curb, Kim returned to the house and started to store the food. She surveyed the general mess and disorder and went looking for Larry. She found him in the TV room. "Larry, you said you'd help me."

"I am. I'm keeping your kid cousin busy. You know, out of your hair."

Jasmine winked. "He's good. Usually by this point in the game, I've beaten my dad."

Kim shook her head. She went downstairs and finished cleaning by herself.

On Tuesday, Kim exited The Talent Agency and walked to where Larry Dare waited on his motorcycle. Ruby and Eric drove up and called to her. She waved. "Hi. What are you doing here?"

They piled out of Eric's new extended cab truck leaving their doors open and the engine running. They each opened a rear door and gestured. "Come on. It's a pool party at Ruby's. Her parents are gone for the evening. We have the house to ourselves. The whole gymnastics team is there and some of the drama club."

"Sounds fun."

Larry Dare dismounted from his motorcycle and put his arm around Kim's waist. "Nah, we're going riding."

"I guess we can't," Kim said. She frowned with disappointment.

Ruby said, "Come on, Kim. It might be one of the last times we see each other. We'll all be leaving for college in a few weeks."

Kim lowered her voice. "Larry, it'll be fun. Let's go. We always go riding. They're my friends. It won't cost anything."

"Ah, Babe, you've got to let go of these people. Why torture yourself?"

"Well," she said looking from Larry to her friends and back again. "I don't know."

285

"Anyway, you have to. We're kidnapping you." Ruby giggled as she hustled Kim around Eric's pickup and into the back seat.

"Yes, it's a friend-napping," Eric said. He muscled Larry into the closest open door. Eric and Ruby slammed the doors, jumped into the front seat, and roared out of the parking lot.

Kim immediately got into the plan, but Larry only gave in when they reached Ruby's elaborate house. "Hey, this isn't a bad place."

"Wait until you see the pool," Ruby said.

The Olympic size pool was large and blue and had both high and low diving boards. Girls and guys were already splashing about. Pop music blared. A few teens danced around the edge of the pool.

Larry nodded his head. "Not bad. Almost like a real Hollywood party."

Kim said, "I knew we'd have fun. I've known these kids since middle school. Some longer than that."

Ruby dangled Kim's bathing suit off her finger. "I slipped by your house and picked this up."

"Thanks, Ruby."

Eric pointed to a cabana. "Larry, there's extra swim trunks in there. Oh, and a fridge. Help yourself."

Larry and Kim entered different rooms in the cabana. By the time Kim came out in a red-checked one piece, Larry was in trunks and standing in front of the open fridge. "Hey, where's the beer?"

Kim said, "We're alcohol free. You don't need beer to party. Hand me a can of that cola, please." She took the can, popped it open, and took a long swallow. She was about to grab a handful of pretzels from a bowl on the bar when Ruby called to her.

"Come on Kim, we're going to have a diving competition."

"Great. Come on, Larry. This'll be fun." Kim dashed toward the pool.

"Okay," he said, "I'm good at swimming." He called to Kim several times over the next hour to watch him dive or cannonball, but somehow, Kim was always surrounded by her friends. Although he was a good swimmer, he didn't stand out from the others, because they were all good swimmers.

Then the guys took over the pool for some water polo while the girls sunbathed. Once the rules were explained to him, Larry held his own, but many of his shots were foiled by the others. After the game, the guys got out and the girls swam races against each other.

Kim caught sight of Larry, fully dressed at the edge of a group of guys, trying to impress them with his upcoming Hollywood role. She pulled the towel around her shoulders so her wet hair wouldn't drip down her back and went to him. "Why are you dressed?"

"The question Babe is why aren't you? I'm ready to go."

"The party isn't over, yet."

"I've hardly seen you for hours and hours, Kim. You've left me hanging here."

"It hasn't been hours and hours. You were playing water polo and then I swam some races. I thought we were all having fun. Aren't you having fun?"

"No."

"No?"

Ruby approached and snapped her towel at Kim. "Come on, we need you and Larry for water basketball."

Larry said, "Butt out, can't you see we're talking here?"

Ruby's face turned red beneath the freckles. She apologized. Kim scowled at Larry and turned to her friend. "I'll be there in a bit," she said. "Go on without me." When Ruby walked away, she added, "You had no call to talk to her like that. It was rude."

Larry pulled Kim along to the side of the house away from her friends. "Babe, this is one of the boring-est parties I've ever been to. No beer, no weed, no nothing."

"I'm sorry you feel that way. I'm having a wonderful time."

"These dudes got nothing interesting to say. All they talk about is their jobs and college courses and sports stuff."

Kim looked at him long and hard. "As opposed to you, your job, and Hollywood? I'm glad we're here. I'm going to miss my friends when I go east to college."

"I thought you were going to Hollywood with me."

"I never said that for sure."

"Well, I'm sure you did."

Kim shook her head. "No. Besides, you don't like these people and these people are me."

"That doesn't make sense."

"Yes, it does. These are my kind of people. If they bore you, then, I bore you."

"No. You see, that's where you're wrong. You have potential to change."

Kim held up a hand. "So, I'm only interesting if I change? No. It's best if I stick with my original plans. You go on to California alone."

Larry stepped back a pace. He put his hands on his hips and nodded his head appraisingly. "I'll do that. In fact, I could leave tonight."

"Do that."

"You'll be sorry." Larry stalked toward the driveway. He stopped, spun around. "Eric!"

"Yo, bro?"

"Give me a ride back to my bike."

"Sure man."

As Eric hustled to comply, Kim noticed none of her friends tried to dissuade Larry. Ruby pulled herself out of the pool and dripping water onto the concrete came to stand side by side with Kim. Ruby dabbed her face with a towel. "Why's Larry going?"

"He's a jerk. I'm sorry, Ruby. He shouldn't have talked to you like that."

Ruby shrugged. "Don't worry about it. It's not on you."

Larry Dare looked back once. Kim put her arm around Ruby's shoulders in an unspoken message that backed up her verbal choice. He shook his head and disappeared around the corner of the house.

"You two love birds have an argument?"

Kim grasped the ends of her towel and moved it back and forth across her neck. "More of an epiphany and a final good-bye. You know, Ruby, different isn't always better."

If Kim missed Larry Dare, it wasn't evident to the people around her. She worked her jobs, spent time with friends, and made school plans with her mother. Only in a few conversations with Trudy did she even mention his name.

Two weeks later, Trudy was lying out in a chaise lounge in the backyard enjoying the sunshine. From a shadier spot, Carol said, "You know, you've spoiled Kim again. She learned to do things for herself and now every time I turn around you're doing the laundry or fixing a meal."

"It'll only be for a few more weeks. Then, she'll be off to college. She can't get too spoiled in that short time. Besides, I don't mind doing all that to pay for the privilege of staying rent free. I'm grateful. I was in a jam. I've got to admit staying with you has been pleasant. I like meal times together and movie night, whether we go out or stay here. I'll miss it when I move out."

"I'll hate to see you go. The house will be entirely empty all at once. When exactly do you move?"

"I take over the lease on Kathy's apartment the weekend of the wedding."

"God really worked that out for you. This summer has been a good one, huh?"

"Hm." Trudy said noncommittally. Because of her police report, Phillip had been jailed pending arraignment for aggravated robbery.

290

Yet, he had the nerve to plead with her to put up bail. She'd refused, saying she didn't have the money, when she knew she would've refused even if she had the money.

Phillip even hinted that she should lie to help him beat the charges. Was the man delusional? He'd hit her.

The worst was, she'd even briefly considered it. If it weren't for her Al-Anon group support she might've caved. The whole episode kept her emotions roiling.

Yes, she'd been brave enough to stand up to Phillip, but not brave enough to tell Carol about him. She felt lucky that Carol didn't read the court reports in the newspaper.

She heard the house phone ring twice. Kim yelled, "I've got it."

Carol adjusted her sunglasses and turned her head toward Trudy. "Trudy, what happened at your old apartment?"

This was it. The time to share. Trudy smeared more sun tan lotion on her arms and snapped the pop top shut. She placed the bottle on the tiny glass-topped table beside her. "It was awful. It makes me angry just to think about it."

Kim appeared at the door. "Trudy, telephone. It sounds urgent."

# Chapter Twenty-seven

At the tone of her voice, Trudy and Carol sat upright. The smile was gone from Kim's face. Her eyes looked serious. She held the phone and lifted it slightly in offering, but didn't move from the doorway. Trudy pushed up out of the chair. "Who is it?"

"Someone called Sarah."

Trudy relieved Kim of the phone and sat at the kitchen table. "Hello, Sarah."

"I hope it was okay to call this number. I couldn't get you on yours."

"I left it up in my room charging. What's the matter?"

"It's your mother. She had a bad cold and then this morning, she sat down to do some knitting and didn't get up. I tried to wake her, but she was gone."

"Gone?"

"She's dead, dear. She's gone." Sarah broke down in tears. "I'm going to miss her. She was such a good friend. What am I going to do without her?"

Trudy let the older woman blubber and ramble. Sarah's worries mirrored her own. Her mom was dead. The last living relative she had, except for Phillip, but Phillip didn't count. He probably caused both her parents' deaths. Trudy didn't think she could forgive him this time. This was her mother.

Sarah's words penetrated. "She'd been missing your daddy so much. She really wanted to go. I guess it's a blessing. It doesn't feel like a blessing. I'm not very brave. Not like your mother."

"Yes, Mom was special. Thanks for calling me. I'll be there as soon as possible."

"Come right to my house. I still have your room ready."

Trudy sat a few minutes to compose herself before she went back outdoors. "My mom passed away."

"Oh, Trudy, no," Carol bolted to her feet and wrapped Trudy in a hug. Kim joined them.

Trudy pulled away. "First, I better call Peter. He'll probably want me to take work with me. I can pick it up on my way out of town. Oh, I don't have a car."

Carol shook a finger at her. "You will not take work. And I'm going with you. Kim's done with her receptionist job. She can come along. We'll take my car."

"Mom, you have to drive me to college. We have all my stuff to take. Dad's not here. You have to do it."

"Oh, nuts. That's right. Of course I'm taking you, Kim. I wasn't thinking." She turned back to Trudy. "What about borrowing the Cavalier?"

"They're using it this weekend."

"Trudy, can you fly?"

"It's okay. It's not like I have no way to get there. The bike will get me there and back safely." Trudy said.

"Motorcycles are cool," Kim added, as if that meant anything.

"You shouldn't be driving yourself. Isn't there someone else you can ask?"

There was no way Trudy would ask Kathy to pull herself away from wedding plans two weeks from the date. She couldn't ask her CMA friends to take off work or cancel vacations. The people at her Al-Anon meetings and those at the karate class were friendly acquaintances that she had never bothered to develop into friendships. Peter was the only other person close enough to be considered anything like a friend and he wasn't that, but a boss. There was no way she'd ask him, or would even want him along.

Trudy had thought she'd put down roots and made friends, but she'd only fooled herself. She'd been reserved with those who would have befriend her. A sense of loneliness and vulnerability blanketed her. She felt like a tiny speck in a very large world.

"No. There's no one else to ask, but I'm fine. I'm used to doing things on my own."

Kim put her hand on Trudy's shoulder. "You aren't on your own. God is right there with you. He'll protect you and help you."

Trudy patted Kim's hand. "Thanks. That's good to remember."

Trudy spent the long drive remembering. She remembered Phillip coming into town on a motorcycle and whisking her away, figuratively and literally.

How angry and disapproving her dad had been about Phillip. He'd yelled and sent her to her room for slipping out to meet him. She would've listened to him when she was younger. As a teen, it seemed he was always yelling at her and she no longer paid much attention. Or maybe she'd stopped paying attention and he felt the need to yell to make her listen. Either way, she'd never considered that he was afraid she'd get hurt, until her mom had talked about it after her dad had died.

He was trying to protect her the way he had when she was a child. He'd yanked her out of harm's way when a goose had chased her, pecking and beating her with its wings. He'd ordered her to stay on the other side of the fence when they brought the bull into the pasture. He'd knocked the sow with a rod sheathed in rubber when it charged her while she slopped the hogs.

They'd spent so much time side by side, working, fishing, riding and roping. They'd gone together to buy Skipper. When they got home, her mother had supper ready, as always. Had her mom wanted to share that special trip with them? They'd never even asked her. She had always stayed in the background.

Of course, there had been times with her mother. She had helped her mother tend the garden and cook, can, and freeze food until Trudy could think of nothing else but how much her back hurt. She'd never once considered how her mom felt or that she might be tired too. Her mom's place was in the home.

Trudy had never really understood her mother. Neither had she guessed her mother had been an advocate, quietly smoothing out the differences between the rough edges of her daughter's adolescence and her husband's strict rules.

Her new appreciation of her mother's behind-the-scenes influence was comforting, yet tinged with regret. If she'd known, maybe they could have had a close relationship sooner.

All those years, her mother had always kowtowed to her husband, and Trudy had looked down on her. Yet, she showed such strength of will once he physically failed.

One never really knew about marriages. What looked like one thing to an outsider, even to someone in the same home, could really be something else, like Brett believing Trudy was moving because she'd looked so happy with Phillip.

For a time, Phillip had fulfilled her childhood dreams of rich living. But it hadn't made her particularly happy or satisfied. Still, she'd have continued that lifestyle, not thinking much about it, if Phillip hadn't created so much misery.

Phillip. Trudy's heart didn't do flip-flops. She hadn't even dreamed about him in days. Of course, his presence was not subtly in Carol's home as it had been in the WC since he was not sneaking in whenever she was gone.

Even so, every time Trudy shifted her thoughts to her parents, the focus returned to Phillip. As bad as it was, she didn't want to be free of him; she wanted things to be different between them.

It was dark when Trudy motored through downtown and parked in front of Sarah's house. June bugs and moths flitted about the yellow glow of the porch light. The curtain moved in the window and Sarah's voice came through the dark. "When you get up to the door, I'll shut the light off so you can sneak in without so many of those pesky bugs getting in."

"Okay. It'll take me a minute. I have to get my bag unstrapped first."

Once Trudy was inside and the bugs shut out, Sarah hugged her. "Have you had your supper?"

"No. I drove straight through, but don't bother. I'm not hungry."

"Nonsense. You come into the kitchen. I've got a plate fixed, ready and waiting on the warmer."

Trudy didn't have the energy to argue. She ate a portion of what was put in front of her, listened to more details of what had happened to her mother, and went upstairs to bed.

The next day, as if eating were the cure-all for Trudy's grief, Sarah cooked a hot breakfast, then served a large lunch after the meeting with Mr. Crombley at the funeral home, and later insisted she eat a snack after talking with the minister. "You have to keep up your energy," Sarah said. "This business is hard work on your body and your mind."

A few casseroles and cakes made their way into the kitchen. "Don't think people are ignoring you. I told the ladies to spread the word not to bring so much since it's only the two of us."

The day of the funeral, Trudy stood before her mother's casket surveying a multitude of flower arrangements. One from Peter Faulkinroy Publicist, a duplicate of the enormous arrangement for her father's funeral, sat prominently at the foot of the casket beside a picture of her mom. This time, there were no whispered comments, no innuendos.

Most often Trudy heard, "Your mother was a saint," followed by a telling of her kindness. Invariably the visitor ended by speaking words of encouragement. Some of them truly touched Trudy.

The ladies from the women's group served their best dishes at the memorial dinner in the church basement. Afterward, as the ladies cleared away the remnants and washed pans in the kitchen, Trudy sat at a table, playing with her empty Styrofoam coffee cup, too emotionally worn out to move a muscle.

The metal chair beside her scraped the bare concrete floor as Beau sat down. She returned his warm smile. "I don't remember people being this kind when I was growing up. Was I such a rebel, I couldn't see that or have they changed?"

"They changed toward you when you changed. Everybody's heard how you've supported your mom. They've forgiven you for running off and breaking your father's heart. They know your husband duped you, and that you stayed away to protect your parents. If he could con your dad, he must've been particularly slippery."

Trudy clucked her tongue against her teeth. "Small town life. Is there anything they don't know about me?"

"Probably doesn't seem like it. Of course there is that skinny dipping time."

"Don't remind me." Trudy chuckled. "It was nice to be part of this community again, even for a little while. I can't think why I was in such a rush to leave it all behind."

"Yeah, there are lots of good folks here. I don't suppose you'll be coming back."

"No. I've got a good job, supportive friends, and a nice church."

"A life." Beau sounded wistful.

Trudy nodded. "A start at a good life."

Beau rubbed his chin thoughtfully. "You know, I've got me a good life right here in Amesville. It's where I belong. I guess it's time for me to quit waiting around for you."

Trudy's lips curved in a half-smile, not sure if he was serious. "I wish you the best, Beau."

He pushed his large frame out of the seat. He replaced the chair with such care that it made no noise. He lifted his hand in farewell and Trudy did the same.

Trudy spent the day after the funeral writing thank you notes for the donations and settling business for her mom, sorting through personal effects, and insisting Sarah keep the month's rent her mom had already paid. There wasn't as much to do compared to when her dad died.

Trudy drove two hours west to Albert City to visit Skipper at the Cooper ranch. She stopped the bike on the road alongside the fence. Across the field Skipper, looking well fed and happy, stood near the barn. It only took a moment before he noticed her. He galloped to the fence and neighed.

"Hey, Skipper, you beautiful boy. I've missed you. I'll see you up at the ranch." She *putt-putt-ed* along the road and turned into the long, dirt drive. Skipper trotted alongside, his mane flying in the breeze. Near the barn, she dismounted the bike and came to the fence. Skipper nodded his head and pushed his nose close to her face. She stroked his neck and told him how sorry she was.

"He's sure happy to see you," a deep voice said.

# Chapter Twenty-eight

Trudy turned. A short, wiry man with a limp approached from the barn. "I'm happy to see him, too, Mr. Cooper. Thanks for agreeing to let me come."

"When you called, well, I wasn't sure at first. I didn't want him getting mopey again. He had a hard time adjusting to being here. He'd stay off by himself. He didn't respond, didn't eat much. He'd spend hours hanging his head over the fence by the road, as if waiting for someone. You, I guess."

Trudy blinked back tears and laid her head against Skipper's neck. She stroked him. She murmured, "I'm sorry, boy. I'm so sorry."

She spoke over her shoulder to Mr. Cooper. "We were inseparable until I married and left home. We couldn't take him with us."

Mr. Cooper continued, "It took quite a bit of attention, but he pulled out of it when our granddaughter starting riding him. She's handicapped, but he seemed to understand right away she had special needs. He's gentle and patient with her."

"He always was a perceptive horse."

"Yah. He knew she needed him. That's what brought him around. He still spends a little time each day at the fence, but he's happy now."

"He looks happy. He's as sleek and beautiful as ever." She stroked him with long strokes along his back and flank.

"Do you want to ride him?"

Trudy whipped around to face Mr. Cooper. "May I?"

"Yah. I can see how attached Skipper is to you. I think it will do him good."

Skipper whinnied. They walked together to the barn, saddled him, and Trudy mounted as easily as if it had been only yesterday.

Mr. Cooper hung over the fence, watching as Skipper trotted, then moved into a canter. After a few turns about the field, Trudy urged him into a gallop. She felt the ease with which he stretched his legs, as if this was what he was meant to do. They circled the field several times, and then pretended to barrel race using the food station and the water barrel. Trudy felt free and joyous. She laughed out loud. Skipper neighed in response. He tossed his head.

She reined in before Mr. Cooper, a little out of breath, but this time it was a good feeling, not nerves or fear. She rested one hand on her jeans. "That was wonderful. I haven't been on a horse since I left Skipper. I wasn't sure I'd remember how."

"Yah. You both looked good out there. Never knew that horse to be prancing and so joyful-looking. At the end of the field is a trail. You can take that if you want to ride longer."

"Oh, yes. Thank you. How much time do we have?"

"I'll be working outside here until supper. Take your time."

Trudy guided Skipper toward the trail. It wound through a woods and met a stream. As he drank, she unburdened all the cares she'd held in her soul. She told him about Phillip, the letters she never got, the good times, and the hard times. She explained how he'd come to be sold. How sorry she was to lose him. She stood, clutched his mane in her hand, leaned into him and cried. He turned his neck and cradled her. She rubbed his nose and face. Finally, she washed the evidence of crying away in the burbling water of the brook.

Walking on the trail again, she told him about her parents' deaths, that Phillip was in jail and would be going to prison. She expressed her disappointment in Phillip's failure to free himself of his addiction to gambling. "I feel that gambling is more important to him than I am and that hurts, but I'm learning to accept that it grips him, he can't control it. It controls him. It's a disease. He needs help."

Trudy told Skipper about her life in Indianapolis, her friends, and how she was growing. As they neared the field again, she said, "It's a good life, Skipper, even if you aren't there. I miss you, but you have a good life here. I hear you're doing important work helping Mr. Cooper's granddaughter."

Skipper bobbed his head up and down. She patted his neck. "When I leave, I don't want you being all sad and depressed again. I have to go back to Indianapolis. You have to stay here. You're needed here, more than I need you. What we had was wonderful. I'll never forget you, but we both have new lives, new jobs. That granddaughter needs you."

Skipper whinnied. She patted him again. They broke out of the woods. "You want to have one last turn about the field for old time's sake? Okay. Let's go." They raced across the field and dashed around the feeding station, looped around the trough and repeated the pattern.

Mr. Cooper stood at the barn door and watched.

Trudy dismounted and praised Skipper. She whispered, "We'll always be best friends. I'll never forget our wonderful time together."

"My wife has supper ready. Will you stay?"

She walked Skipper to Mr. Cooper. "Thanks. That's very kind, but I have to get back." Trudy's voice caught. She stroked Skipper one last time and handed the reins to Mr. Cooper. He removed the saddle and set it inside the barn, then took off the bit and halter.

Skipper watched as Trudy climbed the fence and jumped to the other side landing next to her motorcycle. He watched as she adjusted her helmet and kick started the engine. She raised her hand in good-bye. He shook his mane. Skipper turned and walked into the barn.

# Chapter Twenty-nine

Trudy cried all the way back to Sarah's.

After another hearty breakfast—Sarah wouldn't hear otherwise—Trudy lashed her bag to the back of the motorcycle. She gave Sarah a huge hug. "I'll never forget your kindness."

"Always did like you, girl. You had spunk. Your Mom liked that about you. Don't ever think she didn't."

Trudy nodded, only half believing it. "Sarah, Mom said I was wild like she was as teen. Did you know her then?"

Sarah chuckled. "Oh, yes, ma'am, I did. She was feisty. I remember one time she and some friends tipped over the outhouse when Floyd Witherspoon was in it."

"Old Mr. Witherspoon, the school teacher?"

Sarah laughed out loud. "Yes. Of course, he was young and nimble then. He came out of there, pulling up his pants and chased those kids into the woods, but never did catch any of them."

Trudy flinched. "Oh, uh, Sarah, I'm the one that T.P.'d your house at Halloween."

Sarah laughed. "Always knew it was you."

"I'm sorry about that."

Sarah patted her arm. "Never mind. You always came the next afternoon to clean up all that toilet paper. Yep. You had heart as well as spunk."

Trudy smiled. She put her helmet on and straddled the bike.

Sarah said, "Kind of funny, isn't it? You left town the first time on a motorcycle and you thought it was for good. Now you're leaving on a motorcycle again, and this time it will be for good. God bless you, girl. I know you've had a heap of heartaches, but it's a beautiful world and God has a whole bunch of blessings waiting for you. Follow him. You'll find them. One day, you'll even find yourself a man of God to share your life."

Trudy blinked tears away and nodded, because what was the point of arguing when Sarah was trying to be kind?

The older woman stepped up on the porch and waved. Trudy returned the gesture. The engine rumbled to life and she roared through the little town and left Amesville behind.

The usual six hour trip extended to eight as Trudy stopped every time tears blinded her. By the time she reached Indianapolis, she felt empty, purged of the past, and ready for a fresh start. She turned the motorcycle into Carol's driveway and parked behind the car.

Kim, in a bright blue bathing suit, waved. Wielding a soapy sponge and a hose, she swabbed her mother's car.

Trudy dismounted. "Hey, aren't you supposed to be away at school?"

Kim gave her a big smile. "I decided not to go to Boston. I registered here at Indiana University for a teaching degree. I start in two weeks."

"What happened?"

"Did you ever feel God telling you to do something specific? To go somewhere particular?"

"No."

Kim rinsed soapsuds off the car. "Well, it was a heaviness in my heart."

"Like an elephant sitting on your chest?"

"More like I'd swallowed a stone. I wasn't comfortable with it."

"Was it nerves about being away from home or about leaving your Mom alone? Perhaps it was money worries."

"I thought of all those things, too. It's why I didn't say anything sooner, but the feeling persisted all summer. I thought it'd pass once we were on the road, but it felt so wrong. I finally talked it over with Mom and she said I should do what I thought was best. So, we turned around and came home. I'll go to I.U. and test out of some classes. If I feel I should, I can transfer to Boston next year."

"Staying here has its upside."

"And its downside. It will be cheaper living here, but all my friends are leaving. It feels odd being the one who stays at home. Do you think I'm being childish?"

"You can be childish away at college as well as here. Consider this. Even in America, most people don't go away to college. Doesn't mean that they aren't adult."

Kim beamed at Trudy. "You always know the right thing to say. Enough about me. How are you?"

"Amazed that my mom was still trying to take care of me to the end. When my dad died, there was no life insurance. She went out and bought some on herself. She didn't want me burdened. It took care of her funeral expenses. Her friends were generous, too." Trudy choked out the last words.

Kim put a hand on her shoulder. "Sounds exactly like what a mom would do. She must've been a special lady. Will you be going back?"

Trudy shook her head. "Nothing to go back for. I don't have any other family."

"It's okay, Trudy. Indianapolis is your home now. We're your family."

Trudy covered her face with her hands and sobbed. She thought it impossible to shed another tear, but these tears were happier. They came from a place of knowing that she was accepted.

Kim, who couldn't tell the difference, hugged Trudy and let her snuffle. "I'm sorry. I know it's hard, but you'll be all right."

Trudy hugged her back. "I know I will."

For two weeks whenever Trudy was quiet, they didn't ask why, but would smile and give her a quick hug or squeeze her shoulder. Their support was balm on the scars on Trudy's heart, a tacit acceptance that whatever she was feeling was okay to feel. In response, she tried to be more open and honest about her feelings with both herself and with the Streeters.

When they watched movies or talked fashion or dressed Carol for some seminar or conference, Trudy could join in the fun and silliness without thinking that she was somehow disrespecting her mom.

One night they sat around the kitchen table, making small talk and redoing their nails when Trudy's phone played, "Don't Be Cruel."

"Hello. This is Trudy."

An automated electronic voice identified the call as coming from the jail. It continued. "Will you accept a collect call from inmate—" Phillip's voice interjected, "Phillip Bellafonte."

# Chapter Thirty

Trudy's voice stuck in her throat. The elephant that had been absent, landed so heavily on her chest that she couldn't take a breath.

Across the kitchen table, Carol frowned. Fingers spread wide, she held freshly polished nails in the air and leaned toward Trudy.

Kim's brown eyes widened as she whispered, "What is it?"

Through the phone, the words were repeated in Trudy's ear.

Trudy gasped. "No. No I will not." She disconnected and covered her mouth.

Carol said, "That wasn't a telemarketer."

Kim screwed the cap on the nail polish. "Was it an obscene phone call?"

"No. It was my husband, Phillip."

Carol and Kim yelped. "You're married?"

The look of shock on Carol's face tickled Trudy, but what came out of her mouth was a sob that sounded like a hiccup. She stifled any further emotional display. "We're separated."

Kim pointed at her. "Aha. That's why you don't date."

"Phillip was the one who stole Peter's computer. He's in jail awaiting the trial. It doesn't make sense. I thought God cared. I thought he would bring us together again, not imprison him."

"Oh, my. Oh, dear." Carol put an arm around Trudy. "Kim, give Trudy that box of tissues. What a lot you've had to handle. God does care and I care."

Kim set the box of tissues in front of Trudy. "We both care, Trudy."

"I thought if I waited patiently, Phillip would straighten up." Dry-eyed, Trudy pushed the tissues away with a short jerk of her hand. "Wait here a minute."

Trudy rushed from the room. She returned a moment later and threw an expansion folder on the table. With shaky fingers she untied the string and dumped out the papers. Trudy picked up a handful of letters and waved them at Carol. "Look at all these. First he sent letters through his attorney, which I wouldn't answer. He even had someone stop by to see me at work. Now, he mails me and tries to call. He keeps begging for bail and other money and trying to guilt trip me into visiting him."

Carol and Kim picked through the correspondence, reading a letter here and there. Carol scooped all the letters together and stuffed them in the folder. Kim looked as if she'd prefer to read all of them. She didn't protest, but pursed her lips.

"He wants me to lie about what happened that night and get the charges dropped."

"Would you?"

"I won't lie, Carol. There are times I want to run over there and prove how much I love him by visiting him and giving him money. Hoping then that he'll realize how much I love him and finally change. It's hard. However, I know that giving in is not healthy or helpful. Not for me. Not for him. Not for us as a couple.

"I've been doing everything right since I moved here. Isn't it enough? If God cares, how can he do this to me? He took my parents and is moving Kathy away. Why can't I have Phillip?"

Carol said, "I'm going to make us some hot chocolate. You are going to start at the beginning and tell everything."

Kim said, "Is this private? Do you want me to leave?"

Trudy sent her a half-smile. "That's a very grown-up thing to ask. No, you can stay."

Carol pulled packets of mint hot cocoa mix from the cupboard, emptied them into three cups, stirred in milk, and nuked them in the microwave. The fragrance filled the air as Carol carried them on a tray into the living room.

Trudy followed clutching the expansion folder. She settled into the center of the couch. Carol sat beside her. Kim, with the tissue box tucked under her arm, chose the chair across from her.

"Now then," Carol said. "Tell us."

Trudy hunched over. She looked up, first at Carol, then Kim. "I met Phillip on my seventeenth birthday. He was with the older sister of a friend. He flashed a smile and," Trudy closed her eyes and shivered. "it gave me the shivers inside. I'd seen him around before that, riding his shiny black Harley. All the girls noticed him. None of the parents liked him, but all of us girls thought he was a dreamboat."

Carol nodded. Trudy leaned back and let the memories come. "His hair was black and curly. He was broader across the chest than his hips and it made him look very manly. He wore a black leather jacket and expensive hand-tooled boots. So mature.

Sometimes, he'd talk in an Irish brogue. We all debated whether he was born there and was trying to overcome it, or if he was using it because he knew it was attractive. He offered to take me for a ride on his motorcycle as a birthday present."

"I said yes, of course. He took me out on a long stretch of country road where he could really open it up. A thrill hit my gut when he took off and cranked up the speed. It was so exciting with the wind flapping my clothes and his body solid beneath my grip, the scent of his aftershave lingering on the skin of his neck." Trudy shivered again. "The ride seemed to only last moments, but we were gone for an hour.

"It was only a ride. I was underage and Phillip was twenty-one. He treated me like a little kid, but my dad was sure we were off somewhere necking. My parents were furious that I'd left the party with him.

"Over the next twelve months, he kept showing up at my barrel racing events, ball games, 4-H events. He'd be with various college co-eds or girls who'd already graduated high school.

"We rarely talked, but every once in a while our eyes would meet and he'd smile. One side of his mouth would quirk up and he'd wink or put his fingers to his forehead and give a little salute. If I smiled back or waved, he'd flash a beautiful wide smile that melted my heart. I didn't tell anyone, but he was all I could think about.

"When I turned eighteen, he started coming around. Phillip quit dating other girls. He said he was interested only in me. I felt special and grown up.

"My dad disapproved. He said Phillip was a no-account drifter. Yet, Phillip usually had money, although he didn't hold a job in town. He said he came from a wealthy family and made investments that paid off. He made me feel beautiful and smart and accepted. We sneaked around to see each other.

"I told him how I dreamed of living in the city. He promised me I'd wear sleek clothes instead of cotton dresses and live in a fine house instead of a farmhouse. We started sketching plans for the mansion we'd build. We talked endlessly about which city would be the best. Handsome and daring, he had big plans and was going places. I saw only the possibilities.

"I eloped with Phillip when I was still 18. It upset my parents terribly, especially my Dad. He was livid and said I wasn't welcome back. I think he thought I'd gotten pregnant.

"We traveled a lot for the first couple of years. We had lots of fun together and enjoyed an upscale lifestyle. We shared many adventures and met lots of important people, lots of jet setters.

"At first Phillip made good on his promises, then slowly he gambled it away. After that, I became the chief breadwinner. He couldn't keep a job for long. Always gambling. It was a cycle of feast or famine. We'd bounce around from town to town trying to stay ahead of the creditors and the thugs collecting gambling debts. I did my best to keep up.

"He'd disappear for days or a couple of weeks, but he always came back to me. Each time, he promised me things would be different. For a while they would be.

We'd settle in some new city, then it'd all start again. I wanted to get in touch with my parents, but Phillip discouraged that."

Kim said, "He didn't want you hurt, if they rejected you?"

From the expansion folder, Trudy pulled out the stack of letters with "Return to Sender" printed across them. They were still tied up in a ribbon. She tossed it onto the table.

"No. I think he was afraid I'd leave him. He lied. He didn't tell me my parents tried to reach me. Didn't tell me when my dad had his first heart attack. Instead he cozied up to them himself and took their life savings. He was a conman. It killed my dad, and then my mom."

A numbness descended. Trudy felt as if she were relating someone else's story. She gave all the details of the past couple of years without shedding a tear. "Since coming to Indianapolis I've tried to do what I thought God wanted me to do. I thought some good would come of it. I thought Phillip would change. What more could I have done? Why did God let this happen to me? Doesn't he care?"

# Chapter Thirty-one

Carol settled back into her corner of the sofa and tipped her head up. "Trudy, you seem to think God's far away and uninvolved, but from what you said, it appears to me he's been working in your life all along. You've told your story. Where do you see God deserting you?"

"Phillip took everything. I arrived here with no money."

"And met Spider and Mike who sent you to a temp agency where you got work immediately."

"But, I never knew where I was going to be. I had to drive all over town to go to work."

"Which you could do because Spider and Mike had filled your tank."

"But, I still had to sleep in my car. It was terrifying. I was so vulnerable."

"Yet, you were safe, because you parked in the guarded factory lots. Then, you got a job with Peter, and he pays you extremely well."

"I work like a horse."

"Which you've told me many times over you love. Besides, you got to meet me."

"I remember that I left after our first meeting to go to my father's funeral."

"Which was tragic. Yet, you know your dad knew God and is in heaven right now."

"But, God didn't stop Phillip from cheating my parents."

"Which was the very thing that changed your father's mind about you. Reconciliation with your parents has to make your loss a bit easier."

"But, we had no more time together. I couldn't show my dad how much I loved him."

"I think he knew that, once he knew the truth. Would you prefer that you hadn't reconciled?"

Trudy felt her face pucker like a drawstring bag pulled tight.

Carol pressed on. "No. That would've made everything much worse. In fact, your father understood how you could be misled by Phillip. He forgave you."

Trudy thought about that and nodded. "That was a big relief."

Carol continued ticking items off her fingers. "You said Phillip left you with a broken down car, stole your horse, your diamond ring, and rent money, which caused you to lose your apartment. Still, you weren't destitute. You moved in here, which was a great relief and blessing to me. God wasn't only blessing you. He was blessing me."

"And me," Kim said. "You stayed with me in the hospital."

Trudy bit her lip.

"Finn McCool protected you. Culcallen gave you free legal counseling, which helped relieve some of the debt.

"But, if I hadn't reported the theft, Phillip wouldn't be in prison. Maybe, I shouldn't have said who stole that stuff."

"Phillip did that to himself. What's happened since are the consequences. That's on him. Even Peter didn't blame you or make you pay for the stolen equipment. That in itself is a miracle. Besides, Phillip's imprisonment has protected you from further injury, theft, and who knows what else."

"But, I prayed for Phillip to change."

"Trudy, God doesn't force us to change. He allows situations that create a need for him. He invites us to change and helps us when we ask. You asked for God's help and you changed. You quit letting Phillip take advantage of you. You got better. You smile and laugh more now than when I first met you."

Kim's voice was soft. "You don't look like the whole world is crushing you to death."

"You could tell that? I always thought I was handling it all so well that nobody knew."

Carol said, "Looks to me as if God, because he loves you, orchestrated it so that everything that was meant to hurt you blessed you instead. Even if the end result isn't the one you had hoped for, God still is at work. You've been growing closer to him the entire time I've known you, which makes it easier for him to work things in your favor, like we talked about all those months ago. It wasn't because you earned it or bargained for it."

"You've never talked to me like this before."

"You've never shared anything about yourself before. You were locked up and aloof."

"You think I'm aloof? Phillip always told me I was too open and trusting."

"You were aloof. It's okay. I recognized it for what it was. I knew you were hurting. Now I see you were also trying to protect yourself."

Trudy's eyes stung. The tears she thought she couldn't cry came. She reached for a tissue as Carol continued, "Finally, God orchestrated that we could be best friends. You were there through some of the hard times with Kim, when she got hurt, when she was crazy for that Larry-dude."

Startled, Kim said, "I didn't know you didn't like him, Mom."

"Exactly as planned," Carol said.

"I thought Larry was cool, until I got to know him. The advice you gave me, Trudy, makes more sense, now."

"I don't know what I would've done without you, Trudy," Carol said.

Trudy held up both her hands to stop Carol. "Okay. Okay. Leave it to Carol Sunshine to find the silver lining in every dark cloud."

"And to add the sugar to every glass of lemon juice. At least you're smiling, in a weak, watery kind of way," Carol said.

Kim said, "I'm confused, Mom. Doesn't the Bible say to visit those in prison?"

"Paul wrote that epistle to Christians who were told to help other Christians who were imprisoned for their faith. It was risky and would've endangered those who gave the help. Of course, anyone who feels God wants them to share as a ministry to imprisoned non-believers, should do so. Do you feel God wants you to do that, Trudy?"

Trudy shook her head. "I go all weak thinking about it. Phillip's an addiction with me. When I'm around him, I can't seem to stop falling under his spell. Then, I do things I wouldn't normally do and don't like myself much."

"Then perhaps you should stay away from him," Carol suggested. "You're doing the right thing to say no."

Kim widened her large brown eyes and nodded emphatically. Minnie reared up on her back legs and placed one paw on Carol's arm and one on Trudy's arm. She bayed.

Trudy stroked the dog she was fond of. It made sense. She felt a little stronger knowing they supported her decision.

After that, Trudy remembered what they said every time she was tempted to answer when Phillip called or wrote. She drew strength from it while she sat through his trial.

Phillip pleaded not guilty to robbery, claiming he thought the FAX and the computer were his wife's and, therefore, his.

Culcallen, acting as prosecuting attorney, produced a copy of the signed separation agreement with the time stamp of the FAX. "Your honor, this was signed before Mr. Bellafonte removed the equipment from his wife's possession. It was clear from that moment on that even if he thought the equipment belonged to his wife, he had no legal right to it. Added to the assault on her, which the police report documents, this is clearly aggravated robbery."

"No," Phillip cried out. "Tell them it isn't so, Tru. Trudy, my love, you can make this go away. Don't let them put me in that awful place. Trudy!"

From her place in the gallery, Trudy stared at her hands, clamped together and pressed into her lap. Trudy didn't have the strength to stand and leave the courtroom.

When Phillip wouldn't quiet, the judge had him removed from the courtroom. The jury was advised of their duties and sent to deliberate. It didn't take long for the decision. Within minutes they filed into the jury box to render the verdict. "Guilty."

No matter how many times Phillip called to her, Trudy refused to look at him as he was taken from the courtroom into custody. When he was gone, Trudy pressed her fists to her lips and held her breath.

Peter shook Culcallen's hand and commended him for a job well done. He strode from the courtroom.

Culcallen filled his briefcase and left the prosecutor's table. He placed a steadying hand on her shoulder. He squeezed. "You did the right thing, Trudy. Perjury is a serious business. It's better to tell the truth. Maybe Phillip has to come to the end of what he can do before wanting to change. Maybe this is what it'll take for him to seek God."

"I hope so," Trudy whispered.

The court room emptied. Culcallen put everything in his brief case and sat down beside Trudy. "You'll be okay."

He was a busy man with places to be. She knew that and appreciated the gesture. "Thanks, Culcallen. Thanks for everything." She stood and even though she feared they wouldn't, her legs supported her. She shook his hand and left.

On the drive home, she didn't think of Phillip. Instead, she thought about God and his hand in all the events that had taken place. Unlike Phillip, God was dependable. Phillip had made promises he couldn't keep. He had tried to go straight, but failed. He had loved her, yet he had left her. God always kept his promise and never left her.

She marveled at the revelation. God never left her. The depth of his faithfulness amazed her. He never changed. God knew her with all her faults, and still he loved her, and never, ever left her.

# Chapter Thirty-two

Kathy emptied the apartment Friday night and shared a suite with her bridesmaids at the hotel where the wedding would take place on Saturday. Late Saturday morning Trudy signed the lease and picked up the key.

The single bedroom apartment boasted a kitchenette and a living room with a sliding glass door to the balcony. The entire place was twice the size of the WC as a whole. The only drawback was the bathroom was tiny with a shower unit and a half-size washbowl. All the walls were white, but Trudy counted it a blessing that she had regular walls and a regular closet. Perhaps Carol would help her explore thrift shops to add color and hominess as well as pick up necessities like a desk, table, and chairs.

With the help of Kim and Carol, she moved in a mattress and bed frame and her clothes. She made the bed, set up the work FAX and computer on the floor, and still had time for a nap before dressing for the wedding.

She chose a flowing pale blue and gold floor-length pant-dress that swished when she walked and swirled when she turned. The mirror said she was lovely, but not as lovely as her friend, the bride looked that day. There was no other word for it. Kathy was radiant.

Trudy remembered how she had felt on her own wedding day. Phillip had been so handsome despite wearing a well-used black tie and tails. She'd worn a tight white strapless street-length gown that sported a white feather boa. Somehow Phillip had made using rented clothes and having a ceremony among strangers sound exciting.

Through older eyes she perceived that most of the excitement she'd sensed in the air was not happiness, but manic addiction, the need for thrill and action and a misplaced hope that the dice would be nice even though the odds of beating the house were enormous.

The glitz and glam had revealed itself to be necessary to hide the truth of that gambler's paradise. Eventually, she'd learned that the underbelly of the city was dark and quite unglamorous, lined with broken lives of people who, like Phillip, chased a dream right off the cliff.

But that night, oh how thrilling it had been, standing in one of the chapels of love in Las Vegas with flashing colored lights creating a sense of excitement. He'd held her hand as if he'd never let it go. She'd felt precious. Phillip had looked at her with such love that she remembered feeling all aglow, even as Kathy was glowing as Mike gazed into his beloved's eyes. Kathy sounded breathless when she said, "I do."

Her own bridal breathlessness had only partially been due to love for Phillip since her rented dress was so tight it'd kept her from taking a full breath. Trudy sobered as she considered that she'd had trouble breathing ever since taking those vows.

What had she been thinking? It was ludicrous what she'd let Phillip put her through. If she saw him again, would she fall under his spell? Would she behave the same even though she knew better?

At the thought, that old elephant returned to squash her. Trudy sucked air deep into her lungs and exhaled with a breathy "oh."

The woman sitting next to her shushed her.

Trudy flashed a big smile and whispered, "I'm so happy for Kathy. Everything is so beautiful. She's so beautiful. Doesn't it take your breath away?"

The woman's features softened. She nodded agreement. They both turned their eyes forward and focused on the ceremony.

The minister announced the bride and groom and asked everyone to move to the banquet hall and be seated according to the name tags. Trudy found herself at the 'spares, not pairs' table with three single women and Kathy's married male cousin, Robert, whose wife couldn't make it. At the last moment, another man sauntered up. "Hello, lovely ladies. I'm Joseph G. Espinoza, single, ready, and able."

The three single women giggled. Trudy muttered, "Oh, brother."

Throughout the evening the other women tried to outdo each other for Joe's attention. They weren't the only ones acting up. Joe asked leading questions of Robert then would try to one-up the story by recounting something he'd done.

Through the salad course and the chicken dinner, Trudy counted eight times Joe said, "That's nothing. I did…" and sixteen times he said, "You want to bet?" His attempts to impress the women appeared to be working, but the silly antics disgusted her. She'd never see these people again. If Joe could pile it on, so could she.

As Mr. Single-Man-Who's-Done-Almost-Everything finished up a story that was a little too over the top to be believable, she piped up. "Sure that's adventurous, Joe, but you don't know what daring is until you've ridden a bull in a rodeo and feel your saddle slip sideways."

All five tablemates stared at her. She met their gazes without blinking an eye.

"I was younger then and a lot shorter. I hadn't had my final growth spurt. I tucked in and held onto that saddle and it slid clear under the bull. I was riding upside down on his belly. He was mad as a hornet. He kicked and bucked and jumped. If I let go he'd have trampled me, but I couldn't hold on either. It's a good thing the rodeo clowns were on their toes that day or I'd have been killed."

The women gawked. The married cousin's eyes twinkled and his mouth twitched. Joe made a face. "Naw."

Kathy and Mike were making their way to the dance floor for the first dance. Trudy called them over. "Hey Kathy, do you remember my rodeo medals? These guys don't think I ever rode rodeo."

"Sure. You had a whole wall of them, including five Firsts."

"Thank you for clearing that up."

Joe said, "Oh, I get it now. You're a guy in drag."

Two women exchanged glances and giggled. The other woman laughed outright. The cousin frowned at Joe and shook his head. Kathy slapped Joe on the back of the head. "Don't be an idiot, Joseph Gale."

Joe scowled at Kathy.

One of women said, "Your middle name is Gale?"

He blustered. "Yes. I'm named after an English knight. It's a very respectable English name."

Laughing girl leaned forward and cooed. "I love everything English."

Trudy ignored the rest of the conversation. She stood and hugged Kathy. "I may not get a chance to talk with you later. You look so beautiful."

"Thanks."

"I'm going to miss you."

"I'll miss seeing you too, Trudy. We'll still talk on the phone, though. Come visit us in Phoenix."

Trudy turned to the groom. "Take care of her, Mike. She's pretty special."

"I know it," he said. He looked at Kathy the way Phillip used to look at her.

The music started and the bride and groom moved off to dance to "(Everything I Do), I Do It for You."

The braggart moved his chair closer to the Anglophile. They bent their heads together. Trudy wanted to warn her not to bet on any man who liked to bet. Standing beside her, the cousin said in a low voice, "You never rode a bull."

"Nope. Barrel racing."

He laughed. "It shut him up. I think that's a first."

Trudy glanced back at the table. "Maybe for as long as the song lasts."

"True enough." A new tune began. "I'm Robert. Would you like to dance?"

Trudy studied him. She thumbed the empty placed where her rings would've been. Robert caught the gesture and showed his own gold wedding band. "Yes. I'm married. I'm only interested in dancing. I've taken lessons, so I'm pretty good."

Trudy agreed. She spent the rest of the evening dancing and having a friendly chat. When cake was served with coffee, Joe suggested to Miss I-Love-Everything-English that they split the dry wedding to find the nearest bar.

Afterward, the other two single women moved about visiting with people at the different tables. Trudy introduced Robert to Spider and Denise, which led to conversations about the CMA, and lots of laughter over motorcycle antics.

The bridal couple departed and after several more dances, the band closed down. Robert put his jacket on, swept his tie off the table and stuffed it in his pocket. "Thanks for an enjoyable evening. It's been a while since I had an adequate dance partner."

Trudy shook his hand. "It was fun. You're better than good. You're an excellent dancer. Doesn't your wife dance?"

"Not since a car accident paralyzed her from the waist down."

"I'm sorry."

"You're married, aren't you?"

"Sort of."

A broad grin split Robert's face. "Sort of? Isn't that like being kind of pregnant? You either are or you aren't."

She gave a short, sharp laugh. "Yeah. We're separated, but he's still there, attached to me like a Siamese twin."

"Because you still love him?"

"Wish I didn't. It'd make life a lot easier. I still hope—." She shrugged. She didn't know what she hoped for anymore.

"God has something for you, yet."

She cocked her head and looked him in the eye. "Someone else told me that recently. Only I don't know how to make that happen. My husband is not interested in change and hates that I'm doing everything I can to change myself for the better."

"If you don't mind some advice, quit trying to make things happen. Accept the season of life you're in and learn what you can from it. God will take care of the rest. He's faithful and he never changes."

Trudy nodded.

"I'm serious. Read your Bible. It will renew your hope. That's what my wife and I had to do after her accident. You'll never meet anyone with a sunnier disposition. She's out there doing lots of good. She's dancing through life, even though she can't physically dance anymore." He jingled the keys in his hand, as if he were anxious to get back to his wife, but needed to know Trudy was okay.

Trudy wrapped her golden pashmina over her shoulders and picked up her glittery golden purse. "You know something, Robert. I will. Good night."

He smiled. "Good night."

Trudy watched him stride across the room in his eagerness to get home. His wife sounded like the kind of person who'd make a good friend. She determined to befriend Robert's wife.

Trudy bid good-bye to Spider and Denise and chatted with Kathy's parents before driving to the new apartment. It was late, but she wasn't sleepy or hungry or thirsty.

She found the Bible in the short stack beside her bed and flipped through it. Was God answering all those Psalms she'd read as prayers asking him for justice? She didn't want Phillip hurt. She wanted him back, only different. She wanted him to be the man she saw he could be.

Trudy read other scripture verses that declared God was good, that he cared, and that he called her to walk in obedience. Maybe she needed to be more open to change herself. She'd changed some, but not very willingly.

Next, Trudy read that God offered security. Phillip had been right about her. When she had been safe she looked for adventure, but when life was chaotic and wild, she had longed for safety. Did the two have to be exclusive? Couldn't she be safe and still have adventures that weren't reckless?

For sure, being "carefree" by Phillip's definition was anything but free of care. On the other hand, Robert seemed to think that a life secure in Christ was adventurous. Maybe she'd been looking in the wrong place.

Instead of trying to simply survive, she could live the life she'd described to Beau at her mother's funeral. She already had a good job, a nice apartment, friends, and health. Why not focus on those things and quit thinking about what she couldn't have? Maybe when Phillip finally got out of prison, he'd come to his senses and settle down with her.

In the meantime, she had to admit, it was easier to breathe with him in jail.

# Chapter Twenty-three

The next week, Trudy called up Robert's wife, Susan, and arranged to meet her for lunch.

Susan had a moon-shaped face, laugh lines, and warm brown eyes. She held Trudy's hand in both of hers. "I'm so glad you called. Robert told me how he enjoyed talking with you." Her laughter was a loose staccato of ha-ha-ha. "That story about the bull cracked me up."

Trudy smiled at the memory. "The guy was pompous. He deserved to be taken down a notch."

"Joe always tries to nettle Robert. I think Joe's intimidated by him. Anyway, I'm happy to meet you. Call me Susan, not Sue." In a swift, deliberate move, Susan pulled Trudy's hand to touch the arm of the wheelchair. "And this is Fred Astaire, The Electric Chair. He's my dance partner these days."

Slightly shocked, Trudy fought the urge to draw back. Her eyes met Susan's brown ones. Susan released her hand and said, "I find it helpful to get the awkwardness over with right away. You did well, grasshopper. Ha-ha-ha."

Trudy felt slightly embarrassed, yet relieved. The woman was insightful.

Susan touched a button and the wheelchair turned 180 degrees. "Come on in and sit down. I have the table all ready for lunch."

Trudy took the seat Susan pointed at. Susan parked Fred Astaire at a place setting opposite Trudy's.

Susan was chatty. She filled Trudy in on the charity she was involved in, then briefly touched on answers to questions about her paralytic condition. "I know you didn't ask, but people always want to know. Now, tell me all about your job."

The lunch was over by the time they exhausted that topic. Susan pulled out a tray that had been out of sight on the seat of a chair and loaded the dishes on it. "Would you mind carrying this into the kitchen?"

"Sure."

Susan rolled into the kitchen and Trudy followed. The kitchen was designed to accommodate Susan's handicap. Everything was inches lower than normal. "Set it by the sink. I'll deal with them later. How do you know Kathy? She's a sweetheart. Ha-ha-ha."

Trudy explained, and conversation about Kathy led back to the wedding. Susan said, "Robert said he danced with you. I'm glad he got the chance. He doesn't dance much anymore since the accident."

"I hope it didn't bother you."

Susan's smile belied her words. "Ha-ha-ha. Of course, it bothered me. I'm jealous of those who dance. I'm also disdainful of those who could dance, but don't. Dancing is a wonderful thing."

"I'm sorry," Trudy said.

"Don't be. I'm glad for him. I wouldn't want him not to dance. I'm simply being honest. It's what I struggle with. I miss dancing couples competitions. I miss dancing with Robert. No mistake, I'm grateful to be alive. Some days I struggle more than others to stay positive, even though I have Fred Astaire. Ha-ha-ha." Susan squeezed the chair's arm. "Everybody's got something they deal with. This is mine."

On the way home, Trudy looked heavenward. "God, I know I've been half-hearted about following you. I was mad at you for not working things out with Phillip the way I wanted. For a long time, I didn't understand what the Bible said. Because I didn't understand, I thought it was boring. That's in the past. I'm going to read your word and do what it says.

"If Susan with all her limitations can joyfully follow you, then I can, too. Carol, Kim, Kathy, Mike, Spider, Denise, and Robert are all following you. They're filled with life. They're interesting. I want to be like them. I guess that means I want to be like Jesus. Here's my whole heart, even the part that belonged to Phillip. This woman doesn't need a man to be happy. Just you, God."

Soon after, Trudy began helping Susan with Clothing Kids ministries. Then, instead of merely socializing during the rides and the dinners, Trudy assisted with the ministries of CMA. Her circle of real friends grew.

When Susan mentioned that an apartment in a better part of town was available, Trudy pounced on the opportunity to attend a showing. The apartment was lovely, but priced at the top of her budget. For a couple of days, Trudy wrestled with whether God was gifting her the nicer place or if temptation was presenting itself, offering her to continue a lifestyle she had left.

In the end, Trudy stayed where she was and purchased the Cavalier instead. She didn't regret it. She didn't keep rethinking her choice, either.

It puzzled her that though she had lost so much, she felt satisfied. In some ways, she felt closer than ever to her mom and dad, as if she had found her roots again in conservative living.

As late fall crowded the last few warm weather days away, Trudy continued to browse thrift shops for apartment decorations that were bright and fun. Avoiding urbane black, white, and grey, she chose eclectic, colorful pieces.

One day, Carol and Kim accompanied her to a big sale. Kim held up a bright ceramic monkey that banged tiny cymbals when the key was wound. "Say, this is different."

"I think the correct word is hideous," Trudy said.

Carol chipped in. "She's looking for eclectic, not electric. That's shockingly ugly."

Trudy was still chuckling when she answered the Elvis Presley "Don't Be Cruel" ringtone.

"Trudy Bellafonte?"

"Yes."

"Are you Phillip Bellafonte's wife?"

"We're legally separated."

"This is Reverend Hamil Bunford. I'm the chaplain at Plainfield Correctional Facility. We're sorry to inform you of the death of Phillip Bellafonte..."

Trudy felt as if the breath had been knocked out of her. The room swirled. She gripped a nearby table with her free hand until her knuckles turned white. Like a sinking person looking for rescue, she focused on Carol.

The smile on Carol's face changed to a frown. Her lips were moving. Asking a question.

The disembodied voice on the phone droned on. It did not sound particularly caring. It was asking another question. "Mrs. Bellafonte, do you understand?"

"Phillip's dead. Are you telling me Phillip is dead?"

"Yes. Ma'am."

"How?"

"He was stabbed. I can't say more. The incident is under investigation." The voice continued in her ear. She was sure she responded at some point even though she didn't know what she said. When the call ended, Trudy slowly set the phone on the table. She made a fist and then pushed it against her mouth.

Carol had her hand on her shoulder, squeezing, shaking gently. "Trudy? What happened?"

"Phillip is dead. He must have made somebody in prison as mad as the people outside. They stabbed him."

Kim said, "How awful."

Carol squeezed Trudy's arm. "I'm so sorry."

"But?"

"No buts."

"Aren't you going to say it's a blessing in disguise or that I'm better off without him?"

"You loved him. You're hurting. I hurt for you."

Trudy shuddered a huge sigh. "He's never coming back. I always had that at least, the hope that he would come back for me and it would be good again. Why did he have to die?"

Carol put her arms around Trudy and let her cry. Kim had been observing from a few feet away. She came and locked her arms around Carol and Trudy.

"You are both good friends," Trudy said. "I know God will get me through, but it hurts. It hurts so much."

"I know. I know," Carol said. "Come on let's go home."

Kim picked up the abandoned phone and slipped it into Trudy's purse as Carol guided Trudy out of the store. Trudy buttoned up her suede jacket. "And they want me to claim his body. Do I do that?"

They discussed that during the drive to the Streeter home, but Trudy reached no decision.

In the days that followed, Trudy would often reread the letters from her parents, focusing on the love that shone from each one, rather than the time that had been stolen from them. She could almost feel chips falling from the walls she'd built around herself during her years with Phillip.

Trudy's evenings became as full as her days. On the occasions she found herself alone, she was surprised that grief for Phillip didn't overwhelm her. As the days went on and she didn't have any melt down, she became concerned.

As they approached the airport where Carol was flying out to speak at a women's conference in Alabama, Trudy said. "Carol, do you think I'm a bad wife? I mean, widow? I thought I'd be overcome with grief, but now that he's gone, I'm going on with my life. Is there something wrong with me?

"I loved Phillip to distraction. He was all I thought about for years. My whole life revolved around him. Do you think I'm in denial and it'll hit me later? Or, am I a calloused, selfish, and uncaring person?"

Carol's face filled with kindness. She shook her head. "There's nothing wrong with you. Did you ever stop to think that you've already been grieving for years and years?"

It was as if a lightbulb went on in the dark. Trudy blinked. "I have, haven't I?"

"Yes. You've been consumed with grief for a long time. Now, you're nearing the end of the process."

"Really?"

"Of course, it doesn't mean that you won't get hit by a wave of grief at some point. It's natural that it ebbs and flows."

Trudy pulled the Cavalier over to the curb. Carol unbuckled her seat belt and gathered up her purse. "Now that you know there isn't any future with Phillip, you're free to move forward."

"Do you mean that cute baker? I don't think I'm ready yet."

"I mean God has something else in mind for you. I'm sure you'll be very busy redefining who you are. One thing I do know is that you are unselfish and caring. Also, you are learning that there are people you don't have to be guarded around. You don't have to stuff everything inside anymore."

"That's three things."

"There you go. Progress."

Trudy beamed at Carol. "Thank you. Have a great trip. I'll be praying for you and the women at the conference."

Carol leaned over and gave Trudy a quick, reassuring hug. "Take care, my friend."

Trudy mulled over Carol's words on the way home. She had a lot of work to do to become the person she'd like to be, but all that growing and learning made the present much more interesting than pondering a past she couldn't change.

Her thoughts turned to Carol. The unexpected loss of a loving husband was only one in a string of losses Carol had dealt with. It had hit her hard. Trudy could imagine if Carol had been left in the comfortable financial position that Andy had planned for her, that she might have simply curled up on the sofa with a cup of cocoa and never stopped grieving. Was God using the financial disaster of the embezzlement to help Carol move forward? It definitely had brought Carol and Kim closer together.

It was amazing how God took the crap life threw at Carol and used it to fertilize the roots. Carol wasn't merely a single rose on a thorny stalk, she was becoming a thriving rose bush loaded with blooms. She was moving forward and using her painful experiences to help others. In doing so, she was also helping to heal herself.

# Chapter Thirty-four

The day Carol paid the IRS debt, she invited Trudy to celebrate with her at a day spa. Clouds of steam surrounded Trudy as she sat on a wooden bench. She wondered if this was what it felt like to be in the womb, except for the towel wrapped around her, of course. If so, she knew why babies cried when they came out.

A couple feet away, Carol pushed blonde hair that had darkened a bit from the steam away from her face. "Peter asked me to go with him to a shindig at the Indianapolis Museum of Art tonight."

Trudy tipped her head back and turned it slightly to look at her friend. "What'd you say?"

"I said I appreciated the offer, but no."

"Did you give him a reason?"

"I told him Kim and I had plans and we didn't get much of a chance to be together now that she's in school."

"Ah."

"He's certainly persistent."

"Which makes him perfect for his job. It's why he's successful and continues to grow. He's taken on three new clients this quarter."

"I guess. I wish he'd quit asking me, though. I never say yes and every three months he asks me again. It's like he puts it on his calendar."

"Not on the one at work. I've checked it."

Carol leaned toward her. "You've noticed it, too?"

"You should be gratified that he thinks that highly of you."

Carol wiped her brow. "It doesn't feel like that. It feels like he's poking around trying to find the chinks in my armor."

"Interesting image." Trudy pushed a stray strand of hair back.

"I always feel like I have to be on guard around him. He makes me uneasy."

"He's prickly at times, but he's a good guy. If you're looking for a wealthy man, he's definitely in that category. I got a peek at his tax returns last year."

"How'd you do that?"

"I'm nosy. When he stepped out of the office for a moment, I looked. He's more flush than even I thought."

"Well, I don't care about that." Carol wiped her forehead again. "Do you think I should date him?"

"I think you should do what you want to do. Whatever you do decide, you should come straight out and tell him."

"I'm surprised you're not interested in him, Trudy."

"Yuck. That'd be like dating my brother."

"I thought you were an only child."

"I am. I'm saying he's *like* an older brother. Kinda. Sort of. You know what I mean." A buzzer sounded. They stood and headed to the showers.

As the water pulsed against her back, Trudy mulled over the fact that she wasn't interested in Peter or his money. Surely, that showed progress as well. She wasn't as driven by the desire for material things as she once had been. She still loved dressing well and looking good, but no longer felt she had anything to prove by it.

In front of the mirror, fixing their hair, Trudy picked up the conversation where they'd dropped it. "What are you and Kim doing tonight?"

"We're going to paint her bedroom. We may do some shopping tomorrow. She's looking for a new dress for some occasion coming up."

Trudy chuckled. "That girl is always going to some occasion."

"Yeah. She's good with people and good at organizing. She gets that from me. Come on over if you want."

"I've got a thing at seven, but I might drop by for a bit after that. It'll be good to see Kim. She's so busy these days."

Carol dropped her hand to her side and looked at Trudy's reflection. "Where do you go when you go to your 'thing'?"

Trudy paused a moment. She really didn't want to talk about going to Al-Anon. She didn't want to have to explain why it was still important to her. She returned her brush to the makeup bag. "I get together with people I met when I first came to town. Friends of Kathy's."

"How is Kathy doing?"

"She's great. She loves Phoenix and her new job. They've found a good church out there."

"That's important. Another CMA group?"

"Yes." Trudy paused a moment, then added."And a decent Al-Anon group."

"What's that?"

Trudy explained and added, "No more secrets. When I first came, she invited me to go because of how I was with Phillip. Gambling was his sickness and trying to control him was mine. I still go weekly to meetings. That's my thing."

"Oh," Carol said. "Why is it secret?"

This stumped Trudy for a moment. "I guess I wanted you to see me as capable and self-sufficient, not falling apart because of Phillip. I wanted to be normal."

Carol held a finger up. "Wait a minute. Is that why you elbowed Kathy that time when we met?"

"Yes. She was going to tell you about Al-Anon and I wasn't ready for you to know. Kathy was surprised I hadn't already told you. I kind of implied I had. She understands anonymity, so she didn't say anything at the time, but she encouraged me to tell you."

"That explains it. I wondered what that poke was about. It seemed odd."

Trudy applied lipstick and capped the tube. She cocked her head and mused. "Hmm. The whole secrecy thing doesn't seem so important now. The first time I went I shook so hard I could hardly open the door. I'd have died if anyone knew."

"You've come a long way, then." Carol gave a finishing fluff to her hair. "Kim says she has something to tell me."

"Uh-oh. She's got a new boyfriend and she doesn't think you're going to approve of him."

"No. I'm pretty sure she got an award she was trying for."

"New boyfriend, for sure. Otherwise, she wouldn't wait to tell you about the award."

That night Trudy entered the Streeter home to find Kim and Carol in the midst of an argument. "You are not going on a weekend camping trip in the woods alone with a bunch of guys."

"Candice is going. I won't be the only girl."

"No. Pit toilets. Sleeping bags on the ground. You don't even like to camp."

"It's not like that. It's more like a luxury resort. Steve's father owns a cabin with running water and a Jacuzzi and a speed boat. If I don't go, I'll miss out on all the fun. These guys are safe. We're all friends at school."

"No."

"Trudy, what do you think?" Kim said. "You're hip and cool and know about things."

Trudy plopped down on the couch. "Yep. Sure do. Your mother's right."

Kim made an exasperated noise, turned on her heels, and stomped up the stairs. Carol shook her head. "What happened to my compliant little girl?"

"She grew up and went to college. Don't worry. You did exactly what she wanted you to do."

"What do you mean?"

"If she'd really wanted to go, she'd have gone and never told you about it. This way she can make a stink to her friends about how

344

unreasonable you are, that you might pull funds she needs for college, yada, yada."

Carol blinked and immediately calmed down. She sat beside Trudy. "For not having kids, you sure know a lot."

"I was one. A rebellious one at that. My parents never did find out half the stuff I did and that wasn't easy in a small town. Sometimes I did stuff they'd find out about as a smoke screen to hide the stuff I didn't want them to know."

"You must've been a handful."

"You have no idea."

"Is that what she's doing with this camping trip? Blowing a smokescreen?"

"Hmm. Maybe. Don't think so. Not yet, anyway."

"Thanks a lot. Now I have that to worry about."

# Chapter Thirty-five

Still in the grips of a black dream, Trudy rolled over in bed and flung her arm out seeking comfort. The bed was empty. She came fully awake. "Oh, Phillip."

The desire to sleep evaporated like mist in the sun. She snapped on the light and swung her legs over the side of the bed. This was one of those grieving times Carol had warned her about.

Again, she questioned if she should have claimed Phillip's body. Would that ceremony have given her a way to say good-bye? Would having his ashes sitting in her room or going to a cemetery to visit his buried body given her closure?

No. She'd followed Culcallen's advice and did not claim either Phillip's body or his belongings. It was wise. It was sensible. It was for her own protection. She didn't have the money to pay for a burial, anyway. Phillip was no longer in a position to care, so why do it?

She simply hated waking up every once in a while from that vague black dream and expecting him to be there. She needed some sort of closure.

Trudy padded barefoot across the carpeted floor to the chest of drawers. She lifted down the jewelry case and took it back to the bed. Using one finger, she pushed aside the necklaces and bracelets until she found a picture of her and Phillip in their first year of marriage.

They were sitting on his shiny, black Harley-Davidson, both dressed in black leather, with the colorful lights of the Las Vegas strip glowing behind them. She was laughing, her chin raised, and her ginger hair cascading down her back. His quirky smile was broad, showing white teeth. His eyes sparkled with humor. He was a handsome man. A proud man. He'd loved her.

She smiled at the memory and stroked the photo. Yes, he'd loved her, as best as he could. He'd been broken and rejected help to get better because he thought he could do it on his own. He was proud. Too proud.

Trudy left the jewelry box on the bed and carried the photograph to the well-organized desk. She opened a drawer and drew out a pad of paper and a pen. She sat down and listed all the bad things that had happened, every way he'd failed her or hurt her, and every promise he'd broken. It was a long list that took both sides of two pages.

She turned to a new page and listed all the good things she could think of about him. How he'd waited for her for a year to come of age before approaching her, even though he'd fallen in love with her the first time they met. His patience with her when she was learning a new skill, like snorkeling. His generosity in gift-giving. His desire to fulfill all her dreams. How he kept returning to her, wanting to make her happy. It didn't take long before the front of the page was full.

When she was done, Trudy read it all through again. She folded the papers and put them in an envelope with the photo. She made a few phone calls. The last one was to Peter's office phone.

"Good morning, Peter. I'm sorry for the last minute notice, but I'm taking a personal day. I've called the temp agency to send over a girl to answer the phones. I'll be back in the office tomorrow."

Trudy dressed in a pair of designer jeans, a burnt orange silk blouse, and her black leather jacket. She packed a few things and rode her motorcycle to the Streeter house. Trudy unlocked the door and entered. She called out, "Hi. It's only me."

"I'm in the kitchen, Trudy. You're up and about early. What's up?"

Trudy found Carol still in her pajamas and drinking coffee. "I wanted you to read this. No, I want to read this to you. I want to share this."

Carol paused with the coffee pot in one hand and a cup in the other. She nodded and sat down. "What is it?"

"It's about Phillip. Kind of like a memorial service. I'd like you to do it with me. He didn't have friends or family, at least none that I know of."

Trudy took the chair opposite and put the envelope back in her inner jacket pocket. "Drink your coffee. This has waited this long, a little more time won't matter. I'll have a cup, too."

"Okay." Carol turned in her chair and chose another cup from the mug tree beside the coffee maker. She filled both cups and stretching, set the pot back on the hot plate.

Trudy drummed the table with dark brown fingernails that looked professionally done, but which she'd done herself. "I don't want to simply read it. The setting has to be right. Ritzy, like Phillip was. Will you take the day off from the hospital to go on a motorcycle adventure with me?"

"Sure. I think the claims department can get by without me for one day. Where are we going?"

"Chicago. It's one of the places Phillip and I had planned to visit. It's a three hour drive north on I-65. We'll spend the day sight-seeing in the loop, enjoy fine dining at a ritzy restaurant, spend the night at the Drake hotel, and somewhere in there I'll read what I've written. We'll drive back early tomorrow morning in time for work."

"The Drake. Can you afford that?"

"It'll dig deep into my savings, but it's how Phillip would've wanted it. Besides, it's cheaper than a burial."

Carol looked at Trudy and flashed a quick, understanding smile. She stood. "Okay. Let's do it."

"Don't forget to pack a dinner dress."

Trudy made fried egg sandwiches while Carol dressed and arranged for the neighbor to care for Minnie. She put a note on the table for Kim. They left immediately after breakfast, riding through a glorious red and gold fall day. The sky looked like a bright blue field in which a brisk wind herded white clouds like sheep.

They pulled onto I-65 and sped up. Trudy felt that same thrill that always accompanied a quick increase in speed. It was a feeling she associated with Phillip.

The day went as planned. They visited the Sears Tower and the John Hancock Building, enjoying the views from the skyscrapers. They explored Grant Park and shopped Water Tower Place.

While they talked about other regular things as well, very often Trudy recalled other times and places with Phillip and how he would have thought and felt about what they were seeing.

She asked Carol about Andy and listened while her friend related about the happy life experiences she and Andy had shared and those devastating times they had endured together.

Late that night, they relaxed in a room at the Drake. Carol chuckled. "This has been an unexpected adventure. Kind of exciting. Something I'd never have thought to do on my own."

"That was Phillip. Unexpected. Exciting. An Adventure."

"Everything you told me today is very different from what you told me before. I mean, he sounds like an amazing man. Funny. Personable. Smart as a whip."

"He was. The first few years were particularly good. We had no cares. No house to keep up. We lived free and easy. Who knows? Maybe if I hadn't wanted to settle down and start a family that would have kept on."

"What do you mean?"

"He wanted so badly to give me those things and he insisted on doing everything in a big, flamboyant way. All or nothing."

"Trudy, it's normal to expect to have a home, a place of security, and to raise kids. I mean, you even said you discussed these things before you were married. I can't see how it was your fault that Phillip wasn't mature enough to build slowly, steadily."

"I guess."

"So what changed?"

In that opulent, comfortable, setting Trudy finally felt it was time. She opened up the envelope and showed Carol the photograph. "This is us at our happiest. We were good together. Very good, until we weren't. It happened over time so that at first I didn't recognize there was a problem. I figured it was marriage stuff that everybody went through."

Trudy picked up the bad pages, because she'd already spent the day sharing the good things. "You may have heard most of this already. Some of it I've never shared with anyone because it was too personal."

When she finished, she picked up the leather jacket and tucked the paper into the inner pocket.

"You know, Trudy, I've heard some marriage counselors say after you've made that list you should put it in God's hands, forgive the person, then rip it into tiny pieces and burn it."

"I'm not sure I've forgiven him, yet."

Carol sprawled with her arms spread wide over the back of the couch. She tipped her head back for a moment, then said. "You mean, you haven't put it in God's hands yet and trusted him to take care of it."

"Ouch."

"I'm just saying." Carol's smile was sympathetic. Her eyes looked tired and sleepy. It was a look Trudy was sure mirrored her own. Exhaustion covered Trudy like a blanket. She was blessed to have a friend like Carol who would already be asleep, except she'd never leave a friend unsettled and hurting.

Trudy reached over and patted the hand that was nearest her. "And I can trust you, dear friend, to give it to me straight even if it does hurt."

"'Wounds of a friend are faithful.' Proverbs 27:6."

"Whenever I think I'm starting to know the Bible, you come up with something I never heard before."

"'He that speaks flattery to a friend, even the eyes of his children shall fail.' Job 17:5."

"Now you're showing off."

"'There is a friend that sticks closer than a brother.' Proverbs 18:24."

"Good night, Carol." Trudy moved into the bathroom to get ready for bed. When she came out, Carol was already in one of the beds with the light out on her side of the room. Trudy climbed into the other bed, adjusted the covers, and turned out the light. The room was dark and quiet. Sleep lapped at her like tiny, peaceful waves.

Carol said, "'Iron sharpens iron, so a friend sharpens a friend.' Proverbs 27:17."

Trudy giggled. "I'm going to poke you with something sharp, if you don't shut up and go to sleep."

Carol giggled.

The next thing Trudy knew the room phone was ringing. She picked it up. Her throat was dry as she muttered, "Hello?"

"This is your 5:00 a.m. wake-up call," the male voice said.

"Thank you, I think." Trudy flipped on the light and headed for the bathroom. As she passed the other bed, she wiggled the bump in the bedspread that marked where Carol's toes would be. In a loud, if gruff voice, she said, "Good morning, Carol. Time to get up."

Sleepily Carol said, "'It's considered a curse when someone rises early in the morning to bless his friend with a loud voice.' Proverbs 27:14".

Trudy laughed. "Did you dream that one up?"

After breakfast, they set off on the trip south. An hour later they drove under an iron grey sky heavy with angry clouds. The air turned chill and gusts of wind tried to knock them into the lane of on-coming traffic. Trudy fought to hold the motorcycle steady.

In the rearview mirror, the sky was greenish-yellow. The next time she looked back, a twister crossed the road and disappeared. Trudy leaned forward and accelerated.

As they passed the mid-point on the return trip to Indianapolis the skies lightened a bit and the wind lost its aggression. Trudy spoke over her shoulder. "That was scary."

"Pull over at the next exit," Carol said.

Trudy nodded. Before long she exited I-65 and found a gas station. They dismounted and pulled off their helmets.

Carol rubbed her arms and shook herself. "I thought we were going to be carried to Kansas for sure. A few minutes slower and we'd have been right in that tornado's path."

"This trip is like a metaphor for my life," Trudy said.

Carol wagged her head. Then she and opened her hands in a gesture of helplessness. "For both of us. Come on. I need to settle myself down. Those wind gusts unnerved me."

Carol and Trudy browsed the aisles of the convenience store, not looking for anything, but not quite ready to finish the ride. Trudy left the store first and stood by the bike. She held the papers about Phillip in her hands, staring at them.

She'd already forgiven Phillip for some of the things. She tore out those pieces and dropped them in the side pocket of her jacket to burn later. Carol joined her.

"Thanks for making the trip with me, Carol. I didn't want to do it alone. There's one last thing I have to do." She folded the remaining shreds of paper, creased them, and tore them into little tiny pieces before stuffing them into her pocket.

"That was a big step," Carol said.

"You spoke truth to me. I can trust God to set all of it right. I'm going to let go and let God. I don't want to carry it anymore. Not any of it. Let's go home."

They roared onto the road and Trudy merged into traffic on the highway and opened up the throttle. Her heart seemed lighter, not because she was accelerating, but because in forgiving she felt released from the heaviness of the past.

A sense of gratitude overwhelmed her. She reached in her pocket for a tissue. When she pulled it out, the bits of paper streamed behind her.

Trudy saw them in the rearview mirror. They looked free and easy dancing in the wind. On a giddy impulse, she pulled more of the paper pieces out and let the wind snatch them away. Phillip would've loved that. A streamer of white flagging behind them. She let out a whoop. "Good-bye, Phillip."

A siren screamed behind them. Carol tugged at her. A glance in the rearview mirror revealed red lights flashing as an Indiana State Patrol car closed the distance.

Trudy glanced at her speedometer. She was going the speed limit.

He flipped the siren off and on. Trudy applied the brakes and pulled over.

Both women got off the bike and stood looking back at the patrol car. Trudy pulled out her driver's license and removed her helmet. Carol did the same. The officer still hadn't left his vehicle.

Carol combed her fingers through her hair. "What's taking him so long?"

Trudy drummed her fingers against her helmet. "He's running my plates to see if it's stolen or has warrants on it."

At last, the trooper exited the vehicle and slowly strode with his hand on his gun. He wasn't real tall, but seemed larger than life in the tan uniform and big, brown trooper's hat. "Ladies."

"Good morning, officer," Trudy said. Carol nodded.

"Where are you headed?"

"We're heading home to Indianapolis. I wasn't speeding." Trudy handed over her I.D. He looked at it and studied her.

Carol added. "We spent yesterday in Chicago. It was a memorial service for her husband."

"I'm sorry to hear that." He talked to them a few minutes more. "Ma'am, I'm going to have to ticket you for littering."

"Littering? It was an accident. Well, at first it was." Trudy put a hand to her head. "Then, I got carried away."

"It's part of her healing process. It was a list of things she had to forgive." Carol's voice trailed off at the end.

The trooper glanced up from writing the ticket. "It's still littering. I have to ticket you."

Trudy nodded. She licked dry lips. "How much is that?"

"$200."

Trudy put her hand on the bike seat to steady herself. "$200?"

Carol gasped. "For littering? Snot-balls and boogers."

The state trooper regarded Carol and frowned.

"That's what my little niece says," she mumbled.

"Littering is a serious offense in this state. The fines can run into thousands of dollars. I'd suggest you be more careful in the future."

"Yes, sir. I will, sir," Trudy said.

"Look, Officer. My friend is grieving over the loss of her husband. The memorial was for him and this was part of the ceremony. It was a couple sheets of paper. A letting go. You know, let go of and let God?" Her voice trailed off.

"Next time let go at home by your recycle bin." He finished writing the ticket and handed it to Trudy. The trooper walked back to his car.

Trudy stared at the piece of paper. She wanted to rip it into tiny shreds and let the wind carry it away, but it was on the record and that wouldn't change a thing. "Well, snot-balls and boogers," she said.

Instead, she tucked it into the inner pocket and buckled her helmet. "Thanks for standing up for me, Carol."

"It doesn't seem right, somehow." Carol adjusted the strap on her helmet.

Trudy laughed, a coarse, choking sound. "You're wrong. It's exactly right. It's ironic, even. It's like Phillip got me again one last time from the grave."

Carol's lips moved, but didn't quite become a smile.

Trudy sighed. "It feels like Phillip got me, but in truth, it's the consequence of a choice I myself made."

The trooper drove off. Trudy mounted the motorcycle and Carol sat behind her. Trudy held a steady speed. She didn't need another ticket. Soon they drove into bright sunshine with navy blue skies.

Trudy stopped in Carol's driveway, but kept the engine idling. Being stopped for littering cost them precious time. She would have to go directly to the office. Would Peter prefer her to man the reception desk in jeans or evening gown? She smiled at the thought.

Carol dismounted. "I'll see you later this morning in the office. Peter wants to talk with me about scheduling for the next year. It seems too early to be doing that."

"Nope. It's time. See you, then." Straddling the motorcycle, she walked it in a semi-circle until it faced the street.

"Trudy, this trip was a good thing. You've been brave and truthful. I've been thinking that you're right. I need to bite the bullet and be more direct with Peter. Today, I'll simply tell him I'm not interested in him. Not now or ever."

"That's good. Truth is truth. Peter is not for you. Carol, you may not think so now, but some day you will meet someone and remarry. As for me, I'll always be single." Trudy waved and hit the accelerator.

Over the roar of the engine, she thought Carol shouted something that sounded suspiciously like "famous last words."

The story continues in ...

# God's Love Most Gentle

## Excerpt from Chapter One

### February 14, 1995

Kim Macomb jostled and bounced around the back seat of the jeep. The African sun, like a ton weight, threatened to press her as flat as the grassland. Wind whipped dark silky strands from her thick braid. She tucked them behind her ear, but it only took a moment for them to whip free again.

In the front seat, her husband gestured as he discussed the future of Zaire with the driver. Kim was grateful that most of their discussion was drowned out by the engine's drone. She was too miserable to care about anyone else's future. It was all they'd talked about since leaving the airport moments before the militia shut it down. Like a surreal scene from a 3-D hero movie there'd been people screaming, scrambling, gunfire, yet the three of them escaped unscathed. How did she get here, anyway?

Kurt turned to her and grinned. Her heart leaped in her chest and she smiled back. Beneath the brim of a khaki hat his blue eyes twinkled with excitement. His pale skin, the blight of red-haired people, already showed signs of sunburn. "Hang on. Things are about to get interesting," he shouted. They slowed and veered off the highway, bumping along deep ruts that sliced through dense jungle.

Every jolt felt like the start of a new bruise. Occasionally Kurt glanced back to check on her, his excitement at realizing his dream never dimming. She closed her eyes and lapsed into a weary stupor until the jeep lurched to a stop. The engine's drone was replaced by the buzzing of a fat fly circling her head. She swatted at it and sat up. "What's wrong?"

"There's a tree blocking the path." Kurt pointed. The dirt lane looked like a thin brown belt cinching tall grasses that spread right and left into a full garment of brush and trees. One large tree with leaves dried and brown lie directly across the road.

"I've got a chain we can use to move it. Reverend Macomb, would you give me a hand?" Uzachi's Bostonian accent again surprised her. In a loose white shirt and shorts, Uzachi looked as if he belonged to the land, yet he was decidedly American.

Kurt jumped out the passenger side while Uzachi unfolded his frame from behind the steering wheel and went to rummage through the luggage in the back of the jeep. "Wouldn't you know? It's on the bottom of the heap. This'll take a while. You may as well get out and stretch, Mrs. Macomb, but stay close."

Kim hunched her shoulders and threw her hands out, palms up. "Where would I go?"

Uzachi flashed a brilliantly white smile and offered her a hand the color and softness of a well-used baseball glove. Once she was on the ground, he towered over her. He was maybe eight inches taller, while she and Kurt both stood five-five. He returned to the rear, handing bags and boxes to Kurt to stack on the ground.

Kim stretched stiffness away and rubbed at the sore spots on her lean body. Clutching for a hold during the rough ride hadn't doing her manicure any good. She picked at a chip in the red lacquer on her left thumbnail. She smoothed wrinkles from her pretty pink shirt and tan trousers. Perhaps not the most practical of outfits, but just because she was going to the jungle didn't mean she had to dress ugly. Kurt glanced her way, grinned and winked. She smiled back, knowing he appreciated how she looked.

She wandered toward the obstruction. A path of beaten grass skirted the downed tree and some branches had been stripped away. She scrambled on top of the horizontal trunk, wobbling a bit before balance beam training took over. Everything looked better from up there. She stepped the length of it and back, performing a routine she'd used years before in high school competition.

"Kim," Kurt said. His low tone held a warning.

"Don't worry. I won't fall." One foot poised in midair, she leaned back and held the position so he could marvel at her dexterity. Kim tipped her head back in triumph and looked to him for admiration. His face was tight. Beside him, Uzachi stood motionless, whitened knuckles clutching the winching chain. Each man's gaze was not quite on her, but a few feet to the front.

A thick brown vine hung strangely. She righted herself for a better view. A snake, rising vertically from the tree trunk, was almost as tall as she was. Beady eyes fixed on her. Its smooth, ear-less head flattened. Its mouth stretched wide baring fangs, hissing.